CW00503518

THE NEMESIS FACTOR

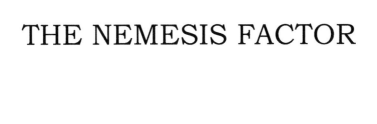

IÑAKI MARTÍN VELASCO

THE NEMESIS FACTOR

*Translated from the Spanish
by Martin Michael Roberts.*

This is a work of fiction. Names, characters, organizations, places, events, and incidents are either product of the author imagination or are used fictitiously. Any resemblance to actual persons, living or dead, or actual events is purely coincidental.

Text copyright © 2018 by Iñaki Martín Velasco

Translation copyright © 2020 by Martin Roberts

No part of this book may be reproduced, or stored in a retrieval system, or transmitted in any form or by any means, electronic, mechanical, photocopying, recording, or otherwise, without express written permission of the publisher.

For my parents, Carmen and Manuel.

"For some reason I can't explain
I know Saint Peter won't call my name"

"Viva la vida" Coldplay. 2008

PROLOGUE

Off the coast of Argentina,
March 5, 2009

He looked at the calm sea astern of *Le Boucanier* and with a touch on the tiller, steered the yacht to sail in line with the coast. The warm Brazil Current was flowing less swiftly than it had done on other occasions, and the coastal South Atlantic waters were as smooth as a millpond.

The southern hemisphere summer was over, and the horizon was turning a reddish hue in the fast-dwindling twilight. The port of Pinamar could still be seen in the distance to starboard, which was receding in slow motion while the harbor entrance was lighting up.

The forlorn loneliness of the sea grew with each passing mile. At his time of life there were few situations left that afforded him a similar feeling of freedom. Guillermo Lavinia stroked his graying hair with his fingers and slowed the yacht down. The powerful engine fell silent, and the splashing of the waves on the hull died down, along with the soughing of the breeze. He struggled to light his umpteenth cigarette with his silver-plated lighter, which was low on fuel, and wrapped his jacket around him to shelter himself from the damp that gripped his tired bones. Inside the main cabin, Anne had almost finished combing their little girl's locks. She fondly brushed her hair, from her forehead down, in slow and gentle strokes. Meanwhile, Angélica enjoyed looking at her face in the mirror. The sun and sea breeze had turned her skin light pink. She wiped her cheeks. Angélica looked at her mother with bright eyes. Anne looked back with all the affection a human being can feel.

"Can I go up on deck with Daddy for a while?"

"Not now, it's bedtime. He'll come down to kiss you good-night when you're in bed. Come on, it's late. The dolphins have already gone to sleep. You'll have to get up early if you want to play with them."

Lavinia poured himself a double Southern Comfort in a coffee mug.

Six hours' sailing, he figured, five-and-a-half if the currents held steady.

The nautical charts showed no special cause for concern to take his mind off watching the scenery, and the few dolphins that followed in the yacht's wake. Further south, by Cape Corrientes, the quirky coastline diverted the cold waters that flowed from the Antarctic all along the Argentine coast, thus keeping the Atlantic warm and calm still in that area.

It had doubtless been a good idea to spend the last days of summer with Anne and their little girl. It had not escaped his attention that they had not been getting along too well for quite a while now, almost a lifetime. Only the first four or five years were full of bliss. The death of Pierre, their first-born, put paid to almost all their illusions. Lavinia's unhealthy devotion to the army and the years spent amassing a fortune did the rest. Love had ebbed away with every phone call from thousands of miles away, with every night spent far from home. Anne suffered in silence, checked her spontaneous smiles, year by year, and slowly stifled the passion that had bonded them in their teenage summers. Not even the birth of little Angélica managed to bring back the old magic. However, above all, she was still his partner and had been there at every twist and turn in their life together. His love for her was so deeply rooted inside him that it was probably greater than ever now, and in the end he had understood that her very existence made his life worth living.

Anne went up on deck. She still had an enviable figure. She flashed her husband a knowing smile, wrapped her arms around his waist and rested her head on his shoulder.

"Angélica's asleep now."

"I'll go down and give her a kiss," he answered, looking into her eyes sweetly. "Tonight will be calm," Guillermo predicted, as he switched on the bow lights.

The breeze cooled down when the sun dipped below the horizon altogether.

"I think we forgot one of the water boxes," Anne said after wetting her lips with the mug of bourbon. "I looked for it in the hold and the closet, and can't find it anywhere.

"Look beside the emergency generators, it might be there. The new marina workers are worse than old Néstor. They turned everything upside-down when servicing the yacht, and the engine hatch is half-jammed. It's a mess," Lavinia grumbled while he checked the nautical chart.

They both stayed silent, lost in the ocean solitude.

The stars began to shine all the more brightly, and stood out against the darkness. There were more of them than any time before, as if the intimacy of that moment had made them cast off their shyness.

"I love you," Anne whispered in an almost unheard voice.

"Me too."

At 10:30 p.m. Guillermo noticed a strange bleeping noise. Anne had just turned in. He felt that it came from the engine. He turned on the autopilot and went downstairs.

Just three steps...

The flash from the explosion lit up the whole coast and turned the sky into a huge fireball. The blast drowned out the whistling breeze for a few seconds, as if the world had been sundered in two. The echo resounded violently all along the coastline. In an instant, the eight tons packed into the 45-feet length of *Le Boucanier* went up in smoke like cigarette paper in a crematorium while the crew's bodies were blown to pieces, and scattered all over the place, among the scraps of iron and other bits and pieces left over from the blast.

Shortly afterwards, darkness engulfed that patch of sea and silence took over, as if nothing had happened.

Only the stars covering the sky bore witness to what merely a few seconds before had been a boat sailing the seas with a family living on board.

The young American woke up after noon.

The daylight seeped through the hostel's shabby blinds. Children shrieking as they ran through the Mar del Plata suburbs brought him back to the land of the living. He was soaked in sweat. Drowsily, he gazed at the walls in his grubby room.

The drugs' after-effects were still squashing his brain, which refused to locate him anywhere on the planet in particular. He looked around him. Papers were spread out and dirty clothes piled up on the other bed.

His memory gradually came back to him.

An uncontrollable dread ran right through him.

He looked for his pills on the bedside table.

He closed his eyes and hunched up into a fetal crouch.

CHAPTER I

Cape Gata, Almería (Spain)
Friday, August 13, 2010

Four hours and a half. Maybe five, if the endless flow of dusty trucks continued to clog up the traffic. The accident on the A92 highway had blocked up the service roads and left the old coast road as the only other way back. More vehicles gushed in from nearby towns and cities, and packed the line of traffic more tightly every second, until it turned into one big, thick, sluggish metallic lump.

"Damnit. It had to happen today of all days," he thought.

For weeks he had been looking forward to his break so much, he could taste it, and he could not get off his mind the thought of dipping his feet into the eternal waters of Capri; nonetheless, the end of season was frowning at him in an unseemly farewell.

Adrian Seaten looked again at the massive hold-up through his windshield.

"Goddamn it's Friday."

The well-rounded August sun shone high in the sky, even after mid-afternoon, and the BMW M6 was a real oven. He loosened his tie and, with his hand and a sigh, he prised the damp shirt away from his back, which was sunburnt from being in Fuerteventura a few days back. "Damned leather seats. Just the job for the Mediterranean sun at its harshest. Sounds like a great idea for the next campaign; sales would bomb," he thought wryly. He smiled and turned on the air conditioning. A powerful blast of cold air hit Laura in the face, while she held back a sneeze twice with her hand, and looked out of the corner of her eye at Adrian, in a mixture of shyness and respect.

"It's time to get out of this dump."

"Does the aircon bother you?"

"No, no, not at all."

Highway 340 skirted the Mediterranean with its six hundred-odd miles of blacktop, from Barcelona to San Fernando, near Cádiz, where it started out. It crossed Andalusia along its southernmost stretch, parallel to the coast, and ran though its beaches, cities, cemeteries and coves. Adrian genuinely worshiped that part of the world, for its people and their surprisingly light-hearted approach to life. A long way from his home turf. The heavy traffic smelled of salt and fish, of cheap suntan lotion, of boiling heat capable of melting anything away, except illusions. Those light and unassuming southerly illusions. Straightforward, half-baked illusions. The other half he had already soaked up as he breathed in the sea air, while the sunlight had branded him from its first gasp.

The burgeoning vacation traffic choked the southern artery and held up travelers. Highway 340 doubled back here and there, alongside the unfinished A7. Gridlock was guaranteed. "The secret is bearing up. Patience is the secret of success, self-control the key." He thought you could write up a self-help book based on that idea, plus a few sentences to back it up.

Just as well the filming had worked out in the end, after countless takes, screaming and cursing. He was worn out. Eight hours under the Cape Gata sun putting up with the feckless agency brats. "Fucking losers." If they spent less effort on all that awful body-piercing and those spiky, streaked hairdos, and more on working hard and setting minimum standards for themselves, then everything would be so much easier. What a generation to belong to! It was not too difficult to have his job and pull in three hundred fifty grand a year. Or maybe it was. Thinking it through, not many could be among the chosen few, otherwise, what would the point be?

He swiveled the rear-view mirror to the right height to steal a glance at himself with feigned carelessness. His brown-eyed look was still intact. He shielded it with his Serengeti Corsa sunglasses, with the polarized Strata 400 lenses, his favorite. It was no ordinary brand, like all of his accessories. Ordinariness kills desire. If everybody has something, it becomes lackluster.

As the minutes ticked by, the temperature inside leveled out at 72 degrees and the BMW's interior was at last a comfortable place to be. The soft touch of the leather upholstery and the contrast between the quiet engine and the opening bars of the Goldberg variations —the Glenn Gould version, of course— soothed him no end.

Laura was dressed in black, which matched her hair and eyes. Long and slim, her face had a certain oriental grace to it, and she squeezed her thick lips to choke back any smile that might reveal the bare broken tip of her left canine. She felt a little uneasy; worse still, she was perfectly aware that her unease could be read in her face like a book. Despite her youth, she was not usually overawed by anything. But that trip was something else. It is not every day that the head honcho drives you in his own car. Creative director Ferri's vacation and marketing director Flávio's careless sprain had conspired to make her his unplanned fellow traveler on this project.

Adrian stole a glance at her full, round, pert breasts, which stretched out her gold-trimmed DG tee-shirt, and he imagined her trying on clothes the day before, a blouse, pants, too contrived, too casual. She looked straight ahead, staring at the highway, unable to hide some of her jitters, which the situation did not warrant. Adrian was well aware of the feelings he awoke in his 'troops', which ranged from respect and admiration to all-out hatred, with only a thin red line between them. He quietly observed looks, reactions and fears, and each time found it all the more entertaining.

The voice of Jill, his personal assistant, suddenly shut up the solemn piano-playing that issued from the thirteen loudspeakers and two subwoofers spread around the car. Adrian pulled a face. The sound was so richly nuanced, so sharp that it stirred the soul. It had doubtless been a good idea to max out the sound with the Logic 7 system. The majestic beemer compartment and its perfect sound insulation made for the ultimate atmosphere in which to enjoy the unique sensation of real sound. The woofer barked out his PA's voice.

"Good afternoon, Adrian. How's everything? I've tried calling you several times. I've got some traffic updates for you. There's a crash blocking the A92. I've looked into available detours."

"Don't you worry Jill, it's too late now. Any important calls?"

"Let me see. Jean-Luc Lavar, from Del Com, called first thing."

"I said important..."

"A certain Sylvie Prévot, from Interpol, called. She wanted to talk to you, but gave no further details. I told her you were out of the office."

Adrian was thoughtful for a few seconds.

"OK, you can go home now if you like. At this rate, we'll be here all weekend. See you Monday. Have a good weekend, Jill."

"Just call me if you need anything, I'll be..."

"Enjoy your weekend, Jill. Bye."

The almighty gridlock chained the line of cars together, as the sun beat down on them mercilessly. The cars moved at random along two lines; first one lane, then another, but they all settled back down again mechanically after a few minutes, when each link in the chain went back to where it had been before. A multicolored showcase of every kind of bodywork, engines and drivers overtook him, or fell back on either side of his car at a tiresome pace. Adrian watched the scene with an interest born of inaction. The bright yellow VW bug driven by two Englishwomen was usually on his left, then it would go forward a few yards, or many more, thirty or forty car lengths, then fall back beside him. In front, a dented, patchy Citroën Xsara had its windows wound down to reveal a knobbly, old rustic elbow. On his right, a BMW X3 tried unsuccessfully to switch lanes, in a bid to overtake an endless line, which bounced him back like swimming against a rip tide.

Soon there would be life beyond those two lanes. More and more cars pulled up by the roadside, so that families could take a breather or seek local traffic news, cellphone in hand. The radio broadcast updates to allay fears and uncertainty. The initial alarm had given way to normality once the drivers en masse had realized that a few hours of gridlock was inevitable. The unexpected is also exciting and, to an extent, the unforeseen lightens up the gray streaks that run through most people's lives, even though it's just the biggest roadblock to hit southern Spain for a few years.

'Who cares!' Adrian thought, while he switched on the windshield wiper for the third time, in a knee-jerk response to remove the thin film of dust that had gathered there. He reveled in his car like an astronaut looking in silence at inhospitable outer space. Inside that cocoon, in the midst of a wilderness, the luxury bodywork was a barrier to the hostile environment, and kept the dirt, the discomfort, the drabness and the masses at bay. What other people do. After Jill's shrill voice had been cut off, the crisp piano-playing had crystallized the air again, and ushered in a smooth silence as its ideal counterpoint.

"I like this music, it's really lovely," Laura commented, by way of an attempt to break the ice.

"Yes. It's more like a cure than a masterpiece. It has an odd effect when you listen to it, you know? It varies from person to person. It takes me away, to someplace else."

"Someplace else?" Laura felt uncomfortable at the closeness of her hitherto distant traveling companion.

"Bygone times."

Adrian had the sudden feeling that he was opening up to the wrong listener and changed the subject to more down-to-earth matters.

"Bach composed it for a sleepless count. You might say it was devised to make people sleep. Legend has it that Count von Keyserlingk asked Bach for a composition to lull him to sleep. Every night, Goldberg, one of his pupils, would play the piece behind a divan, skillfully and softly, until the count fell asleep."

"A nice story. I can understand the count. It's such relaxing music."

'Relaxing? Did she say relaxing? Gazing into a fireplace is relaxing.' Adrian looked at her in pitiful tenderness. He watched the young woman's face reflected in the car window, in which a smirk was drawn while he could not stop his own from beaming a broad smile in sympathy.

Laura had joined Boreal Life three years before. Back then, Adrian used to have a brief chat with applicants at the final stage of the selection process. He trusted fully in the headhunters and his recruitment team, or at least he liked to think so. His little quirk rarely led to vetoing the new hires. He never liked to undermine his team's work arbitrarily, but he did indulge in getting to grips first-hand with a future employee's profile and potential. He asked them about their ambitions, the whys and wherefores of past decisions, their values. Finally he would say goodbye and offhand ask them a rhetorical question: 'Well, thank you for your time. I guess that you have already been asked this if you've gotten this far. I understand your English is fluent and you have no problem reading through an earnings statement. Furthermore, I take for granted you have a grasp of Little Misty, don't you?' The comment triggered an automatic reply: 'Yes, yes, of course I do. I would just like to take this opportunity to say again how much I'm looking forward to joining this great project.'

In truth he was enormously proud of how qualified his team was. They could boast of an endless pile of masters degrees, double degrees, languages, specialty management courses and high-level experience. But what he found most telling was having an impressive group of professionals who swore they were fully familiar with Little Misty.

Adrian still sadly remembered Little Misty, his American boxer puppy, that kept him good company in his senior year at Four Peaks High School, Ohio, when Big Misty, his mother, was run over by a car and died.

He was overwhelmed by the lasting impression the tragic tale of his little boxer had made on his executive staff.

As it happens, he never rejected candidates for that reason. The LMEs (Little Misty Experts) are also needed in organizations, in fact, they make up the vast majority of them. 'We won't let a trivial detail get in the way of my goal. I'll find out about that new software, or whatever it is. We'll just let appearances cover up for our shortfalls.'

More than fifty people had joined the firm in the past four years. Only ten had boldly asked what the hell all that Little Misty stuff was about, stressing it was the first time they had heard tell of such a thing. On the few occasions it happened, the meeting room adjacent to his office, where he interviewed the candidates, brightened up with a virginal white light and everything was flooded with an innocent freshness that made him smile on the inside. Laura, dressed in an ordinary pink

Benetton polo shirt bought specially for the occasion, was one of them. A girl with a sweet look, he recalled.

Variatio 17 of the Goldberg variations struck up, which was where they came closest to being heavenly.

The English girls had not appeared on his left for quite some time now. Instead, the ugly visage of a black Renault Laguna mostly made him company. The dreadful combination of brand, model and color made him fear the worst before he let his gaze settle on the occupants. His worst fears were confirmed when he saw a scrawny individual at the wheel of that conceptually challenged contraption; he was fifty-something, shamelessly wore a short-sleeved, flesh-toned shirt, had sideburns trimmed above the ear and three days' stubble. It did not stop there. The shirt's collar had buttons to hold in place a light rather than dark gray tie, maybe somewhat two-toned and straight cut, which hung down to well below his waistline. The rush of correct guesses stunned him, so he had to look back in front of him for a few seconds. He needed a break. But morbid curiosity got the better of him and he turned around to look at that man again. He imagined snub-nosed patent leather shoes, with tassels. He imagined ankles and wrists sporting silver bracelets. 'Yes, he got his just deserts.' Adrian smiled.

The man chain-smoked and returned his gaze. Maybe he was upset. Adrian looked at, but did not see him. He could not stop mulling it over. 'The short-sleeved shirt was already overdoing it.' He wondered who the man had spoken to over the past fifty years, how he had seen himself, what he had filled his own private heaven with, what criteria he had used to chisel out his heart's desires. He stared the man in the eyes. 'Yes, look at me, that is what I'm wondering; that's why I stare at you in pity, with contempt. But take a good look at me. Because it happens to be a constructive, sincere contempt.' The man looked into his eyes and avoided his glance, as if he could read his mind; Adrian closed his. 'I mull over whether I am a bad person. At times I wonder. I don't want to hurt anybody. I bear him no ill will. I simply look at and despise him. I don't think that makes me a bad person.'

He felt like smoking, although he had decided to quit just ten hours before.

The cellphone's cheesy ringtone heralded an incoming call on the hands-free speaker, from his fiancée, Helena. The wedding was coming up in less than four months' time. Like tomorrow.

Laura remembered that woman's voice and the stupid haughty pose she struck when she came to pick up Adrian at the office, before the Thursday concerts, and could not help frowning suddenly. The profile of a dutiful and dependent female was a far cry from her ideal of womanhood, and Helena seemed to fit the bill.

Helena oozed devotion to her husband-to-be. Atop the highest podium in her panoply of gods, garlanded by the most beautiful ornaments and flamboyant flower arrangements, stood Adrian Seaten. He epitomized all the needs and desires of a well-heeled girl like her, from a traditional and eminent family, and who had a child-bearing drive, to boot. Adrian came from a well-to-do American family, was smart and fulfilled with flying colors the requisite charisma and success demanded by her and his future in-laws. When they announced their engagement and named the date of their marriage, Helena thought she had found true bliss.

Laura was still brooding, and staring at the countryside through the car window. Her life had unfolded light years away from the dumb preppy girl and her distant and smug boss.

"Adrian, darling, how are you?"

"Fine, Helena, plumbing the depths of hell." Laura listened in amused discomfort; indeed, she thought to herself she had never heard the like before. Helena broke down into gory detail the myriad variations of center table decor, and went about shamelessly explaining the unthinkable ins and outs of protocol upon entering the church.

Adrian saw at a glance, and not without some concern, the smirk on his companion's face, who discretely kept staring straight ahead.

Finally, a half-hour later, he managed to steer the inane conversation with his fiancée to an honorable close. He sighed and prised his shirt away from his back again. Laura was chatting on the phone to what sounded like her sister. She had not been able to help feeling somewhat claustrophobic after listening to the conversation about Adrian and Helena's future wedding. Her personal expectations did not stretch to such long-term commitments. She did not have any relationship on the cards, and those she had had, usually lasted no more than a week, her highest threshold for withstanding boredom. The usual kind of guy that took an interest in her was common-or-garden, the sort she met in neighborhood bars and restaurants, of few words and limited ambitions. She had figured that the density of jerks per square foot might be the subject of scientific research. But she could not care less; she did not need anybody by her side right now.

The first dark hues in the sky heralded nightfall and draped the landscape with shadows, slowly, and in step with the setting sun as it dipped below the horizon. The carnival procession had not sped anything up at all, and spending the night stuck in a traffic jam was not exactly what Adrian had in mind.

'Don't even think about it.'

He turned off the engine after ten minutes of not budging an inch, and switched from the CD to the radio in search of some good news. The melody of 'Here Comes the Sun' came through on FM radio rather than any longed-for news. He decided to listen in awhile before tuning into a local news channel. He had never understood why George Harrison did not write more songs. The man was a genius. Obviously they did not let him. Bottom line, he was a lesser Beatle. The first time he heard that song, it did not move him. Now, however, it infused him with optimism. He remembered that Harrison had also composed 'Something,' obviously up to his gills in acid, because a song like that cannot be written without the aid of God or the right drug. An oasis of divinity sprouting in the midst of mediocrity. You can be a genius for a second, then quit forever.

The chafing on his back was killing him. 'The Fuerteventura sun lashes you like a whip. All they have is sun and sand. What's the point? What's the point? The quiet island. And then some! I won't go back.'

CHAPTER II

Paris (France), Saturday,
July 31, 2010

It was not the first time he had had to interrupt his vacation for some pressing matter or other, but even so he was still mad about it. Denis Martel sat in his window seat in business class aboard the Airbus 321 bound for Athens, and grudgingly handed the coat from his linen suit to the stewardess, who wished him a great day with a forced smile.

Of course, so much responsibility came at a price, but he could not stop thinking of Olivia's disgruntled face at the Charles de Gaulle airport terminal. He felt that lately he had made the grade when it came to letting everybody else down. They had been looking forward to their vacation for months: those ten days were going to be for just for the two of them, to spend with his little girl, Cécile.

His ex-wife Alana was not overjoyed, either, to hear about his surprise assignment. A whole eternity spent licking her wounds then, at last, after she happened to bump into someone she had forgotten about for many years, she had started life afresh with an old buddy from college. Alana was happy again. Cécile had been the most important thing in her life since she had split up from Denis, but a few days alone with her new partner were much needed —indeed vital, for her relationship— and she was aware it would not be the same with her daughter around.

The passengers consisted mostly of couples and families with children. They took their seats noisily, their eyes brimming with joy over their forthcoming vacations. Denis watched them traipse toward the economy seats. In reality they were just bit-players in the background. He only had thoughts for his young girlfriend.

Olivia's patience must surely be wearing very thin. It seemed obvious that at thirty, she had better things to do than run around an old Interpol hound, on the rebound from ups and downs, his spirit wasted by cigarettes and booze. A girl like her would have better options, no doubt, and he only gave cause to make them look brighter. He furrowed his brow in resignation, while through the window he watched the Air France ground crew finish off mechanical checks and stow baggage.

"Something to drink, Sir?"

For the first hour of the flight he sank into a deep and drowsy state, caught up on his sleep and washed away his troubles with a relaxing gin and soda.

The juddering plane, shaken around like a toy by the whimsical turbulence, brought him back suddenly to reality.

He wiped his face with his hands and turned to look at himself in the window. The reflection was blurred, but good enough for him to make out his hairless head and the bags under his eyes. He was worn out. Denis had chalked up four flights in two days and he was not up to it any more. He cursed his advancing years and asked the stewardess for a much-needed black coffee.

Before opening his briefcase, he checked he was safe from prying eyes. An old hand's instinct kicking in. On the other side of the empty courtesy seat, a stout man with a mustache gripped the armrests while sweat poured from his forehead. Denis grinned. Then he thought there was nothing funny about turbulence, and set about reading the documentation the department had forwarded to him. Estimated time of arrival in Athens was 18:45 hours, local time.

From the terminal he would head straight to the harbor in Piraeus, where Georgios, his contact at the Interpol National Central Bureau in Greece, would provide him with a ticket for the superfast ferry to Naxos. The initial plan was to stay on the island for three or four days, although that would depend on how the investigation progressed.

He checked the documentation thoroughly to see that all was in order. Without that, it would be tough to get the unconditional cooperation of the country's authorities, who would go over each and every paper with a fine tooth comb, as usual, in an open bid to find some fault to enable them to send the outsider back home, legitimately. Hard-bitten local cops never liked an intruder authorized to stick his nose into their business, and for an officer from the Interpol General Secretariat, knowing how to handle them deftly and diplomatically was all part of the job.

He sighed in resignation. When he had begun work six years previously at the main office of the world's biggest international police organization, he thought he had drawn a line under his haphazard career in the Paris Police. Lyons was doubtless a great city to live in, and Interpol headquarters a nice, straightforward place for a retirement gig before settling in some out-of-the-way refuge, where he could find something like peace and quiet.

When his transfer was made official, he truly looked forward to a quiet stint of tedious bureaucracy and paperwork for, as opposed to common belief, Interpol does not report to any state authority and neither does it have executive functions. The operative organs in each country were made up of their own police forces, for activities on their territory, in keeping with their own laws.

The officers and criminal information analysts at the General

Secretariat, based in Lyons, were experts in multiple fields of criminology, but they confined themselves to coordinating the fight against international crime by availing themselves of their privileged standpoint and global outlook. They analyzed criminal behavior patterns and trends on a global scale, but rarely did they work at the coal face. It was sheer, blissful housekeeping.

Denis Martel had left behind his glory days and would not go back to them for anything in the world. In the wake of the disastrous outcome to the Le Bon case and two years of forced leave afterwards, the chance to reinvent himself in the Secretariat was the answer to his prayers.

To begin with, he joined the Criminal Intelligence Unit, where he monitored databases of more than two hundred fifty thousand criminals, analyzed tracking, links between crimes while spotting patterns and *modus operandi*. His experience in investigating pyschocriminal behavior and organized crime led him, very grudgingly, to the Organized Crime and Terrorism Unit. Since then, he had conducted three times as many inspection visits and spent most of his time away from home.

A pinging sound turned off the signs mandating the use of seat belts and announced that the turbulence was now behind them.

Denis came back to the present and began to leaf through the dossier.

The item seemed to be especially important, not just because of the facts —at the end of the day, violent crimes are run of the mill— but because it was cataloged as *red*.

An old Serbian military officer had been found hanging in his hotel room. Any verdict of suicide, very common amongst retired soldiers who had been on active service, collapsed like a sugar cube in water due to the fact the victim's arms and legs had been hacked off.

He examined the photos in the dossier.

At first it looked like a *pre-mortem* dismemberment: The edges of the cuts had hardened and separated due to slippage of the dermis. 'Poor guy, that's no way to go,' he thought.

Of course it was not a surgical amputation; a blunt ax may have been about the sharpest thing to cause such rough cuts.

There were also stab wounds to the torso.

'They went to town on him.'

The dead man had been identified as Vinko Miletić His details on file were very sparse: born in Belgrade about sixty-six years ago. No known family. Miletić and his troops had taken part in the siege of Srebrenica in July 1995.

Denis figured they would not have to look hard to find out whether the man had had any enemies. He looked out the window.

The noonday sun spread over the airplane's fuselage. Lower down there was an endless layer of cloud, like a bed of cotton, which strongly reflected the sun's harsh rays, by blocking their way to earth and flinging them back upwards. Denis pictured the towns, streets and woods tinged with gray below the pall of cloud, those gray days that benighted people's souls.

He took a deep breath. Most definitely he was not in full possession of all the facts, at least not right now. It was a *red* case and, therefore, access to information was restricted. Interpol, from its very inception, and given its neutral character, kept out of any crime that did not affect several of its member countries, and likewise avoided those that were by nature religious, military or political. Therefore, any item that, for whatever reason, clashed with that foundational principle, was tagged *red*.

It was not the first time he had handled restricted cases, and took for granted that information would reach him in dribs and drabs.

He closed his eyes and drifted back to remembering Olivia, which he did until the Airbus landed in the Greek capital, several hours later.

The meeting with Georgios was swift and confined to handing over tickets and a transfer to the port of Piraeus. They agreed to meet again upon his return, in three or four days' time.

After fifty minutes of exhaust fumes and gridlock in downtown Athens, he felt a pleasant sense of relief when his eyes beheld the waters of the Aegean Sea. A gentle breeze kissed his cheeks. The sea was a huge blue bathtub, sullied only by the enormous wake churned up by the ferryboat's powerful propellers.

The great multicolored mass of passengers took up almost all the seats on the top two decks, and clung to the welcome blast provided by the numerous air-conditioning vents. Children ran wild up the stairs and along passageways, while their parents dozed and took a break after a long wait and tiresome lines in Piraeus.

Denis preferred to watch the scenery from the stern, on the open deck, where groups of smokers milled around the cars, as well as other passengers that admired the impressive sight of the sunset reflected off the sea.

Most of the passengers got off when the ferry pulled into Mykonos. The majority of travelers were headed there or to Santorini, the last stop on the route.

The racket of car engines as they drove down the forward gangways shook him out of his musing. He found that approaching land had also brought his cellphone back to life, and a wailing noise told him he had new voicemail messages.

"Hi, it's me, I guess you're still on your way. I'm off to Saint Tropez tomorrow. I'll spend a few days with Marcel and Marion. Take care. Bye."

The coarse voice in the next message came in stark contrast to Olivia's dulcet tones.

"Denis, it's Al. Call me when you can, any time, I'll be

around."

He returned Olivia's call, but got no answer. A second later he called Al Coburn on his secure line.

"Al, it's me, Denis. What's up?"

"Have you reached your destination yet?"

"No, there's another stop. I'll be there in about... I don't know, in an hour, I think. I hope."

"Come on Denis, I haven't much time. Did you receive all the documentation?"

"Yes, they've given me the lot."

"I'll be in touch tomorrow."

"Talk to you tomorrow, then." The line went dead.

"Shit," Denis hung up and cursed to vent his frustration.

He guessed Al Coburn was in no mood to talk about vacations cut short or any of that nonsense.

The ferry cast off and set sail again for Naxos. Denis lit a cigarette and watched the island of Mykonos dwindling in the distance. It was the dead of night by the time the boat and its throbbing engines headed into its final port of call. The taxi waiting for him in Chora took him straight to his hotel. He barely opened his luggage, flopped onto the bed and fell fast asleep.

Fifteen hundred miles away, one of the dog days had dawned. From early on, Lyons' streets were bathed in baking heat, made muggy by the Rhone and the Saône rivers coming together. The forecasts of soaring fiery temperatures in the Rhône-Alpes region had been borne out fully, and the *Cité Internationale*, the area where Interpol's headquarters was located, soaked up the bright sunlight in all its harshness.

The air conditioning had broken down again and the fan was having fun blowing papers off Al Coburn's desk.

"We're on the case, aren't we?"

Coburn turned around to face his companion.

"We're working on it.

CHAPTER III

The gas station was crowded.

Adrian instantly regretted having turned off the coastal highway. He got out to buy drinks and something to eat while Laura waited in the car. The hundred-degree heat smacked him in the face.

The first glance was not what you might call encouraging. Endless lines of cars were waiting by the pumps that, by the minute, were running out. Dozens of cars were parked around the service station with their doors and windows open. Trippers were milling around in groups, chatting away, pooling their personal tales and pondering how many hours they would be trapped for. A bunch of children ran after a ball in the most brightly lighted part of the parking lot, as if they were still enjoying a day on the beach. People crowded outside the restroom, waiting their turn. He looked at a young woman next to the door cradling her baby, to calm its shrieking. The stench was unbearable.

Adrian did not have to go far to realize that the line for the food and drink counter was even more crowded: it went out the door and right around the premises. The mosquitoes were having a feast thanks to the crowd.

He had seen enough already. He turned around and headed for the car.

"We're going."

"You brought water?"

"No, this is just hell. Let's find someplace else. Can you hang on?"

"I guess so, don't worry."

He looked through the windshield for a few seconds, and then started the engine. Getting back onto the highway was out, because getting back into something solid and motionless was impossible. He was overwhelmed by a sudden feeling of claustrophobia and anxiety. He could not bear to be trapped in that place another minute, or be surrounded by all those people.

He crossed slowly to the back of the service station, while zigzagging to dodge the families sat on the ground and eating sandwiches. In back was a half-open gate. The opening appeared to lead to a dirt road between the pine groves. The glare of the gas station lights did not reach far, and he could only see its course by the light of a full moon. He opened the gate wide and, after a few seconds' hesitation, drove right through. Laura did not utter a word. She could see in Adrian's eyes that he had reached breaking point. She guessed any rational comment would be counterproductive and, she guessed right, as usual. Moreover, what the hell? She was enjoying this. Stuck with the big boss man in the middle of nowhere, with no way out. Life played tricks on you at times, and she wanted to play along in the most unpredictable and reckless way. A day to remember. And God knew, it was not over yet.

The first stretch of the dirt track was in good condition. At a cautious speed and with the aid of the much appreciated moonlight, it could be covered without trouble. The GPS situated them at the back end of nowhere. The satellite had no knowledge of that road. Then again, nobody had any knowledge of that road. He decided to share the current scenario with Laura. Both concurred they would turn up somewhere sooner or later, and amused themselves for a while with guessing games: maybe they would find a country hotel, lost in the mountains, in which to spend the night until the chaos subsided at the break of day, or a back road that would take them to some city or other or, who knows, maybe even a pig farm. Adrian told tales of his nights out at Harvard, when he would drive nowhere in particular with his buddies, to look for a party in an unknown house. Laura did not listen. With a distant look, she silently remembered a summer night, bang in the middle of her teenage years, which she could never forget, although she had wanted nothing else for years.

The farther they went, the narrower and more winding the road became, and the less certain they were. Only the M6's comfortable interior soothed the sneaking suspicion they were well and truly lost. It had been forty minutes since they had left the stinking gas station and sleep was already beginning to weigh on her eyes. The curves were sharper and sharper, the terrain rougher and rougher. The thickening woods wove together the treetops, which had shown the way but now blocked out what little light was cast by the moon.

Laura had been asleep for a while; she had nodded off altogether, worn through by a long and peculiar day. Her hair partly covered her lips and gave her a look of peace. Adrian gave her a look of healthy envy. He had not slept soundly one single night in the past ten years. At last he chose to end his rash and short-lived resolution to quit, lit up a cigarette and wound down the window. It had gotten considerably cooler.

He would never know how long it took, really, maybe only a few seconds. When the two front wheels lost touch with the ground, he sank into a fleeting dream-like state, which for him stretched out for several eternities. His gaze lost in the void, the image of the trees stuck in his mind as they floated in mid-air, their branches swaying and shaking the vehicle.

A chain of earth-shattering bangs hit his brain, while a white light suddenly covered everything. At last, all the lightning flashes gave way to a silence that hurt his ears.

Silence and emptiness.

In the distance, a child walked toward him. He could not see its face when it came close: a blurry shadow covered its head. It stopped in front of him. Stock still. Then everything went dark.

From the depths, memories and images came back to his mind from the not-too-distant past. From just a few years ago.

A red sky began to form in the darkness. The sun was setting. Several figures took on familiar shapes. From nowhere. Slowly. An old house. A long, coarse wooden table.

Three young men sat around wagging their chins, although nothing they were saying could be heard. Music. Louder and Louder. Dim candlelight lit up the room.

CHAPTER IV

Cambridge, Massachusetts
June 4, 1999

Jeff lit another cigarette with one of the candles strewn across the table in the old living and dining room. The effects of the 'angel dust' were beginning to unhinge him and his feeling of invulnerability was *in crescendo*. He felt proud. The phencyclidine was a crap shoot: the trip could be blissful or highly destructive.

The other shit was more predictable. Cocaine was for old fogies that had sold out, who needed to liven up their egos and forget about the decline of their unfulfilled lives. Not that stuff. It was sheer organic chemistry. He knew what he was up to —just a few hours before he had graduated *magna cum laude* in chemistry from Harvard. Once PCP reaches the brain, it inhibits dopamine and adrenaline uptake and causes dissociative anesthesia; it depresses the nerve centers responsible for making the body experience pain, and disconnects bodily awareness from cerebral sensations. You are air.

A feeling of peace spread throughout his body, rising from his back to his temples. There were still several hours left before the big party at The Ocean House. Everybody would be there. Again. One last night. Jeff saw the way William and

Peter focused their attention on the absinthe, and took great pains over filtering it. The sugar cube had to be small enough, so as not to stop the liquor falling into the little glass container, but big enough to dissolve slowly and sweeten the mixture.

"It's good," Peter acknowledged. "Distilled in Mulhouse." Peter Caldwell was the youngest of five children born to James Caldwell, one of the world's leather industry magnates. The foundations on which his father had built his empire were laid by his lucrative business dealings with groups of African poachers that hunted down highly endangered species, doubtless the most valuable ones on the planet. After that he expanded his business into lucrative arms deals with guerrilla armies in Central Africa. Caldwell controlled much of the black market in the Dark Continent. But Peter did not lend too much credit to those tendentious rumors. True or not, he would rather spend his days enjoying the $7,000 monthly allowance with which he could afford to live large while on campus at Harvard. There was no reason at all to bother himself with stupid questions.

The candlelight shadows flickered on the ceiling. William poured icy water into the mix. It was not at all easy to get hold of absinthe distilled with extra thujones, and even less so to have a blend shipped from France that exceeded the U.S. legal limits. Peter, nonetheless, was well aware by now that the extent of difficulties depended very much on the amount of money you slapped on the table.

Adrian had not shown up yet.

Jeff could still express himself coherently, cogently, even. He looked at his legs but felt they were not his. He cracked an absent smile.

William Atkins had now stopped feeling dog-tired after several sleepless nights. Four or five hours' sleep was not enough to recharge his hyperactive mind. Although he had graduated in economics with flying colors, he was an expert in computing and networks, and was capable of building a computer with his bare hands, designing innovative operating systems or destroying software systems with lethal logic bombs. Ready for anything except his girlfriend dumping him. That cruel woman.

"Time for my song," William cried out.

There and then, he turned to the Bang & Olufsen, and right away, the sound of "Bizarre Love Triangle" filled the room. He took a gulp of absinthe. The old New Order hit was just what the doctor ordered for his grief. Only old techno lovers remembered the band, but William felt that track was awesome. 'Among the top twenty of all time. The top ten,' he thought. He used to like getting high while listening to 'Hotel California', which doubtless enhanced the effect of marijuana. 'Wrapped around your finger' filled the brief silence that ensued after the track finished playing. He reckoned that Police hit was not among the all-time greats, and neither was any of their others, except perhaps 'So Lonely'. He felt like being sick.

"Forget about her, buddy. She doesn't deserve you. Let her rot in hell. She's a fucking bitch, like the rest," Peter was trying to keep the mood right, according to his standards, while preparing his PCP fix.

William was in no state to be consoled by any argument. It was not his first come-down, but neither had he been through many, which dated back to his spotty adolescence. He remembered that huge, gaping hole he could not explain, and how much he cried. He looked at his stomach in the mirror, in search of for the butterflies that ran riot, would not let him eat or sleep, and caused physical pain, but could not be found when he probed it by hand; he cried without knowing why, and cried all the more for crying without knowing why. He cried over cartoons, over documentaries about lions eating fawns, over the endings of dumb TV sitcoms. Those were weird and spiteful days. By this stage of the game, however, he could take the bad breaks more easily. Alcohol and drugs made everything more bearable, although he often vomited blood of a morning. He would soon be moving to San Jose, California. He had ended up accepting a job offer from Cisco Systems, one of many corporations that had been head-hunting him the past year: it was the one that offered the best located apartment.

"I hope Adrian doesn't take too long. If he isn't here in an hour, we're off," Jeff said in a broken voice, although he was aware that as far as his friends were concerned, nothing could get going without Adrian.

"Relax, Jeff, relax. Enjoy your last nights in the Cave, you'll miss it."

At last Adrian parked his vintage car in the Cave's driveway. It was one of the best houses on campus, a Victorian-style mansion surrounded by a huge garden, equipped with the latest in home automation and decorated entirely by William's mother. He could afford such luxuries. At $6,000 a month, between four scions of powerful families, the rent was no more than chicken feed.

Adrian entered the room and sat in the remaining empty chair at the table.

"How'd it go with the old man?" Peter asked.

"You all know Rosewood," he replied offhand while he watched the PCP and the glass which showed the bright green color of the absinthe. "Where d'you all get it from this time?"

"Olivier Gervais," Peter answered with a smile.

"I cannot but admire your family lawyer's skill. I tip my hat to you," Adrian admitted, while he imagined that stuffed shirt Gervais sneaking in unadulterated absinthe among bills of sale and court orders. Adrian Seaten looked in silence at his roommates of four years' standing. All four were there. Will, Peter, Jeff and him. Conflicting feelings swirled around his head. While a feeling of release ran through him, he knew he would miss them and his years on campus. A way of life that was now coming to a close.

He closed his eyes. He could not get the conversation with

Rosewood, the old professor, out of his head.

William played 'Bizarre Love Triangle' again. The loudspeakers throbbed with the full force of a heart about to break.

"Quit that damned song, will you?"

"Today's our last day."

"A great day."

The Ocean House was one of the emblematic medium-sized mansions where the Coleman twins —who were now in their senior year— lived, along with two of their cousins. The Coleman family, who were big in the Texas oil business, were among the Republican Party's leading donors and their vast fortune could only be matched by their political influence. Chris and Leonard Coleman, for their part, had become very popular among the upper crust on campus, and the pride and joy of their acclaimed family.

Their farewell party had, no doubt, been elevated to the biggest event of the year on the social calendar. The select guest list separated, in the callous eyes of university civilization, who was somebody from who was nobody. Because in the fledgling lives of the students on campus, being considered somebody or nobody gave their very existence meaning, and was the basis for self-esteem among the offspring of high society. For months past there had been much horse-trading to land a formal invite to the event. Now the great day had come and bunches of the chosen few began to show up in the nearby streets.

When the four friends joined the party, the night sky was shrouded in purple and the stars began to come out, like bright little specks set free by an enormous full moon. They parked Peter's old Mustang behind one of the lengthy lines of cars along both sides of the street. The bustle and music could already be heard there, from hundreds of yards off. They drank a toast of absinthe and vodka before climbing out of the car. They drank to themselves, to the future, to friendship, and to themselves again, and so on, until they had drained both bottles. When they crossed the gateway into the Coleman residence, a burst of light and music sharpened their senses like a full-on electric shock.

Between the garden, the pathway and the hall, a throng of multicolored bodies shook their bodies like crazy. Adrian saw that the *crème de la crème* of the major families on campus had turned up, as had the members of the leading fraternities, who were forever surrounded by pretty freshman girls, putting away vodka and cocaine in industrial quantities, as if they were going out of style. John Butler, the massive president of the International Economics Society, was snorting angel dust off a table in one of the corners of the main room, surrounded by his sidekicks: the same old crowd and their usual special escorts. Butler always invited one or two bits of freshman arm candy for his personal pleasure, usually scholarship girls, who were dazzled by an invite from 'Big John' and driven by their longing to rub shoulders with the in-crowd they so admired from afar. Adrian watched them from the corner opposite, and smiled back at one of them. She was slim and beautiful, with shiny black hair, but her old, orange- and turquoise-checked Guess shirt was three or four seasons out-of-date and she did not fit in. 'You're giving yourself away, cute stuff,' he thought. Then he gave her a concerned look. 'Be careful, kid.'

The other guests, three or four hundred-strong, streamed in and turned the mansion into a temple of excess, bursting with smoke and people, drenched in music, drugs and dancing, of close-ups and shrieks going up and down, from room to room. The smell of burning hashish drenched every room, engulfed the mezzanine floor, rolled down the stairs and into the garden. The music thudded off the walls that, like huge sounding boards, amplified the sound until it was an unholy ruckus that dinned itself into the temples like a drill. The atmosphere was a thick blend of stolen kisses, arm-waving, upstairs racing, nipping behind bushes, leaping about, cigarette papers, bourbon, broken bottles, acid, jimsonweed and Moroccan resin fumes. Adrian, Jeff, Peter and Will did not see much of each other that night. Lost in the den of pulsing humanity, they spoke, laughed, smoked and drank their fill, as their young bodies were still immune to excess. At times they bumped into each other, or their paths crossed amidst heaving bodies, and they swapped greetings in the thick of the crowd.

Whilst leaning on a banister rail, Adrian tenderly kissed Sarah Lynch, as he drew her hair away from her forehead. Although they only dated for the first semester of their sophomore year, they were still as thick as thieves and —so she fondly believed— always would be. That special chemistry was a privilege they ought not to have lost; the only problem was that it came along too soon in their lives, but they knew that.

Hand-in-hand, they walked upstairs to the bedrooms, wending their way through gaps in the corridors packed with dozens of other bodies dressed like them. He smelled a blend of feminine fragrances —jasmine, orange blossom, seaweed— watered down with bodily secretions, making up a syrupy and dizzying scent that wafted down the stairs. Adrian felt Sarah's cold hands on his back, below his undershirt. Their lips met in a blaze of passion, drinking in each other deeply, savoring the feeling of pleasure that came with possessing the body of a kindred spirit.

There were five bedrooms on either side of the corridor on the second floor. Amid laughter and signs to hush each other up, they found an empty room. Adrian half-opened the first door warily. Lying on the bed, unconscious and naked from the waist down, was the girl in the orange- and turquoise-checked blouse. She had passed out; too much alcohol and drugs for such a slender body. John Butler was enjoying himself on top of her. Adrian slammed the door. 'Son of a fucking bitch.'

"What's up, Adrian?"

The next bedroom along was empty, they went in and shut the door.

"Nothing, sweetie," he replied. "We'll be fine here."

Sarah looked younger naked. Her breasts were small and round, and her hips gently curved. Her white, unblemished skin, was soft to the touch and smelled of moisturizer. Adrian stroked her legs, from her ankles to her navel. He smelled her back, her neck, her breasts. Sarah breathed deeply. She felt safe, secure and wanted by the one who set himself up to be the sole owner of all her passions and desires. They drenched the sheets in sweat while they probed every hidden inch of each other's skin and flesh, inside and out, everywhere that fingers, tongue and lips could reach, until they fell fast asleep.

Hours later, when the first light of dawn shone through the bedroom window, they made love again. Then they lay in each other's arms. Adrian found a tear rolling down Sarah's cheek; whether out of joy or sadness, he could not tell. He held her tight and they fell into a deep sleep again. When he opened his eye again, she had already gone.

'Better that way,' he thought.

The hangover kicked in like a thousand knives cutting his neurons and the daylight battered him behind his eyes. He remembered his unfinished business. It was late, he had to hurry back to the Cave. He threw his clothes on and crossed the corridor. His clothes smelled of smoke and sweat. The bathroom door was ajar and he went inside.

He saw John Butler kneeling, his hulking body prostrate in the bathtub under the faucet, from which water gushed onto his head.

Adrian lit a cigarette and watched him in silence.

'Big John' did not feel the liquid pouring down his back.

Neither did he notice the strong smell of alcohol spreading through the bathroom when Adrian took the lid off the sky blue tin. He only began to wail when he felt his back burning.

CHAPTER V

Denis had not finished his breakfast on the little café terrace at the Château Zevlogi Hôtel when Yanis Mitroglou showed up on time for their appointment. He was with a young uniformed cop who introduced himself as Gallis, the local chief of police. Mitroglou was an old acquaintance, one of those in charge of the Interpol National Central Bureau in Greece. They had already worked together on other occasions. Denis grinned to see his friend's rotund figure again, stuffed into a light linen suit and topped with a white straw hat, more suited to a sugar cane plantation owner in Panama than a Greek police office. The last he remembered was a few years before, when the two of them were seated in a *taverna* in the Thissio neighborhood in Athens, along with a half-empty bottle of ouzo and a pouch of rolling tobacco.

"Yanis!"

"Denis! I didn't expect to find a guy like you in the Cyclades,"Mitroglou jested.

"Hmmm yes, it's a swell place. I didn't know they hacked people to death around here, either."

Gallis cleared his throat, making it plain he did not find that funny at all. His baby face and hair parted straight on the right were in contrast to his West Point marine stance. Denis took no notice and sipped his cappuccino in delight.

"Well let's get down to business. Gallis, why don't we go

over the facts that brought this gentleman here?" Mitroglou asked.

Gallis nudged his glasses with his forefinger and started to speak in solemn tones, in a failed bid to downplay his greenhorn, know-it-all look.

"The facts are that on July 26th last, a white male was found dead by cleaning staff at the Sofi guest house, around 11:30 a.m. He was identified as Vinko Miletić, of Serbian nationality. He was sixty-six years old. The forensics estimate the time of death was between 3:15 and 3:30 a.m., and the autopsy report determined asphyxiation as the cause of death."

"Hanging," Denis added.

Mitroglou nodded.

"The body had an enormous bruise to the head," Gallis went on. "And also the hands and feet had been amputated."

Denis sipped his cappuccino and set about spreading white cheese on his toast, thereby interrupting the young officer's explanation.

"No fingerprints or physiological traces were found at the crime scene, just Miletić's blood and remains," he continued after pausing, while he placed a Manila folder with photographs in it on the table.

"Anything of note amongst the belongings?"

"Nothing special. Clothes, a couple of books, a toiletry bag."

"This confirms the amputations were *pre-mortem*," Denis asserted while he inspected the photographs.

"Correct.

"Well now," Denis asked. "What have we got?"

Gallis looked at Mitroglou before answering, as if seeking approval, which he was granted with a dip of the head.

"We'd better start with what we don't have: no weapon, no motive, no prints, no witnesses. The weapon could have been a surgical saw. According to the forensic report, the victim didn't quite bleed dry before they hanged him with a metal cable."

"No witnesses? How did they get into the hotel? Was nobody on the door? People don't go unnoticed at that time of night."

"There was only one guy in reception, Markos. He's been on the night shift for four years. There was nobody else. He stated that he saw nothing."

"Nothing? Do you see why I love him?

"That's what he says. It's in his statement."

"He'll never say otherwise. It's more than his job's worth." Denis reckoned.

Gallis shrugged his shoulders and proceeded with his report.

"The perpetrator escaped through the window, and then jumped over the perimeter fence. Nobody saw a thing."

"There must have been more than one of them," Denis concluded. "It is unlikely anybody could have immobilized and tortured that poor guy alive by themselves. The perpetrator did not act alone."

"We're not so sure about that," Gallis interjected in a mysterious tone. "The autopsy found races of curare in his blood."

Denis lit a cigarette and slowly blew out smoke. He looked perplexed at Mitroglou. Curare was a powerful muscular blocking agent, in the right doses. They had planned the torture down to the last detail. Whoever it was, wanted to see him suffer and die in agony.

"It was payback time," Denis figured. "It's got to be revenge. They knew exactly what they were doing."

"There's something else," Gallis interrupted. "The severed hands and feet were placed on the table, arrayed in a circle, and..."

"And what?"

"In the middle of the circle was a flower, a yellow narcissus," Gallis explained, as he proffered a photograph from the file showing the scene.

"Great, just what we needed. A crime with a calling card," Denis asserted with deep irony.

He was aware that that tiny detail opened up a whole range of possibilities and lines of investigation. It would be no mere formality. He sensed it was going to wreck his vacation plans. Back at Headquarters, they wanted quick answers; the special *red* tag meant top priority. The sun began to beat down and although the faded 1980s Cinzano parasol shielded their heads, the heat was starting to drill through the pores of his skin with a vengeance.

"Come over to the precinct first thing tomorrow," Mitroglou suggested. "Naxos is a small island, it isn't easy to come and go without leaving a trace. We have an exhaustive list of every visitor to the island. Statements have been taken from a lot of tourists."

"And?"

"Nothing. For now."

"I'll be there first thing tomorrow."

When Gallis and Mitroglou left the café, Denis opened up his BlackBerry and called Sylvie.

Sylvie Prévot had been on his team for years. When she joined Interpol it was in the Criminal Psychology Unit. An expert in criminal profiling, in her department she spotted criminal behavior patterns and psychological profiles of wanted delinquents. In her detailed reports she assessed the conventional crime variables; geographical profile, scenario, *modus operandi*, victim and motivation. When she had a police sketch or photograph of the suspect to hand, she would set aside an exclusive section on an analysis of the criminal's physiognomy, despite her boss, Jean Boidi's reservations. Although many deemed physiognomy a pseudo-science, she firmly believed that studying facial features, both temporary and permanent, provided an X-ray to the soul. She had become eminent in the field. She received invitations to congresses and conferences and, for the devoted followers of that technique, having an Interpol agent among the brethren was quite an asset in affording them the utmost credibility. On occasion, she worked with museums and experts in painting, who sought her expert assessment on anonymous models portrayed by famous artists, who even today had yet to be identified. She determined their social status, their concerns and the message sent by their looks. Sylvie was fascinated by lifting the lid and revealing the inside.

She did not think twice when Denis invited her to join his unit. Hers was no more than a support department and the new post would at last allow her to make way 'in the field'. An unfortunate comment by Jean Boidi on the uselessness of her technique when it came to choosing a husband, went to speed up the process. Although Denis was completely skeptical about the 'psycho' department's contribution —he attached as much credibility to it as to newspaper horoscopes— Sylvie had always struck him as a woman with character, intelligent and valuable, doubtless head and shoulders above the rest of the mediocre crew. As time went by she had become his personal assistant in investigations, and his right hand.

In reality, his personal assistant in everything. She was the one to turn to when he sought advice, from his personal fate to his endless queries over how to behave with his daughter Cécile. His private Delphic oracle.

Sylvie was in her early forties —ten years younger than her boss— but had clocked up a hectic life, with two ex-husbands and three children, and was almost maternally devoted to Denis. She considered him a good man, a dying breed, and somehow admired his approach to life, so far from the rationality and strict responsibility she imposed on her own. A loose cannon that fell foul of the rules, as did everybody who bucked the system. She never dared try to unravel the feelings that man stirred up inside her. She told herself that it was no more than the inevitable trust and complicity born of so many years of working together, although she knew she was kidding herself, that it had begun to be somewhat more for a while. Maybe she was too thoughtful to admit it, and felt abject terror at opening up the cracks in her armor plating. On the other end of the telephone, she listened intently to her boss, her green eyes as wide as saucers. After the usual chit-chat about his entangled personal life —Olivia, Cécile and other sundry matters— Denis brought her up to speed on the reason for his trip, the case's priority, as well as each and every detail surrounding the crime in Naxos.

After hanging up, Sylvie got to work right away on the case. Vinko Miletić. A narcissus. Two starting points.

Before he quit the café, Denis phoned Olivia, who had begun to enjoy her days off in Saint Tropez in the company of Marcel and Marion, a couple with whom she was friends. The conversation was terse and trite. He preferred not to take much heed of his fiancée's distant tone: he understood perfectly that he had more than earned it.

Next thing, he called Alana. His ex-wife greeted him with her indelible Irish accent before handing him over to their daughter. Finally, she and her new partner had decided to stay in Paris and postpone the journey.

Everything under control.

It was lovely sunny weather and the whole day lay before him: he had an appointment with Gallis the morning after and had entrusted Sylvie with the legwork. He thought of approaching the Sofi guest house, but dismissed the idea. Denis knew that asking around on his own behalf would not go down well with the Greek cops.

Therefore, he decided to stroll around Chora, walk along Agios Prokopios beach and enjoy some good wine and a *saganaki* in one of the restaurants near Portara, the temple of Apollo.

When night had fallen, with his skin reddened by the sun, he went back to his hotel and fell fast asleep, laid low by a bottle of Jameson.

CHAPTER VI

He left the hotel early the morning after. The Mediterranean sunlight was all over the place. Denis wandered through the city streets, which were coming back to summer life along with the daylight. The Chora police precinct was stuck in an old, low building, right in the middle of town. The whitewashed walls reflected the sunlight onto a large bunch of passers-by who came and left the place, or loitered in small groups around the doorway.

Denis greeted and showed his ID to two young cops guarding the door who, with obvious disinterest, showed him the way to Gallis's office before getting back to their lively chat.

Once inside he felt like he had gone back thirty years in time. A worn-out, dusty counter functioned as a reception desk, which led to a small room where two lines of people waited to be admitted to the same number of offices. The noisy fan that hung from the ceiling swirled the hot air, which stank of tobacco and sweat, and made the month of August flap on a rancid calendar pinned up under a clock, which would have been more at home in a *taverna* than a police precinct.

Yanis Mitroglou was already in the office with the young commissioner. Denis greeted the two men affectionately and gratefully accepted a black coffee before getting to work. After some small talk about the unusual precinct building, Denis sat back to listen to the two Greek officers explaining the logistics of accessing the island.

Naxos had an official population of around twenty-five thousand, a number that rose considerably during the summer months. Although the island had a small airport, there was only one flight a day, by Olympic Air to Athens, at 10:40 a.m. The little Bombardier Dash 8 Q-400 turboprop that covered the route could seat sixty passengers, and Gallis stressed that it was usually half-empty.

Most people, therefore, made their way to the island by sea. Visitors usually arrived on board the numerous ferries linking the Cyclades Islands to each other and the mainland. Eight ferries a day and the occasional cruise liner docked in Naxos's seaport, although the latter usually sailed off the same day with all passengers aboard and, according to their operators, no passenger had gone missing.

Yanis Mitroglou described in detail how pains were taken to check departures from the island in the days following the murder. The special security detail had monitored the seaport as well as the airport. The officers had asked tourists for details of their stay on the island —entry date, reason for visiting, hotel, home country contact details— and, in some cases, a more extensive interrogation if there was the least cause for suspicion. Apart from having caught a well-known French opium dealer on the run, nothing had been found that could be connected to the crime.

The three officers knew how ineffective that sort of operation was. The outcome was more intimidating than anything else. Furthermore, there was always a chance that the killer had stayed on the island, a chance the three deemed —no need to kid themselves— very remote.

Gallis, nonetheless, was extremely confident that the investigation would work out. Naxos was an island, after all. It was not so easy to arrive, wait for the night, kill somebody then go home, just like that. Yes, OK, it was the biggest of the

Cyclades Islands, but also the least visited. Quite the opposite of Mykonos or Santorini, the stars in the commercial tourist firmament that was the Aegean Sea, Naxos was a backwater, easygoing and calm, and its dogged and faithful visitors only sought a bit of peace and quiet.

Miletić was one of them.

The old man went back every year, relentlessly, and always put up at the Sofi guest house. The staff described him as a quiet and friendly guy who tipped generously. He kept pretty much to himself, spoke little and whiled away the hours reading on the beach or in the cafés in central Chora. He stuck to a Spartan routine. Every morning at 5 a.m., he left the pension in sporting gear to go jogging, had breakfast at 7:30 a.m., and went up to his room after 11 p.m. He had no known friends in Chora and neither had he fallen out with anybody, at least as far as anyone could tell.

What the young Greek officer was convinced of was that, whoever had killed Miletić was not local. He had been chief commissioner for three years and on the Naxos police department for seven, and knew the island inside out: its people, its families; he even knew their pets' names. For him, it had become a matter of the utmost importance. The local police, led by the young officer, had thrown themselves body and soul into the case. It could not be otherwise. Somebody had come to sully the honor and image of their turf, their home. A white speck in the vastness of the Aegean Sea which exuded peace and dedication to the quiet Mediterranean lifestyle, and whose harmony, aside from a few petty thefts from tourists, had not been stained with blood for decades. His team had pulled out all the stops, but found nothing: no uncorroborated alibi, no apparent motive.

Denis glanced over the passenger lists. He would have time to look at them carefully later, although he felt it would not be easy to glean anything clear from them. It would not take a painstaking investigation into a man like Miletić, with war crimes in his past, to come up with potential enemies. Hundreds, if not thousands, would at least welcome the news of his macabre demise.

'What about the amputation, the narcissus, the odd array of the limbs?' he thought.

He sighed in resignation. Obviously, the peculiar crime scene, flower included, did not preclude premeditated murder in revenge for his alleged atrocities, but doubtless it also led to other possible scenarios: a psychopath, a ritual criminal, or even a crime of passion.

He looked at his watch. They had been holed up in that cubbyhole for two hours.

Sweat cloyed his skin and stuck it to the fabric of his shirt. He decided to get out of there as soon as possible and call Sylvie from the hotel pool bar, dry Martini in hand. He had not had a proper one in months.

"If I wanted to go unnoticed in Naxos, or at least less noticed, I would have stayed on board my own boat."

Gallis had at last attracted his attention.

"Until a year ago, hardly any tourist boats spent the night in the seaport," the young cop continued. "It is noisy and uncomfortable, the ferries maneuver just beside the harbor mouth and the boats are exposed to the Etesian winds. Only fishing smacks used the moorings. But last year the new Naxos marina was opened. It is run by city hall and under the watch of the local port police. It is our pride and joy. It has every amenity and in recent months arrivals of sailors have shot up."

"Where is the new marina located?" Denis asked.

"Beside the port. Near downtown, the hotels, everything. Everything is nearby here. We've looked over every single boat moored at the marina. On the night of July 26, sixty-three out of eighty available moorings were occupied."

Denis invited Gallis to proceed.

"Most were chartered. They usually plan sailing cruises for six to eight people, to take in four or five islands. Some include specialized crew and even catering. They usually tie up for a night in Naxos, two at most if weather conditions force them to. We found nothing irregular or suspicious: families on vacation or groups of youngsters on a booze cruise. Nothing of note, in general."

"I see. Anything of note in particular?"

"Maybe. There were two boats that sailed from the port early that morning, before dawn, from which we haven't been able to take statements. The information we have from the port roster is the departure of a Dufour 38 with a Greek flag, at 5.38 a.m., registered as My Own, captained by a man with a U.S. Passport, William C. Atkins. It had docked two days beforehand, on the morning of July 24, at 11:13 a.m. A likable guy the port workers said. Thirty years of age. Sailing alone. A lone wolf who didn't go back to sleep on his boat until the Captain Morgan had closed. Nikos the bartender told us he didn't stop flirting with the waitresses or downing one whiskey after another."

"I don't blame him," Denis smiled. "What do we know about the boat? Can it be located? Even if it's only for a routine inquiry; we have to narrow down our options."

"We've tracked it down. The boat is registered in the name of a Greek company. Neotour Sails. They own eight sailing boats, between thirty and fifty feet long, which they rent out for Aegean cruises. They have confirmed that Atkins handed the boat back at the Alimos marina, their home port. Alimos is to the southwest of Athens, five miles from the port of Piraeus and twenty from Venizelos International Airport. Our friend is probably on the other side of the pond by now, and it'll be impossible to find him."

"You think, young man?" Denis asked in a defiant tone.

Gallis held the old officer's glance, saw his wrinkled, blue eyes watching whoever he spoke to like a hawk; he saw his wrinkled temples and the sparse gray hair draped on his skull, and felt he was X-raying his mind. He grasped that he was pondering the experience in person, and that perhaps it would not be so hard to find Atkins, not for that guy seated in front of him. He did not look the sort to give up without a fight, although he sensed that his interest in the American sailor would dwindle right away.

"The second boat to cast off that night was a Formosa 40," Gallis added. It is registered as the Discovery. A wooden throwback to the seventies, forty feet long and with a Croatian flag. It docked in the new Naxos marina three days beforehand, on July 23, at 4:40 p.m."

"Who was sailing it?"

"A married couple. Osmanović by name: Kemal and Jasmina. It was their first time in Greece. Both with Bosnian passports. Their own boat. Croatian registered, based at the Split marina, in Croatia. According to the authorities in their home port, the mooring is still empty, they have yet to tie up."

"They are still at sea."

"Yes, we think so. If Split was their final destination, then it is quite possible that they have a day or two of sailing left, if they don't call in anywhere else. All ports in the southern Aegean have been alerted, but none has yet given any report of the Discovery. As far as we know, everything suggests they will sail straight back to Split."

"And how do you know? What have you found out about them?"

Denis asked, while he reluctantly breathed out the smoke of a Karelia Light that he had just borrowed from Mitroglou's pack.

"Jasmina Osmanović got on well with Olga, one of the local port police. They're the same age and quickly hit it off. Olga recommended several places for them to eat and some trips inland, they even invited her one morning to have a drink on board their boat. A charming and cheerful couple, she said. They had been married a couple of years and were on a belated honeymoon. She described Jasmina as a sweet, smiling woman who was most interested in the history of Naxos and its customs, and ever attentive to her husband. She liked to joke with the kids on the boat moored next to theirs, a French family; she confessed to Olga that she wanted to have kids soon and bring them up in Mostar, where they lived. She never stopped talking about how beautiful her city was, her home, the medieval streets in the old town, the Neretva River, the old clock tower. She mentioned on a couple of occasions that they would head home as soon as they left the island, in fact, they stocked up with enough supplies to last the journey."

"And what about him? What did our friend Olga say about Kemal Osmanović? Do we know where they were on the night of July 26?"

"We know exactly the same about Kemal as his wife: the guy was a paragon of virtue and charm. And we know little more about that night. Their neighbors moored next to them say they were both on board about 8 p.m., getting ready to sail. The watchmen didn't see them leave the premises until they set off."

"Good. That'll do for today."

Denis had had more than he could take of the atmosphere in that cubbyhole. There were many loose ends he was beginning to tie up, and he would rather do so in an open-air sunlit terrace café than the cramped Chora precinct.

"I've been in touch with Lyons to see what we have on Miletić. If you don't mind, I'd like to have a copy of all the statements."

"We've prepared a full dossier for you," Gallis interrupted, handing him a cardboard binder. We'll be in touch if there's any progress. On both sides," he noted.

58

Denis nodded and shook both his hosts by the hand; they stayed behind after he left.

Walking out of the precinct was like crossing the border into another world. All his senses rushed back to him: the fabulous Mediterranean light, the shy morning breeze impregnating the atmosphere, the strong sea smell, the tinkling of bicycles, the murmuring of voices from the antiques market.

A bunch of little girls giggled their way across the street, chasing each other. Denis thought of Cécile, his own little girl. He reproached himself for all those childhood memories he had lost forever, that had been banished to the graveyard and replaced by hectic workdays and ridiculous priorities that had once pretended to be vital. He sighed. How many casual things obscure what is essential, and how many winters it takes us to realize.

His hotel terrace stretched out along the street there, but he decided to walk past it. The nice morning enticed him into taking a stroll. The narrow, stony back streets crisscrossed the old town. It was encircled by the remains of the inner wall of an old fortress that, centuries ago, the Venetians had built when they occupied the island. Stores selling souvenirs lined both sides of the street: hand-woven mats, copper kettles, little copies of sculptures, fake sunglasses, olive oil and honey. Also, there were the *kafenios* —little bars completely filled with aging men— which began to buzz with heated chatter over a mid-morning coffee.

He spotted a sign on the right which showed the way into an old market, in Greek letters. A stocky woman beckoned him, arms waving, into her antique store, while she showed him hand-woven, colored cloth, but Denis kept looking ahead, as if transfixed all of a sudden.

'The Sofi.'

He walked over to the gate.

He was aware that he ought not to do any investigating by

himself, or at least not without forewarning his colleagues in the local police, but he could not help walking through the door. A routine visit to the guest house where the crime took place would do no harm. Creeping ivy covered the front of the building, so you could barely see any of the white wall underneath. The entrance was arched after the fashion of a Mediterranean porch, and shaded a row of plant pots that lined both sides to show the way. He went through the wooden front door. The little lobby barely had room for a couple of sofas and some dark, wooden chairs around a coffee table, where the morning's newspapers were stacked up. It looked like it would be hard to leave unseen. He asked the receptionist if there were any rooms free. A friendly girl served him. It looked like Marko, who was on duty the night of the crime, was not at work that day.

"I'm sorry, Sir," answered the girl, in English with a strong Greek accent. "We have no free rooms. Please call back later in case we have a cancellation."

"Very well, I'll do that, thank you. It's a lovely guest house. Tell me, how do I get from here to the new marina?"

Denis went out of the old market and followed the girl's directions. The pontoons were little more than walking distance away from the bijou guest house: you only had to go 200 yards to run into the harbor area. On his right, at the end of a long, stone breakwater and on top of an islet, stood the imposing Portara. He admired the spectacle offered by the enormous marble portico. It was all that was left standing of the unfinished temple of Apollo, the unstinting witness to every single sunset for more than three thousand years. Twenty feet tall and twenty tons of pure history. Restaurants around the port were scrubbing up ready for the first sitting of lunch. Decked in traditional decor, they competed in detail in the daily struggle to lure as many tourists as they could. The terraces were packed with tables draped in checked tablecloths, with jars of olive oil on top, and garlanded with rows of octopuses drying in the sun.

The new Naxos marina had been built just beside the old port entrance. The pontoons stretched out and were taken up entirely by small and medium-sized vessels.

He watched two girls in white uniform walking toward the port police station. He figured that Olga, Jasmina Osmanović's short-lived friend, was one of them.

The marina was open to the public and not a few tourists were strolling along the quayside, which was a hive of activity: families having lunch in the aft cockpit, owners mopping the decks or cheerful fishermen preparing their tackle. He realized that the premises lacked any kind of supervision, and its main entrance led to the street with the most bars and restaurants per square foot in Chora. Foot traffic would be considerable in the high season, even in the small hours. The herds of boozy tourists would be enough by night for nobody to notice another individual or two going through the open entrance to the new marina.

'Even though they were covered in blood that was still warm.' Sylvie was pounding his cellphone.

Time to get back to the hotel.

CHAPTER VII

The intense heat bore down on his eyelids as if somebody were shining a laser at them. His slow and forced breathing fought to keep his body going, and he could barely overcome the half-clotted blood blocking his nose and running down the back of his throat. He realized that his brain confined itself to his vital reflexes. It neither obeyed his commands, nor opened his eyes, nor moved his limbs. His ears picked up signs of a dull, repetitive throbbing He felt as if his soul had departed from his body and had lost all control, while he wallowed in a painless, peaceful feeling that dulled his wits and numbed his senses.

A succession of images began to run through his mind, well-known faces that smiled at and talked to him. Helena, Professor Rosewood, Peter, Laura, Ferri.

One after the other.

His mother cradling him in her arms and giving him baby-talk. Adrian wanted to touch her, but could not reach. His arms waved in the air and swiped her face, which slowly faded into nothing.

Everything went blank around him.

Thousands of people made way along a big triangle of frozen ocean. The deafening noise of thousands of footfalls cracking the ice dinned his eardrums and rattled his insides. Some fell unawares, struck by pain, above all children and old people, whose feeble bodies ran out of breath while the crowd tramped on, leaving behind a trail of bodies that were covered within seconds by the snow dust the sky poured down on them relentlessly. He saw in the distance how the coastlines burned in flames hundreds of miles high that lit up the night sky, although they barely shed any heat. He walked on in silence while around him he saw the silent exodus of all those gray-clad bodies. Occasionally, the noise made by the march was so loud it shattered huge blocks of ice and hundreds of people fell through the cracks, to be buried forever.

"Adrian, Adrian."

Laura's broken voice rang through his head.

"Please wake up."

He vaguely made out a face among the shadows. He understood he was lost in a dream. The same old one. He wanted to wake up with all his might. Consciousness came back to him this time, fraught with a sharp pain that rose in step with the senses coming back to his body.

The sense of touch was the first to rouse itself. Then he saw that a bundle of bandaging covered his left leg. His body was covered with blankets from head to toe. He could now hear the voices more clearly and memories began to trickle back, steadily, in dribs and drabs: a hellish tailback, a dark and lonely dirt road, Laura's voice. A forest. The void.

"Adrian."

He whispered something mute. That woman's voice sounded familiar.

"Talk to me, please. For God's sake, say something! We've had a terrible crash."

Adrian could see the girl a bit more clearly: she had some scratches on her forehead and her eyes were awash with tears.

'That sweet look.'

He recognized Laura's face.

"I'm alive, I guess," he muttered, haltingly.

Countless questions assailed his mind —the crash, the car, the bandages— and, nonetheless, his mental processes could only yet run at half-speed. He looked up: the sky was high and dark. An artificial light rebounded off the rocky walls, and cast a bunch of shapes and shadows around him.

"Where in hell are we?" he asked, at last.

"Safe," a male voice thundered behind Laura. "Thank God you're both alive I don't believe in miracles, but maybe you should begin to."

Adrian saw a stocky figure in the shadows, with a bushy beard and long hair.

"I don't know what made you come along the old cliff-top road last night," the guy added. "God alone knows why you're still alive. The old pine grove cushioned your fall before you landed in the cove. If miracles exist, then this is a fucking miracle, believe me." And turning to Adrian, he added. "You have a bad leg wound, but you'll make it. Now get some rest."

The man vanished into the shadows.

Adrian looked at his colleague in a desperate bid to find answers. Laura lay down beside him. Her boss needed to rest, he was still in a state of shock.

"We're alive, Adrian," she cried out nervously.

"Yes, that's a fact, and could you... Could you enlighten me? Where are we?"

"In a cave. A kind of cave in a rocky cove." Adrian understood nothing.

"And where did 'Jesus' come from?"

"I don't know. They dragged us out of the burning car, you passed out, they dressed your leg and now they've brought us here. There's two of them."

"And the other one?"

"At sea."

He had little energy left to force his neurons to work. Pain was making itself felt more by the second.

"Where am I and who the hell are these guys?"

Laura gave him a pill and paper cup of water.

"It's a tranquilizer, it'll dull the pain."

Adrian hesitated for a few seconds before swallowing. God alone knew what was in the pill 'Jesus' and his friend 'at sea' gave him.

He relented in the end.

What did it matter, if really, he could not be sure he would wake up tomorrow?

The tranquilizer was not slow to take effect and he fell into a deep sleep. When he opened his eyes, hours later, he was overwhelmed by the impressive scene around him.

CHAPTER VIII

The hotel's outdoor terrace café was cute, not very big, but enough to accommodate a dozen round tables surrounded by Greek sculptures and a collection of dwarf cactus plants. Denis took the only free spot left in a corner sheltered from the sun, which an Italian couple had just left. A young waitress with a winsome smile and deep brown eyes served him right away and, in the blink of an eye, he had a bowl of olives and a dry Martini on his marble table top.

Some years ago, he would have struck up conversation with the girl. He would have told her all about the origin of that mythical gin-and-martini cocktail, back in 1862, when it was known as the "Martínez cocktail" in San Francisco. He would have gone on about the common mistake of putting in lemon peel instead of an olive which, no doubt, spoiled the taste on the palate, and he would have dubbed as heresy the stupid habit of using vodka rather than gin, which not only adulterated the flavor of the mixture, but also the magical feelings it aroused. He would have asked her out to dinner in some seaside restaurant and they would have toasted the Mediterranean with some dry white wine. Later on, after a romantic walk through the marina, he would have tasted her lips by moonlight and stroked her skin until dawn.

Denis looked back at the cellphone screen, while the young waitress and her deep brown eyes went back inside. Reality hit him like a punch in the stomach. He smiled somewhat wanly and savored the bittersweet and creeping feeling that he was perfectly stuck on the way back.

"Sylvie?"

"Denis, I've been trying to reach you all morning. Where have you been?"

"In a meeting in a dive of an office with the local cops. An unforgettable morning. But a quiet one. Right now, I'm perfectly provisioned to give you all the attention you deserve."

"I can well imagine," Sylvie answered, picturing her boss just as he was. "Any progress?"

"It's all very raw. We have a few clues that need looking into, but nothing solid for now. Have you come up with anything?" Denis asked as he sipped his cocktail.

"I've sent off the photos of Miletić for analysis. Jean and the Criminal Behavior and Psychology team agree that our nutcase wanted to send a message, and that the victim wasn't chosen at random. It was not a madman he chanced to meet the night before in a bar. This was a premeditated crime. The sedation with a paralyzing agent, the array of the dismembered limbs, the murderer's *modus operandi*. Every detail confirms that idea. Whatever the motive, they had planned his killing down to the last detail.

Denis agreed with Jean Boidi and his gang: it was too clinical, too cold-blooded. A straight-forward, well-thought-out execution. The 'psycho' team were very accurate when it came to telling him what he already knew.

"You're former colleagues are just brilliant."

"You shouldn't be so hard on them. They're just doing their job."

"Don't you miss them?" Denis asked wryly, to hide his inner fear that she would one day walk out on him.

Sylvie ignored her boss's question. Deep down she found it odd that by this stage he had yet to figure out that she would never leave him.

"As for the flower that appears between the amputated hands and feet," she continued.

"The narcissus."

"Correct. Although that term covers a vast range of varieties. There are eight families commonly called narcissus, all very similar. They're bulbous plants from the amaryllis family, very common in the Mediterranean. The flower which appears in the photo is a *Narcissus Poeticus*, the only one of the eleven species that flowers in summer. Most of them do in spring."

"It flowers in summer. Any other peculiar traits?"

"Not really, just when it flowers. Apart from that, it's like the rest of its species. It's easy to recognize: its stalks have just one flower, flat white petals, a little open, orangey crown, and often with a red edge to it."

"Maybe our guy had decorative leanings," Denis jested, as he tried to forget the disgusting taste of Mitroglou's Karelia with a Marlboro.

"I've also been looking into the etymology and symbolism of the narcissus, in case our sicko wanted to send a message."

"Tell me more."

"It's name has deep roots in Greek and Roman mythology. It comes from Narkissus, or Narcissus, son of the river god Cephissus and a naiad called Liriope. There are several versions of the story, but all tell a similar tale; the best known is by the Roman poet Ovid, from the first century A.D."

"Ovid. When I was seventeen I read *Ars amatoria*, a treatise on love, twenty centuries old. A visionary, that guy."

"You and your precocious sensitivity."

"Useless sensitivity. You know I've never been very artful in that regard," he joked.

"You can say that again," Sylvie whispered quietly enough for Denis not to hear her.

"OK, tell me about our friend Narcissus. I don't remember

his story, if I ever knew it. Mythology was not my bedtime reading."

"Our Narcissus was a handsome and conceited ephebe. His unique and extraordinary beauty seduced maidens and boys alike. A vain creature condemned by the goddess Nemesis to fall in love with himself. He drowned when he plunged into a pond, while trying to embrace his own image reflected in the water. On the spot where he fell a flower sprouted, which was dubbed narcissus in his memory."

"Doubtless a tale with a lesson. Ponds are plagued with flowers these days."

"Folklore has it that the flower symbolizes vanity, conceit. Other interpretations link it to homosexuality," Sylvie continued.

"Hacking Miletić to pieces out of vanity or conceit would be like jailing Hitler for tax-dodging."

"If we are talking about somebody in their right mind, maybe, but that doesn't appear to be the case," Sylvie corrected him.

"That sounds like rushing to conclusions."

Sylvie fell silent for a few moments. She preferred to move on and not give her opinion again about her boss's stubborn skepticism when it came to expert psychological opinion.

"In any case, we have found nothing on file about crime scenes where there was a flower or anything like that. I've sent a memo to our contacts in the central country bureaus. You never know, there may be similar references at local level."

"And?"

"No reply for now."

"Let's move on to Miletić," Denis suggested after a skeptical silence.

"No known family. Nobody has claimed the body. He lived in a modest apartment in the Terazije neighborhood, downtown Belgrade. Nothing unusual was found in his apartment: a bit of old-fashioned furniture and some old books. No documents, no photos. Definitely no trace of his past. He eked out his existence on a meager pension he'd drawn since retiring from the military twenty-five years ago.

"Twenty-five years ago? But didn't he fight in the Bosnian war?"

"Correct. But not in the army. He had been pensioned off years before due to some heart complaint —heart failure according to the Ministry's medical records. Afterwards, when the war broke out, he joined a paramilitary group called the Scorpions, a special unit set up by the police, which reported to the Serbian Interior Ministry. Miletić worked his way up to lead a division of more than a hundred men in the Croatian conflict in 1991, and for three years after that in the Bosnian war. A nasty piece of work."

Denis had heard about their doings. They were out-and-out death squads. They hid their faces behind black masks and terrorized towns and villages in Bosnia and Kosovo, looted, raped and murdered indiscriminately. They were reputed to be the armed wing of ethnic cleansing.

"In July 1995," Sylvie continued. "Miletić and his squad took part in the siege of Srebrenica. When the city fell and for a week after that, thousands of Bosnians were executed: men, old people, women and children. The men were shot indiscriminately then buried in mass graves. The women were separated from their families, many were raped and then also executed, or sold. The massacre's perpetrators are wanted by the International Criminal Tribunal for the former Yugoslavia that the United Nations set up in 1993.

"Miletić too?"

"No, not Miletić. Several sentences were handed down for genocide and human rights violations; today, many of the accused are still at large. In Miletić's case, despite testimony gathered from witnesses, no firm evidence was found to make the genocide charges stand up in court, and neither was he sentenced for crimes against humanity. After the trial he went back to leading a quiet life: he literally vanished off the map. He has no known friends or partner. Neither has he been active in any extreme-nationalist political group, like many former Bosnian-Serb army leaders did after the war. A veritable ghost."

Denis sat back in his uncomfortable metal chair.

The waitress with the deep brown eyes served another table with her ever-present smile, oozing an energy that can only spring from happiness. Gentle oboe music wafted over from two small speakers hung on the outer wall of the hotel terrace, which mingled with the murmuring of chattering guests enjoying an aperitif. A child darted between tables on a little plastic scooter.

He figured that one thing he could be grateful in life was not living through a war first-hand.

"Denis."

"I'm still here."

"Do you need to know more about Miletić?"

"No, not for now. I just want you to look into a Bosnian couple and an American citizen. They left the island that same night, hours after the crime, each sailing on their own boat. No big deal, but worth checking off the list. I've instructed them to fax you all three passports. Take care, Sylvie. See you when I get back."

"You take care, too."

After a brief stopover in Athens, where he had a pleasant old boys' dinner in the Monastiraki neighborhood with Yorgos and Mitroglou, Denis flew back to Lyons, which was still reeling from a heat wave.

CHAPTER IX

The office looked deserted.

Most of the staff took their time off in July and August, and the few officers still wandering around the office spent their days in lively discussions on the ground floor cafeteria, instead of dealing with the handful of tasks that required some serious attention at that time of year. The receptionist told him that Al Coburn wanted to see him as soon as he showed up. Denis took note, but preferred to spend his first hour catching up with Sylvie over breakfast.

An hour later he was seated in front of Coburn.

Albert C. Coburn's office could easily have passed for that of an Oxford literature professor. Going through that door was like entering a whole new world, by moving from the excessively minimalist modern office world of glass and steel, to one with the stuffy atmosphere of the last century. The right wall was covered with mahogany bookshelves from floor to ceiling, filled with countless rows of legal tomes, tracts and books on international politics. Every inch of the wall opposite was covered with diplomas, testimonials and photos with heads of state and other big hitters. At the back was an enormous dark, wooden desk behind which Coburn spent most of his waking hours, and upon which stacks of files and mounds of reports were piled up. The big window opening in the rear wall shed daylight across to the other end of the room, where a long meeting table completed the furnishings.

The old man was quite an institution in the organization. Discretion personified. That diminutive and reserved man hid his gaze behind round spectacles and, at first glance, did not look like much behind that report-laden desk. Coburn was old school, and always kept himself at an unbridgeable distance from his interlocutors. He never uttered a word too many, never gave away more than needed and rarely had he been heard to make a value judgment. It was said that his deafening silences made the loftiest of people feel stupid. In his job he handled more classified information than anybody, as he had done for the last three decades. Having a discussion with him was like a round of poker with somebody who you know from the start plays with marked cards. He never mixed with the team, and seemed to have been born devoid of feelings. Coburn was now pushing seventy and the corridors buzzed with endless rumors and tales, true or otherwise, about the enigmatic life behind a character with a somewhat mysterious side to him.

After a cool greeting and small talk about the heatwave, Coburn quickly went to the point. He wanted to know all about the Miletić case. Denis went into full detail about the progress made on the case, his meetings with the Greek police, possible leads and the next steps to take. The old man listened carefully to his report from beginning to end without a word, staring at him, without a flicker from his face muscles. He then ordered his secretary to make coffee and kindly asked Denis to take a seat by the long meeting table at the end of the room.

"Interesting, Denis. Good work," Coburn said, in a much warmer tone than usual.

"Thank you. We've only just begun.

We expect to tie things up soon."

"An unpleasant business, no doubt," he asserted in a hesitant tone as he stirred his coffee. "This is not the first time it's happened. It is always the same story, the same situations crop up."

Denis kept his mouth shut, astonished at Coburn opening up and sharing his thoughts on the case without warning and out loud.

"The same situations that always have the same consequences, don't you think? It's sad that man never learns from his mistakes but, then again, that also helps to predict behavior and solve cases. Cases like this."

"What do you mean?" asked Denis, intrigued.

"It all revolves around the motive, finding the hidden reason that prompts violence, in any situation. We all scatter stimuli around us among the people with whom we interact every day, every hour. It is best to sort what is essential from what is tangential, to retrieve the original motivation that provokes the act. That is the key."

Denis sipped his coffee and kept quiet, waiting for some concrete message to materialize out of the old man's airy musings.

"From what you say, in his last years Miletić had nothing to do with anybody, right?"

"Indeed. He had no known connection to anybody. Everybody says he was very much a loner. His phone had no registered outgoing calls, except to some takeaway food establishments. He had no friends. He gave the impression he did not want to know about the human race after the war."

Coburn stayed quiet for a few seconds, and slowly nodded his head while he removed his glasses.

"Right, Denis, right. That's what I mean. With no interaction at all, no stimuli are produced, at least none necessary to spark responses of the caliber seen in a crime like this. Not even the sickest psychopath, the most mentally deranged person farthest removed from logical thought processes, prepares a murder with this degree of rigor and detail to execute somebody they don't know, that hasn't given them any stimulus, albeit an irrational stimulus. But our reports suggest that he had had no links to anybody for years."

Denis followed Coburn's line of argument attentively, lulled by his sparse tone of voice.

"His cruel execution is due to his part in the war; any alternative in his case cannot be other than remote. He had no life, thus (we agree on this much) he cast no stimuli in recent years to bring about his murder, so his death is down to his past life."

"A reasonable hypothesis," Denis agreed. "Nevertheless, there is always the possibility that his killing was a serial murder, no more. We must not dismiss anything. Moreover, Miletić was acquitted on all charges."

Coburn nodded reluctantly.

"A serial killer. You're not listening to me, Denis. You're missing the key stimulus. In most cases, the simplest and most obvious explanation is usually the right one. Think of the motive again. His acquittal does not make him less guilty, his trial was a farce."

Denis kept quiet."

"Miletić was acquitted twice on the charges brought against him by the International Tribunal," Coburn added. "Because there was no hard evidence. But tell me, who in their right mind could think that Miletić took no active part in the outrages, even if he was merely following orders? There were survivors, witnesses. There is testimony. There were people who suffered from his atrocities, who saw his face, who heard his voice."

"The Tribunal was aware of the witness statements and passed judgment. He was acquitted. That's a fact."

"But not a relevant fact. The goal of the International Tribunal is not to sentence small fry like Miletić, his acquittal doesn't let him off the hook," Coburn corrected him, as he looked out of the window to watch the clouds go slowly by.

Denis began to understand those who said the old man's

silences made you feel stupid.

"The International Tribunal's goal was to salve consciences, Denis. To salve nations', governments', the United Nations' consciences, and of all those that allowed the savagery to go on under their noses, of all those who looked the other way. Of those who abandoned all those poor people at the gates of the biggest and most barbarous mass sacrifice the world has seen since Hitler's day."

"Please continue."

"Let us interpret history. Let us get back to the subject. Let us seek the original cause. Throughout the whole Balkan conflict, the response from the major powers to human rights violations was lukewarm. In the case of the Srebrenica massacre, the international community ignored it at first, and when it wanted to react, it did so slowly and awkwardly. Too many competing interests, you know."

Denis knew the story very well. Sylvie's dossier was meticulously complete. In 1993, on April 16, the United Nations Security Council approved Resolution 819 declaring the Srebrenica zone a safe haven, and sent a contingent of U.N. peacekeeping troops to Bosnian areas. From a military standpoint, it would have taken more than forty thousand troops to effectively safeguard the zone, but the international community deployed only seven thousand five hundred, which moreover were authorized to use force only in self-defense, and not to defend the citizens they had been sent to protect. During the Srebrenica siege, nobody did anything to prevent the Serbs from stopping convoys of humanitarian aid entering the city, where more than sixty thousand Bosnians began to starve, deprived of food, running water or medicine. When the Serbs stormed the city in 1995, there was only a contingent of four hundred Dutch soldiers there who fled in panic and let them have their way. NATO turned down all requests for air support. The whole world stood and watched, like those with front row seats at a slaughterhouse.

"The outcome was eight thousand dead," Coburn continued. "Thousands missing. Mass rape. Written and pictorial reports of the massacre by the mass media went around the world, public opinion in every country began to ask questions; it was then, and only then, when the international community became aware of the horror, of their inaction, of the savagery. Afterwards, the International Criminal Tribunal for the former Yugoslavia acted. Against who? Against those that suit them in order to spread the media message, the message of security, the message of, 'Listen, peoples of the world: we won't allow impunity, we will protect you.' How? By showing the leaders' heads. Milošević, Karadžić, Mladić. Amongst the other, lesser accused, only those with documentary proof have been charged, despite harrowing testimony from the victims. None of them, those like Miletić, matter much. Their acquittal isn't relevant. It wasn't a matter of judging the guilty, but salving consciences and sending the message that the U.N. and international community are there."

Coburn took a sip from his glass of water and wiped his eyes before he slowly put his spectacles back on.

"One of Miletić's victims did the work the Tribunal neglected to do," Coburn finished. "And we know who his victims are."

"The 'psycho' team's report affirms that the killers didn't know Miletić personally. The type of execution, the way the limbs were arrayed, the flower."

"All very reasonable. The killer must have thought just that when he arranged the crime scene that way, don't you think, Denis? It is still a good way to cast the net wider. Moreover, many of his victims didn't know him personally and they will surely be thanking heaven for his death."

Denis Martel made no answer. He was still perplexed by his interlocutor's uncommon personal implication in the case. Be that as it may, Coburn's words made sense.

77

"The Osmanović couple. Follow that lead; something tells me it's a good one."

"I'll do that."

"And another thing. When you interrogate them, don't treat them like victims. Prejudgment impairs objectivity."

Denis gave no answer.

"Thank you, Denis, you may go."

CHAPTER X

Two thousand square feet of area that whimsical nature had hewn out of the rock face. He saw, at the front, the gaping entrance that let in the dawn's early light and lit up every nook and cranny inside.

Adrian could not believe it.

The cave floor was lined with a great, long black cushioned tarpaulin that covered the whole area except the back corner, where boxes of various sizes were piled up and full of belongings, tools, packaged food and water flagons. On his right, an enormous mosquito net hung from the ceiling and covered two huge air mattresses, where the two men were snoring away: 'Jesus' and another individual with a ponytail. On the left side wall were some climbing hooks, from which hung neoprene divers' suits, goggles, pipes and a map of the coast. A dozen oxygen tanks lay on the ground, next to several harpoons and assorted fishing tackle.

Laura was still asleep.

Neither his instinctive urge to explore that natural dwelling nor the limp caused by the sharp pain gripping his left leg could dampen his burning desire to get out of there.

Adrian hobbled along, dragging his splinted leg until he crossed the cave's entrance to the outside. It took a few seconds for his pupils to adjust to the bright morning light, and for his retinas to begin to make out the fabulous scene before his eyes. The sandy beach reflected the first rays of sunlight and the waves broke to dump lines of foam on the shore, again and again.

The beauty of that enclave dazzled him.

The cove was not big, just a hundred yards across. He looked up. An impressive rocky cliff sheltered it from end to end. Erosion had chipped away over the centuries at the vast walls of volcanic rock and hollowed out an area that was inaccessible by land, like those coves on the Costa Brava or the Peñas Cape which he sailed around in the summer when he was young, on board the Liar, his father's old forty-footer.

He could barely see as far as the wall's end. On the south side, a pine wood and broad bushes stretched down the crags and stopped dead, ten yards from the sand. He guessed that 'Jesus' was talking about that place when he spoke of the miracle: they had plunged down that slope and the vegetation had given them a soft landing.

Adrian could not take another step, the pain was unbearable. He struggled to scrabble up a rock to try and find the wreck of his car in the area. Not a trace. He only thought he spotted some black tracks in the sand, like the faint marks of a fire. 'My M6 burnt to a crisp.' He took a deep breath, he was too befuddled, too dazed to think straight, and so he hobbled back to the cave. Laura had woken up and gone outside to look for him.

"Tell me, Laura, what's going on here?"

"How are you, Adrian?"

"I've been better. Tell me everything."

"I fell asleep in the car, and woke up when we crashed. We fell down the slope and then into the ravine, I was hurled out when we hit the beach." Tears welled up in Laura's eyes. "You were trapped inside the car. I couldn't get you out, your legs were in the way, I thought you'd died. God, how the car burned, Adrian. It was horrible."

Laura burst into tears. Adrian hugged her. She was distraught, with her nerves on edge.

"You were going to burn to death and there was nothing I could do."

"Take it easy."

"Then this man came along, with the other guy, they came out of nowhere. They forced the door open with a crowbar," Laura said between sobs. "They got you out."

Adrian stayed quiet, giving his colleague time to calm down.

"They brought us to this place, to this cave, they treated your wounds and put your leg in splints. They also gave you tranquilizers."

"But who are they? Where the hell did they come from? And what are we doing here?"

Laura shrugged her shoulders. God alone knew.

"Tell me," Adrian pointed to the beach, right to the area just below the wood that ran down from the cliff. "Where did we land? There?"

"Yes, just there."

"And the car? What about my car, Laura? There's no sign of it. Nothing."

"Well it was there yesterday, on fire," she answered, drying her eyes.

"On fire, but not burnt to a cinder."

Laura did not reply. She had neither answers nor the strength to find them. She was dizzy. It was Saturday. Under normal circumstances, she would be back home after a day's work. A quiet weekend, as they all seemed to be recently. She would go to the movies with Eva, her room mate and only friend, or spend time reading a book at home. She was light years away from her comfort zone, and had not even begun to digest what had happened in the past few hours.

"We have to call home, they must be fucking worried."

"My cellphone was in the car," Laura said.

Adrian was disappointed to realize that his was, too.

'Call home.' Actually, he only needed to talk to Helena.

He was an only child and the nearest thing he had to a home was his apartment in the Tuileries neighborhood, in Paris. His mother had died when he was eight and his father, Roger, lived in the Harper House seniors home, in Lincoln, Massachusetts, in a very advanced state of Alzheimer's. He usually went to see him every two months. He would sit next to him and show him photos of the two of them; old photos of father and son sharing moments of their lives since Adrian was a toddler: birthdays, fishing trips to the ocean, high school graduation. His father always looked at the photos in silence while his son told him thousands of funny stories about the good times they had together. He told them enthusiastically, and tenderly, as if unaware that the man no longer recalled anything; he didn't even remember him. At times, Roger would shed a tear. Adrian would hug him and the old man felt the young stranger's affection and warmth. When he left the home, a sense of anger overwhelmed him from head to toe.

His father had doted on him when he raised him, sheltering him from any hint of grief over his mother's untimely demise. He had borne the brunt of the pain at her loss, letting his son's eyes see only looks of happiness and hope, while he soaked up all the downheartedness that ate away at him from the inside, day by day. Adrian consoled himself at times by thinking that his father's illness also washed away the past grief and wiped out the dark places in his heart. Sometimes, life hit you with twisted jokes. Roger Seaten was a recognized specialist in Modern History. For more than thirty years he had been a lecturer, researcher and emeritus member of the governing body at the JFK School of Government at Harvard, and his vast knowledge of international relations had led him to work on foreign policy with two presidential administrations. Whenever Adrian saw those half-lifeless eyes, he could not help but think how many secrets and mysteries had withered away in that dried-up brain.

'Jesus' spoke and interrupted his thoughts.

"Good morning. How are you?" he asked in a thick Portuguese accent. "My name is Flávio."

Flávio gave Adrian his hand, and returned the greeting and the introduction. He guessed the man was no more than thirty. He had a serene, mysterious stare. The outlandish figure from the night before could at last be seen in the light of day. That guy looked to have been crafted by Da Vinci. His body was wiry and his skin, smooth and dark, making his torso and leg muscles stand out. He had a long mop of light brown, sun-bleached, shoulder-length hair while a golden fringe fell down to his thick lips, that were cracked by the salt water.

Flávio sat down on a rock, next to Adrian and Laura.

"How's your leg?"

"Better," Adrian replied. "It's properly immobilized, although the pain is unbearable at times. Listen, Flávio, I don't know who you are or what you're doing here, but I would like to thank you for saving our lives. Had you not been there, we wouldn't have lived to tell the tale."

"You're welcome. Life is the most precious possession there is," Flávio's voice was mellifluous and serious. "It is an honor to have the chance to save it for somebody."

The other guy appeared from behind and sat next to him without a word. He was a clone of his buddy. He may have had curlier hair, maybe he was a little shorter, maybe stronger, but both looked like they had been cast in the same mold.

"May I introduce you to Paul."

Laura and Adrian greeted him shyly, overcome as they were by the situation. Paul kept his mouth shut. Adrian began to feel worried and intrigued by that odd couple.

"Paul, Flávio, thank you very much again, thank God we're fine. Now we'd like to make a call so we can be picked up. Do you have a phone we could use?"

"Sorry, we have no phone," Flávio replied. Adrian took a deep breath.

"OK, well then, how do we get out of here?" Flávio and Paul swapped glances.

"You cannot get out of here," the former said. "This beach is inaccessible by land, and doing so by sea is dangerous," he added. "The currents and rocks make entering and leaving very difficult."

Adrian understood none of it and began to lose patience. He had a sudden urge to leap at the throat of that hermit fellow with prophet-like airs, and felt a sharp ache in his leg. He grunted in pain.

"Listen carefully to me. I don't care who you are or what you do. I don't care if you're drug traffickers or smugglers. It makes no difference to us, and neither will we say anything, we just want to get out of here and go home. What part of that don't you understand?"

"And we're telling you it's impossible," Flávio said slowly.

"Sorry if I'm not explaining myself. What..."

"You're explaining yourself very well, Adrian. You've landed in our private beach, our home. You have trespassed on our private universe. We have rescued you from your burning car and treated your wounds. Getting away from here is impossible without outside help. You cannot leave by yourselves, and you can believe that we can't do anything to help you, either. Moreover, we don't want anybody to come and disturb our home, or sniff around our beach or poke their noses into our business. I hope to have made myself clear now," Flávio replied in a calm and plain voice.

Adrian counted to ten so as not to blow up. He took a deep breath. Aggression got you nowhere and he did not know his weird interlocutor very well.

"You have nothing to fear," Flávio continued. "We just want

to live in peace, in our habitat."

"Your habitat?"

"The sea," Flávio noted, and pointed in front of them. Adrian looked silently at Flávio's face. That kid was a freak. A moron. A recluse who was leaking lithium by the pound. Laura stayed quiet, while waiting for Adrian's reaction.

"Listen, Flávio," Adrian began, adopting his new host's calm tone of voice. "We don't want to disturb your relationship with your habitat, the sea, or anything. We have a life out there. There are people who will worry about us. People who love us, who don't want us to suffer and whom we must get in touch with to tell them we're OK, that we're alive and have not vanished off the map. Unless you mean for us to stay here for the rest of our lives.

Flávio looked at him without moving a muscle in his face.

"We will take you home, but not now. That is impossible. We have our reasons. It won't be long. Just three weeks. People will come for us and we will leave together. We will drop you off, safe and sound, in the first port we see, but you must obey the rules. We don't want you drawing attention to strangers, we don't need anyone snooping around here. Take it as a trade-off for saving your lives."

Adrian had trouble remembering what day it was: it was in the middle of August. 'Three weeks.' It all seemed so surreal. He thought of Helena, their upcoming wedding, the ton of unfinished business at his agency that could not wait. Those thoughts raged through his head. His mind gradually settled down and he began to think collectedly. Two people cannot disappear that easily. They would doubtless have already been reported as missing, and a search party would have been sent out with all available means at its disposal. They would comb every inch of the area, and uncover the remains of the car. It was only a question of hours, maybe less.

'The remains of the car,' he thought.

Adrian recalled having seen nothing on the beach.

"OK, I don't think we have any options,"

he said, pretending to be convinced. "We hope you reconsider, because the whole thing is quite pointless. By the way, we need to find the remains of the car. Some of the luggage may have been saved, and there were some tools that may be of use to us."

"There's nothing left. The car was burnt to a crisp, just dirty scrap metal. Rest assured, we have clothes, food, water and shelter. You need nothing more, just rest."

"But that's impossible. You can't..."

His mysterious hosts did not bother to answer and headed inside the cave. Shortly afterwards, they re-emerged clad in black neoprene suits, dragging along diving gear; oxygen tanks, flippers and goggles. Without a word they walked toward the shore looking straight ahead, as if in a sort of trance. They knelt down by the sea. Flávio covered his face with his hands, while Paul merely looked ahead. It took a few minutes for them to disappear into the waves, swallowed up by the sea depths.

Adrian and Laura watched the ritual carefully. In silence. Any comment was futile.

"Don't worry, we'll get out of here. We have time to think of a way. I'll take care of everything," Adrian winked at Laura and smiled for the first time since the crash.

Laura smiled back at him. She calmed down for a moment. She had always thought of him as conceited and aloof, but in some way that she could not explain, she felt safe beside him. She had never needed anybody to make her feel safe. Laura knew how to take care of herself and, nonetheless, she did not shirk that new feeling, on the contrary, she embraced it less reluctantly than she would have imagined.

They decided to take it easy that day. The bruises from the crash needed rest, and their ideas, clarity. Their strange hosts had left them a wicker basket. Laura found two straw hats inside, as well as sun cream, a gallon flagon of water, and a plastic container with fruit and dried octopus in it.

"There's just one thing that bothers me, Laura."

"What?" she looked at him, feeling a little queasy.

"I hope you like fish, because we're going to gorge on it."

Laura took a second to overcome her disbelief before she burst out laughing.

It was the dead of night when Flávio and Paul came back to the cave. They took off their wet suits and hung up all their tackle on the wall hooks. Adrian and Laura were fast asleep on their air mattresses. Paul went up to Adrian. He saw that his blanket had slipped off and tucked him in, up to the shoulders; next thing, he fell on his camp bed and collapsed, as he was worn out.

Flávio grabbed a bottle of vodka and a clean towel, and went out on to the beach. He sat down on the sand and stared at the horizon. It was a clear night and the moonlight lit up the crests of the waves, which rolled shoreward to turn into foam. He plugged the earphones of an old Discman into his hears and took a swig from the bottle.

The days of asking God for answers were over and done with. A song filled up his ears. The light westerly breeze ruffled his hair as a thick tear began to trickle down his cheek. He waited a few seconds for it to come.

Patiently. Eyes closed.

Until at last that grief began to well up; it was so familiar and heart-rending. He clenched his fists and welcomed, as he did every night, the fireball that festered in his life like a terminal cancer.

Hours later, the vodka had knocked him out and he huddled up into a ball on the sand, anesthetized and unconscious, with the moon as sole witness.

CHAPTER XI

The Lufthansa flight from Paris landed in Sarajevo on time, in keeping with Germanic precision. After waiting for a half-hour, his hire car was finally ready and he turned onto the M-17 highway, toward Mostar. He had not planned to drive for two hours and a half with no air conditioning, and even so he had had to put up stoically with the unhelpful attitude of the girl at the Hertz counter.

But his reflexes were still dulled by the Chablis lingering in his veins.

As he did just about every time he went back to his old city, Denis had taken the opportunity to have dinner with LeBoeuf. He enjoyed Paris much more as a visitor than a denizen. Too many years caught up in the big city's iron beat. He always stuck to the old drill. Yves LeBoeuf, his old lieutenant in the Paris Police, would pick him up mid-afternoon at the entrance to the Le Meurice Hotel, then they would chat for hours in the Marly café and relive endless old stories for the umpteenth time.

His old friend had for years been his second-in-charge, and whereas now he was the operating chief in the Paris Police, he still felt his old boss pulled rank on him. In the their meetings, Yves would bring him up to date on department news and ongoing investigations, and ask his friend for his opinion and advice. He did not need them, but liked to make him feel that he still valued his thoughts, as a token of thanks and for old times' sake. In between cups of coffee they would rake over their lives from top to bottom, as if they had not seen each other in ages, instead of every two months, which was how often they usually met. When darkness came they would pay homage to the inevitable dinner at the Drouant, down on the Place Gaillon, where they would delightfully savor a couple of dozen number 3 *huitres creuses* from Brittany, washed down with Chablis. They would make an evening of it until past midnight, and then tightly hug each other good-bye until next time.

A dilapidated Opel honked its horn and brought Denis back to reality.

The Sarajevo exit on the M-17 highway led to Meše Selimovića Boulevard. Most of the buildings lining it had been built after the war, on top of the rubble left by the enormous concrete blocks shelled by the Serbian artillery. The old boulevard was now commonly called 'Sniper Ally', in macabre homage to the Serbian marksmen who, during the war, used to hide on the rooftops to shoot at the 'ducks', which were usually pedestrians walking along the avenue. Only one huge semi-collapsed building was left standing, pock-marked by shrapnel and bullet holes, to bear uncomfortable witness to the brutal hatred between brother communities.

The Sarajevo to Mostar highway had only one lane each way and was full of bends. After going down a bleak mountain pass, flanked by canyons and lakes, he followed the Neretva River bed all the way to his destination. In the course of the two hundred miles between its source in the Dinaric Alps until it flows into the sea in Croatia, it breathes life into the land that it irrigates, to form a long, rich and fertile valley, while its basin channels mountain water that is very pure and chilly, even in the summer months.

The traffic was dense, packed by countless German and

Italian cars touring the area. He reckoned it would take three hours to reach his destination.

Sylvie had easily tracked down the young Osmanović couple. They had returned from their Aegean cruise, and Jasmina raised no objection at all to helping with inquiries. Sylvie's call was the first she had heard of the Miletić murder, or at least she said so convincingly. She had an appointment with Denis at 5 p.m. in the café at the Bosnian National Monument Muslibegović House Hotel.

The countryside on both sides of the M-17 was spectacular. The slow traffic allowed him to savor every last detail. The mountainsides showed cuts revealing layers upon layers of different colored earth, to which clung small towns and villages, whose wavy fields were dotted with piles of hay, patches of cabbage and other vegetables. All along the old highway, the water was dammed up in lakes and ponds, which prompted visitors to go bathing, so some stopped their cars on the banks to have a dip and enjoy the scenery.

Denis recalled the French Foreign Ministry's recommendations to visitors to Bosnia-Herzegovina. One of them advised travelers not to turn off the highway or stop in clearings that had been in the firing line during the war, in order to avoid mines. They also warned of the countless mobile speed traps along the highway. He kept an eye on the speedometer to check that would be no problem.

As he approached his destination, groups of young goatherds stopped to look at the cars go by, as if watching a gala parade, while their tribes gamboled in the meadows. On both sides of the highway he saw the remains of what had once been farms, gutted by fire, shamefully revealing their flanks that were battered by shrapnel and full of different-sized shell holes. The walls —or what was left of them— were covered from top to bottom with every kind of graffiti; Cyrillic and Roman letters, painted in red and black, one on top of the other, as if each wanted to have the last word.

It was not hard to imagine what scenes had been played out on that same ground, not so many years before.

Despite the sluggish traffic, he got to Mostar earlier than expected. He still had a couple of hours to himself before his meeting with Jasmina Osmanović, and parked in between the old town and the famous *Stari Most* bridge. It was a baking hot day, well above one hundred degrees but, despite the boiling heat, the city was buzzing with life. He only had to take a glance to have the feeling he had left behind Europe to enter head-long into the Arab world. A rowdy street market stretched along the alleys of the old town and had numerous souvenir shops and stalls. Denis delved into it and wandered around. The sun's harsh rays bounced off the light, slippery marble floor. There was rather little shade under the shops' awnings, and tourists milled around the counters, among the wide range of wares and keepsakes the sellers hawked loudly: veils and headscarves for belly-dancing, Aladdin's lamps, copper pots of all shapes and sizes, and all sorts of other goods. As though in a peculiar, throwback dream, buyers snapped up Soviet-era and even war-time goods, from shell cases to caps, posters and military decorations.

He retraced his steps to cross the *Stari Most*, the symbol of that beautiful city where for centuries different communities and religions had lived side by side. Divers plunged from a great height into the waters of the Neretva for a few euros, and drew a round of applause from onlookers. He looked at the old bridge in admiration. That pile of stone had seen so much history that it seemed to peek over the shoulder of all around it. So much history that people had not yet managed to take it all in.

It dated back to the 16th century, during the time of the Ottoman Empire. It was destroyed during the war and rebuilt afterwards. A photography exhibition by the entrance showed snaps of before and after it was resurrected. It was barely twelve feet wide and flanked by two beautiful towers —the Halebija and the Tara— one at each end, and which marked the border between two worlds: Catholic Croatia to the west, and Muslim Bosnia to the east.

Denis sat down in one of the restaurants near the river. A jug of ice-cold beer helped to balance his body temperature. He sampled a delicious *pljeskavica*, along with a kind of beef sausage called *sudzuka*. That, followed by a dry sirloin steak, assuaged his appetite before he headed off for his appointment with Jasmina.

The Muslibegović House Hotel was within walking distance of the bridge —well, everything there was within walking distance— and it housed a small museum inside. The Ottoman-era building impinged on all five senses with flashes of the old East. A friendly gentleman with a bushy mustache showed him the way to the inner courtyard.

He sat down at one of the wicker tables, where lush creeping vines grew to form a sort of roof to provide some wonderfully refreshing shade. He phoned Sylvie to check up on the latest data on Jasmina and to find out about any developments in Lyons: they had yet to receive a fax of Atkins' passport from the Greek police.

At which the woman he had sought showed up at the appointed time: she was so young that Denis thought he had the wrong person.

CHAPTER XII

"Mr. Martel?

Denis swiftly hung up on Sylvie.

"That's me. Mrs Osmanović?"

"Please call me Jasmina," she answered as she shook his hand politely.

Denis gently asked her to sit down by the table after they had completed the formalities. The waiter took their order of one sparkling water each, with ice and lemon.

According to the report Jasmina was pushing thirty, but the women in front of him could have passed for several years younger. Her features were still those of a teenager. Her skin was very white, almost clear. Not a single wrinkle showed on her face, not even around her eyes or mouth; she looked to have been fashioned from China porcelain. She had medium-length, pitch-black hair, which draped across her shoulders. Her big, expressive black eyes shed sadness and joy in equal measure. She wore a black tee-shirt and faded jeans which accentuated her youthful look even more.

"How was your journey, Mr. Martel?"

"Please call me Denis. The journey was fine, thank you, very pleasant. I didn't know Bosnia-Herzegovina. I'm impressed by the beautiful countryside and the speed at which new buildings rise up. I have seen a country proud of its roots and committed to reconstruction."

"There's a long way to go."

"I have no doubt it's worth going all the way. Jasmina, before we begin, I should like to thank you for your help. You know the reason for my visit. We are investigating the murder of Vinko Miletić, a Serbian citizen."

"I'm all yours, Denis," Jasmina interrupted.

"Miletić was found dead in his hotel room in Naxos, just ten days ago, in very violent circumstances."

"I know, your assistant gave me the details. As I already told Ms. Prévot, I don't think I can be of much help. Anyway, I have agreed to see you, in case I can be of some use."

"I believe you have both just got back from Naxos, haven't you? You and your husband. Kemal's his name, isn't it?"

"Indeed. Kemal and I got back to Mostar two days ago from Split, where we have the boat moored. We don't use it much, it belongs to my husband's family. We were married two years ago and have barely had a chance to take a break and spend time by ourselves. We decided this would be a good time for a quick trip to the Aegean. We spent two weeks away. In particular, I believe we were in Naxos for four days."

"Was it the first time you visited the island."

"Yes. Some friends had recommended it to us as a nice, quiet place, ideal for a get-away, and of course they were right."

"I wholeheartedly agree with you. It is a lovely island and, no doubt, a quiet one. What did you do with your time during your stay?"

"I'm sorry, Denis, but I don't quite understand the question."

"I mean, what activities did you undertake, what was your daily routine."

"No, no," Jasmina smiled. "I don't believe I made myself clear. I understood your question straight away. What I don't understand is what this has to do with the Miletić murder, unless the reason for your visit is that there be a shadow of suspicion falling on my husband and myself."

Denis was taken aback by the young lady's cool, direct approach. She did not drop the sweet —naive, even— smile, while she looked at him with her wide-open, teenage eyes.

"No, Jasmina, you're not suspects. But you must understand that we have to follow the usual procedure in our investigation. You and your husband left the island on the night of the crime. The victim was a well-known ringleader in the Scorpions, and we know you took refuge in Srebrenica during the siege. We must interrogate you, as we have done many people in Naxos."

Jasmina took a sip of her sparkling water.

A slight breeze blew through the hotel courtyard, and rustled the leaves on the luxurious vine.

"We saw the sights, went on trips, went down to the beach at sunset a couple of times," she answered at last. "We usually ate in restaurants in downtown Chora, or the port. We spent hours and hours on the boat, reading and chatting to the crew tied up next to us. Nothing special, as you can see."

"What do you and your husband do for a living? I understand you live here, in Mostar."

"Yes, we moved here two years ago. Before that we lived in Hamburg. Kemal is a chemical engineer and, after he graduated, he moved to Germany to work for an oil major. I met him after the war, on one of his trips to Sarajevo, we fell in love and I went to live with him. After our wedding we decided to come home. I was born in Mostar and spent my early years here. I wanted to come back and help to rebuild my country, give back everything this land gave me. Now we have a small animal feed and fertilizer business, we work on community education projects and workshops for children and teenagers."

"You are also a member of the Belgrade chapter of the Women in Black group.

Jasmina smiled. Those Interpol guys had really done their homework and had a detailed run-down on her life. Even so, that did not bother her at all.

"Yes, I am. Although not as actively as I would like. If we allow the atrocities and horrors of war to be forgotten, we run the risk of repeating them. I do my utmost to make sure that will not happen."

"Did you know Vinko Miletić?"

"Not personally. I know, as you just said, that he was one of the ringleaders of the Scorpions. And he was tried by the International Tribunal in The Hague. But you already know that."

"And do you believe he was guilty as charged for ethnic cleansing, crimes against humanity..."

"Absolutely," she answered, without raising her tone of voice a bit, and added. "Although, to tell the truth, I'm not happy he's dead. I don't care. I've been through so much pain that I won't allow rancor and hatred to embitter my life and my family's. I won't let them. It's something that you may well not understand."

Denis made no comment. She was surely right that he was unable to understand certain things.

"You and your family lived in Srebrenica before the war."

"We used to live in Bratunac, a small town near the Serbian border. When the Serbian offensive began in 1992, we were forced to flee to Srebrenica. My parents ran a small hotel on the outskirts of Bratunac, and my father was reluctant to leave until the last minute. That hotel was his life's work, and he had sweated blood to build it. Father rebuilt an old warehouse with his bare hands. He worked around the clock to manage and run the accommodation. He took care of everything personally, down to the last detail, as if he were sculpting a statue that was never finished. Mother helped out with the cooking and cleaning. My siblings and I lived there. Father made our home on the top floor. I remember that I had a view of the mountains from my bedroom window, and of the little brook running downstream to our patch of land. Shepherds used to cross it every evening with their flocks, and my siblings and I used to go over to see them, after school. We went to the central school. I used to take part in theater groups. They were happy days... until that spring came."

"When did you decide to take refuge in Srebrenica?" Jasmina fell silent for a while.

"Our lives changed altogether. Rumors began to spread among the Muslim community in the spring about disappearances and killings. Brutanac had been an example of Muslims and Orthodox Serbians living side by side respectfully in the former Yugoslavia. Families and children, we all mixed and in reasonable harmony; we were a tight community. But after the declaration of independence, fear began to stalk the streets and people stayed indoors. It all became a ghost town. I fell out of touch with many of my Serbian best friends. Some paramilitary Serbian army units began to raid Muslim family homes at night. The stories doing the rounds became more and more terrifying: whole families disappearing, killings, rapes, looting. Every night, from my bedroom window, I could see columns of smoke rising from the rooftops in the middle of my town. Many decided to flee to safer places. My father, however, was unwilling to let them throw us out of our own home and allow the reign of terror to succeed: that would have meant sacrificing everything he had fought for. He did not want to give in. He always told us to hold fast to our principles, our ideals, because that was the only thing that gave our existence meaning, above all else. Without that, we were as good as dead."

"Even so, you finally decided to flee to Srebrenica," Denis inquired.

"It was the first week of April. It was my older sister Alma's birthday."

Jasmina broke off her tale.

Fifteen years had gone by and she remembered that night

with chilling accuracy, as if her worst nightmare had been branded on her memory with a red-hot iron. The images came flooding back in an outburst of feelings which prevented her from speaking a word.

"Sorry, Denis..."

"Take it easy, take your time."

"My sister Alma had turned nineteen and my mother had cooked a special meal. That night, in the small hours, there was a dull thud on the door, then more and more knocking, louder and angrier. The hotel was closed. Now and again my father had taken in a frightened family fleeing their homes to escape from the continuous looting in the town center. When he looked out between his bedroom curtains, he saw a group of six or seven Serbian paramilitaries waiting outside the door. They were very young, armed and completely drunk; they could barely stand up. One of them wore a blood-stained uniform.

Jasmina recalled the screams that were more and more hateful, more and more impatient, demanding that the Muslim rats serve them alcohol. She could not wipe away the memory of the moment when her father roused the family and took them all into his room, or when she and her sister hugged their mother, quaking in fear, huddling next to her.

That feeling of dread came back to her and tightened her stomach once more.

She took another sip of her sparkling water.

"My older brother Amir was all for going downstairs with my father, grabbing his old rifle, the one he used to go hunting with in the woods, and doing away with those bullies that had come to harm his family. But father convinced him to stay in the room, to mind my mother and his sisters.

The voices outside that filled the whole house rang inside her heard once more. They threatened to burn the house down with everyone inside it. The ringleader shouted louder and louder. "I want to smell that Muslim scum's flesh burning!

Today we're having rat barbecue!"

At last, my father went downstairs and opened the door. He got a rifle butt in the face and several kicks to his body.

"What took you so long, scum?"

They entered the cafeteria and grabbed several bottles of liquor. They sat down at one of the tables. They forced my father to serve them on his knees and play Serbian music on the old record player.

Jasmina's voice began to break up just then and she went quiet as she relived that terrible racket. In their upstairs room, they could clearly hear everything going on downstairs, the insults, the blows. She was no more than a girl and deeply wanted silence to swallow her up. Amir said repeatedly that he wanted to go downstairs, that he would kill them. They heard one of the gang ask their father about his daughters. Her mother began to cry. Then, footsteps coming upstairs. After an eternal silence they kicked the door down. They took them away at gunpoint and dragged them down the stairs.

"Now we have women! Party time!" Those fiends' whooping cries exploded inside her head again, mingled with the gut-wrenching sobs of her sister, who was in the grip of an anxiety attack.

After a long pause, Jasmina continued her story.

"Two of the soldiers stayed with my brother upstairs. They took us downstairs. They had tied father to one of the wooden beams. His face was swollen and covered in blood. One of them, who had a scar on his cheek, laughingly poured a bottle of liquor over his head.

Jasmina suffered in silence so as not to cry. She did not want to shed any tears in front of the inspector. She went back for a second to the body of the girl she had been, who, scared to death, watched those soldiers' faces. Their eyes brimmed over with hate and liquor while they egged each other on.

"The infidel needs purifying!"

That night, one of those faces looked familiar, that of the stockiest among them, one that had not opened his mouth and watched the whole scene with detachment. The ringleader, nonetheless, was the skinniest; he had a bony face and predatory features. They called him 'Dogo'. His sidekicks laughed at his wisecracks while he boasted of his ability to inflict the most abject cruelty, in a macabre way, to score points with the devil.

One of them approached her father and yanked his head up by the hair. "Who do we start with?" Their father muttered through bloody teeth that they should leave them alone, they could take whatever they wanted, but to leave his daughters alone. "Perhaps you'd like us to start on your wife?" But their father could barely speak because his lips were so swollen from the blows, and he could only proffer a meaningless wail. Two of the men dragged her sister on to the table, grabbing her by the feet and hands.

Jasmina carried on with her tale after calming down.

"They tortured us there for hours. They humiliated and abused us while they drank liquor. They aimed their pistols at us and battered my father and sister."

She could see her sister right now, before her eyes. Alma had stopped crying, and was just panting and gazing into nothingness. She was trembling and quaking. They tore her pajamas off so she was completely naked. "We'll fuck the infidel, she's asking for it." The soldiers surrounded the table and grabbed her by the wrists and ankles, laughing all the while as they watched her bare body shiver. Her mother began to pray on her knees and was floored by a kick in the face. The stocky kid looked Jasmina in the eye, gulped and gritted his teeth. She remembered that look.

It was so familiar. That expression.

At last she recognized it. His name was Marko Bilić, and he had been to elementary school with her. She had not seen him in years. Her best childhood friend, with whom she had spent many an afternoon after school playing in the woods, then snacking afterwards in his home on bread pudding that his grandmother made for them. They same boy with whom she had run and played on the street in town. He had moved to Belgrade four years before, and now he had the look of a wild animal. He had grown up a lot, while his stockiness had turned to muscle and doubled his size since she had last seen him, when he bid her farewell. His hair was close-cropped and his uniform stained with dirt and blood. He would not stop looking at her.

Jasmine began to beg him.

"Help us!"

Marko looked at her without changing his expression, and gritted his teeth again. Jasmina's distraught sister began to shout, as if she had woken up again.

A few seconds later, Marko fired his gun into the air. "That's enough!"

The rest of the group turned round and taunted him. "What the hell got into you? Have you switched sides to this fucking scum? They're just Muslim whores. Come on, Marko."

The next shot passed within inches of the ringleader's bony skull. Then he aimed at his head. "Get out of here. Enough is enough."

Jasmina breathed in once more to sweep away her thoughts, and spoke to Denis Martel again.

"The morning after, at dawn, we loaded up father's old pick-up with some belongings. My brother had survived a brutal beating. Before we set off, my father set fire to the hotel. I remember we didn't speak a word until we reached Srebrenica. My mother merely cried now and again in the front seat."

Denis managed to comment, after a deep silence.

"I'm really sorry. It must have been horrible." Jasmina made no reply.

"In Srebrenica we lived packed in with other families for

nearly three years; then we were transferred to the United Nations safe haven, in Potočari. The rest is history."

"What about your parents? Your siblings?"

"When the Serbian troops entered the city, almost the entire Muslim population was inside the Potočari haven. One morning, Ratko Mladić and his Serbian soldiers came. They took all the men away. We didn't see my father and brother again. My mother died of grief a week later. Alma was kidnapped one night along with three other girls by the Scorpions. I was deported to Tuzla in a bus full of women."

"Have you heard anything about your sister."

"No. I only hope she brims over with bliss in paradise."

"Did you ever bump into Miletić? Do you remember him?"

"No, I don't remember him..."

Just then Kemal entered the courtyard and wrapped his arms around his wife.

Jasmina was all smiles again, as in a reflex action meant to keep her husband from suffering over her own grief. Kemal had been traveling much more recently. He told her they had to open up new markets, that there were opportunities out there. His absence made the moments they could spend together all the more valuable.

The young Bosnian greeted Denis and sat down. They whiled away the evening. Denis listened in interest to a few tales about rebuilding Mostar, and the ins and outs of his booming family business, which Kemal explained in enthusiastic detail.

They spoke of their voyage around the Aegean, the majestic sky by night as they sailed in calm winds. They guffawed to recall how they struggled to catch a little tuna fish that they had trolled with a boathook, but it got away.

The young couple radiated an absolute complicity Denis felt he had never had in his relationships. Kemal's every word and gesture toward his wife brimmed with sheer devotion.

An hour later Denis headed back to Sarajevo, and declined

with thanks an invitation to spend the night at the Osmanović home. They would be in touch should Interpol ever need anything.

The highway was deserted. Darkness blotted the landscape and every trace of humanity had vanished: tourists, goatherds and travelers had all taken shelter and plunged into silence what had been the busy blacktop just hours previously.

His thoughts went back, again and again, to his conversation with Jasmina Osmanović. Her bravery. The struggle for her ideals and her family's. "Exceptional courage," he thought. And as on so many other occasions, he began to feel petty and worthless. He remembered his brother's face: a shiver of bitter, severe anger ran down his spine. One of those that only arise when you are not at peace with the departed.

The flight left on time.

At two in the morning he collapsed from exhaustion in his Lyons home.

CHAPTER XIII

Adrian woke Laura up as soon as he saw Flávio and Paul go off to commune with nature in the Mediterranean. That morning the sea had turned into a blue flatness, a mirror whose glass showed a perfect reflection of the sky. The day was fit for enjoying their surroundings, but there was work to do. They left their half-finished cups of stewed coffee made by Paul, got washed, as usual, in sea water from one of the jerrycans stored inside the cave, and a bar of Marseilles soap. Fresh water was for drinking only. Adrian prodded his splints that, made with sticks, string and bandages, immobilized his leg as well as a plaster cast. The pain had died down due to the pills, although he still had a noticeable limp. He held on to Laura's arm as they walked out of the cave and onto the middle of the beach.

There they could spy the crag's surface and tried to spot any way to escape by land, as well as the place where the car had crashed in the sand. The huge basalt cliff shrouded them like a blanket. The volcanic rock had been eroded by the sea over thousands of years. The top of the cliff edge was at a great height and sheltered the beach's whole surface with its backward slope.

"A fortress," Adrian thought, as he shielded his eyes to examine their surroundings.

The drop was deadly all along the edge, even for the M6's reinforced cabin, except on the southern slope, the place where they plunged into the air, where a few clumps of pine trees, palms and cypresses gave way to thick bush down the slope, and dwindled into bare rock face a few feet from the ground.

Laura drew Adrian to that spot slowly and carefully, like somebody handling fragile goods. They examined the area in disbelief. They could still see some traces of tiny burnt cinders and ash, but nothing else. All the sand in the area had been raked over very carefully, meticulously, with a watchmaker's precision. There was no trace of the car. Not a sign that a car had ever been there throughout history.

Laura stood in silence, waiting for Adrian to fully digest the scene. Those two had dismantled the wreckage overnight and got rid of it, to make the place as clean as a whistle. Their unwilling hosts were serious about their convictions, and were not going to allow any chink in their armor to put them at risk, or leave any sign that could lure intruders into their natural stronghold. What strange reason or mental illness afflicted those guys' minds?

Adrian was convinced that a search and rescue operation would be under way. Everybody leaves behind a trail of clues and tracks wherever they roam. He wondered whether anybody had seen them in the gas station, amid the ruckus, as they drove through the fence and out along that dark track. Somebody must have noticed them. Pictures of them must have been doing the rounds thereabouts, with detailed descriptions of the car and, doubtless, their steps would be retraced painstakingly, but it was obvious that while the car itself had been a box of tricks that could have given away their location, finding them without it was another matter.

"Do you think they'll find us?" Laura asked.

Adrian smiled at her calmly, although his quiet resignation was only skin deep.

"Of course, and if not, we'll get out of here. Make no mistake. Sit down," he said, sitting down as best he could on the sand.

She sat down beside her boss with her back against the rock.

"Laura, it looks like Flávio and Paul are out of their minds. I don't know what strange madness has addled their brains. They're not criminals, or at least I think not, but we have nothing to gain by confronting them. We will find a way out of here. We must be patient and get it right."

Adrian closes his eyes and relaxed for a few seconds while listening to the waves lapping the shore.

"They go out diving every morning," he continued. "And don't come back till the evening. They leave us alone all day. Naturally, they are convinced we can't escape from this fucking beach, but I'm not so sure about that. What I am sure of is that we have time and will give it a try. We will look among their kit, to see if they have any tools; we'll scout for escape routes in the rocks, we'll swim to the ends of the cliff."

Laura did not need a pep talk to convince her. They had nothing to lose.

"We'll find a way to signal our presence to anybody that glances at the beach; soon I'll be able to move my leg some more and everything will be easier."

Adrian raised his chin to look her in the eye. Laura met his gaze with her brown eyes, then looked down to his bare chest. His muscles were clearly defined beneath a thin layer of hair. She was surprised to see a scar underneath that ran across his torso.

"Everything will turn out fine."

That evening Flávio and Paul came back earlier than usual. They normally returned at nightfall from their mysterious trips to the undersea world, but at that time of the day the sun still had some way to go before it set.

Laura, was on the shore, saw them land on the beach clad in their neoprene wetsuits and hauling a fishtrap full of fish.

"Where is Adrian?"

"In the cave. His leg hurt and he took some painkillers. He's been asleep for hours."

"It's time for dinner. Ask him if he's ready to eat anything."

Paul went inside the cave while Flávio emptied out his catch on to the shore; sea bream, red porgy, sea bass and a grouper. A score of fish in total, of varying sizes. He used a clasp knife to gut the fish, one by one, scraped off the scales and threw the guts on to the shore, which the seagulls swooped down on within minutes. Adrian came along with Paul's help, while the latter carried some bags, then he sat down on the sand, beside Laura. They swapped glances, quietly. He was still under the influence of the tranquilizers and groggy, but awake enough to admire the remarkable catch.

Paul dug a hole in the sand and placed a good-sized, old round tin in it, into which he emptied a bag of charcoal and some dry twigs. He effectively lit up a lively fire with the help of a gas lighter, and in seconds it had burned up the pine shoots and formed a generous bed of burning embers. On top of that he placed a gray-black metal grill, worn and charred by use. Flávio, meanwhile, had boned the fish and sliced them with surgical precision, and he set about arranging the fillets of his tasty catch on a rudimentary aluminum tray, after drizzling virgin olive oil on them. Next he sprinkled coarse salt on top and laid them down carefully, side by side, making sure none overlapped the other.

Adrian watched the proceedings in amazement. 'Well I'll be damned, 'Jesus' is a chef.'

A few minutes later, the embers had reached the right temperature. Paul used a wooden stick as a poker to turn over and smooth the embers, in order to spread the heat they shed evenly over the tin's whole area.

The smell of fresh fish cooking on the grill whetted Adrian's appetite. Three days of painkillers, fruit and cold food was too harsh for his demanding stomach, which was still getting over his injuries. He slowly savored the soft, golden flesh with transports of delight. He had to admit, the taste was spectacular, a delicious mouthful of the sea that allowed him to hold heaven itself in the palms of his hands. 'These hermits sure can look after themselves,' he thought.

Flávio offered them a glass of sweet wine that Adrian turned down gently. What the hell, they were prisoners, after all. He could not hold back his astonishment when, next thing, Laura accepted the offer gladly, and he darted his colleague a withering glance that was lost on her, receipt not acknowledged. The young lady was relaxing and enjoying her dinner on the beach. The last seventy-two hours had been tough and intense, and she had no intention of sparing herself any pleasures. She closed her eyes as she savored the taste of the *garnacha* grapes and felt the warm evening breeze on her cheeks. A fantastic sea bass and wine that, under the circumstances, tasted like the pick of the world's most sumptuous cellar.

"Did you eat well?" Flávio asked politely.

"Wonderfully. Everything was delicious," Laura answered, as he held her glass out level with the neck of the bottle Paul held, so he could serve her a refill.

"You don't have any tobacco, do you? Mine was burned up in the crash," Adrian shivered on the inside to see Laura getting familiar with those fellows.

"Yes, wait," Paul rolled a few cigarettes with Golden Virginia tobacco from a tin he had, and offered them a pair.

"Where are you from? What brings you here?" Laura asked boldly.

Paul and Flávio looked at each other before answering.

"We're from Brazil, São Paulo," Paul answered. "Although we haven't set foot there for four years."

"And what about you? How come you were driving along these roads?" Flávio said, turning around the question right away in his strong Portuguese accent; it was obvious he wanted to cut out Laura's questioning.

"That's what I ask myself," Adrian protested.

"We had been filming a spot in Los Muertos beach," Laura added. "We work in an advertising agency. We were stuck in an unholy traffic jam that blocked up the freeway, and took an exit to a country road. I guess we got lost. Night fell. Then, you know: the ravine, the crash..."

"Where are you from? Flávio asked Laura directly, assuming Adrian did not feel like chatting to them.

"I'm Spanish, I was born in Málaga but moved to France when I was fourteen, and now I live in Paris. Adrian is American. We work together, he owns the company."

Laura gave her boss's face a sideways glance and understood right away that he did not like anybody speaking for him.

"Four years away from home. Don't you have any family in Brazil?" Laura insisted.

"We have no family," Flávio answered blunty. "It's getting late, Paul, I think it's time for bed."

Paul looked at him in silence and breathed deeply.

"Not yet. I'd rather to stay up awhile. Take it easy, buddy, let's go see the sunset. I'm right here."

His words faded into an uncomfortable silence and the four banqueters decided to enjoy being lulled by the refreshing sound of the calm sea waves lapping the rocks. The cool breeze made the summer heat more bearable, although even at this time of night it bore down on the Mediterranean coast. Air currents swirled around the vast cliff face and turned into whirlwinds that ventilated the whole surface of the cove, like a natural fan, and caressed the skin in a gentle massage.

After a while, Flávio and Paul went to the cave and turned in, but not without cleaning up the grill.

Laura and Adrian stayed put, lying down on the sand.

"Why did you do that? I don't think it's a good idea to get close to those goofballs."

The young lady saw his annoyed look and smiled. She did not need to be a mind-reader to see that he did not like either those guys, or the situation, one tiny bit. For a minute, she felt somewhat softhearted to see him lying there, with his leg in splints and frowning in annoyance. She never could have imagined she would come to have a soft spot for Adrian Seaten.

"Well I think it's a good idea. We don't know who they are. It is best that they see us a people, not objects. You yourself said we had nothing to gain by confronting them."

"It is one thing to stand up to them, quite another to invite them to brunch at the George V, my dear. I just want them out of the way. I don't like mixing with scum, I can't help it," said Adrian, who could not remember the last time anybody had dared to contradict him.

Laura tried to picture what brunch would be like in the George V.

Adrian snorted. The effect of the painkillers was wearing off and his pain barriers had reached rock bottom. He found the feeling of helplessness was even more painful than the throbbing that gripped his leg.

"You need to get some rest."

Laura settled her boss's head on a backpack containing a neoprene wetsuit, then she put one of the cigarettes Paul had rolled into his mouth and lit it with the gas lighter. She lay down by his side. The smell of his skin washed over her immediately.

Adrian breathed in the tobacco smoke and sighed with pleasure.

He could not remember having seen so many stars in the sky.

CHAPTER XIV

Sylvie Prévot finally saw her boss's door open at 12:30 a.m. She could never quite tell whether it was a rare skill or inborn instinct, like *déjà vu*, but each and every time the day brought particular chaos to the office, she knew Denis would stroll in at noon, never before, spruce and fresh as a daisy.

She figured it was definitely a natural instinct.

"The old man wants a word with you," Sylvie strode in to Denis' office, while he looked at her still half-asleep. "He wants a detailed report on the conclusions of the Miletić case for tomorrow's commission."

"No way. What conclusions is he talking about? He knows very well that we're still working on the case."

"I've told him that, but you know what he's like. It's like talking to the wall."

"Wait," Denis said, as he picked up the phone.

His talk with Coburn did not last one minute. The case was classified and the commission was taking a special interest in it. Coburn had to report and that is all there was to it. He wanted the report by the close of business, naturally. Denis cursed as he hung up. 'Damned bureaucrats,' he thought. The commission was composed of representatives from the central bureaus in four countries, as well as Coburn himself, and God knew he had powers aplenty to manage the case as he sought fit. By late afternoon, after including some corrections that Sylvie had added, they sent him the report.

After a hard day —to put it mildly— they both agreed that a couple of beers were called for to clear their heads. And that was not to mention the unfinished business they had backed up. Cedric, Sylvie's ex-husband, had not paid his alimony for months and what hurt even more, was that he treated the kids as if they did not exist. Olivia was still in Saint-Tropez. She hardly picked up Denis' calls, and when she did it was like she was shelling peas. Doubtless, after a breathless week, it was time to call a summit meeting and catch up.

Like every Friday, live Celtic music blared out over the customers in the *Saint James*. The waiters could not keep up with orders from the dozens of executives who were packed two or three deep at the bar. What better way to end the working day than with Irish whiskey and beer? The atmosphere was livening up at the same pace as the Guinness barrels were being drained one after the other, at a rate of knots. Sitting in their little artificial bubble, at one of the tables farthest away from the small stage, Sylvie and Denis picked over the day's agenda, item by item. His impressions of the Mostar trip were not on the agenda to begin with, but after a few pints, inevitably, they always ended up talking shop. Denis was still chewing over that meeting. Neither could he get Coburn out of his head. 'Prejudgment impairs objectivity'. Sylvie listened carefully to the details of his interview in Bosnia. After she heard the harrowing tale of the Osmanović family, for a second she stopped thinking that her own problems were important.

The beer began to take effect on her diminutive body.

The band's music blended the sounds of a *bodhrán*, bagpipes and fiddles, while the audience sang along to 'Whiskey in the Jar.' They clapped disjointedly, in a decided bid to beat time. Within seconds, the place became an unrestrained dance floor, with leaps, twists and claps all the way from the stage to the door. Sylvie wished Denis would take her by the hand to the dance floor, but her boss would not stop talking about that woman and how exasperatingly slow the Greeks were: four days and they still had not managed to fax Atkins' passport.

Tomorrow morning he would talk to Mitroglou to speed things up.

Two hours and a few pints later, they decided to call it a night. Denis gave his colleague a ride to the doorway of an old apartment in the Presqu'île neighborhood, behind the Saint-Nizier church, where she lived with her three children.

Sylvie looked at herself in the mirror. As she always did when she said good-bye to him, she had a bittersweet look on her face.

CHAPTER XV

"Good morning, Denis," Mitroglou's voice sounded blunter than usual.

"Yanis, good to talk to you."

After a few minutes going over the pleasant dinner they had had in Athens a few days before, Denis cut to the chase.

"We still haven't got that fax of Atkins' passport; the boys in the Naxos police seem to be taking things very easy."

Mitroglou stayed silent for a few seconds on the other end of the line.

"Denis, the case has been kicked upstairs. For us, it's closed," he answered finally.

"What did you say?"

"I thought you knew," Yanis insisted.

"No way!"

"The commission has decided that the investigation into the Miletić case is closed now, within Interpol's operating remit. They have uncovered new data and Coburn has transferred its follow-up to a new level. Just today we've had official confirmation by memo. That's all I know." Denis could not believe his ears. He was well aware that Coburn and the top brass handled classified cases any old how, but that was going too far. They had not even sketched out the first lines of investigation.

"Got it. I'm sure there's some explanation. I'll talk it over with Coburn. But I still need Atkins' passport."

"I'm not authorized to send it to you, Denis. I have received specific instructions about sharing information. I'm truly sorry."

Denis counted to ten. He had known Yanis for many years and knew that the old Greek cop would have helped happily, unless he had received a concrete warning not to do so.

"Yanis, I've always been there for you when you needed and you can trust me totally. I've never let you down and..."

"Denis," Mitroglou sounded even angrier. "Why don't you drop it? You know what your problem is? You take everything personally. It's just another case, that's all."

"I doubt that. I have the feeling there's much more to all this than meets the eye. You're an old hand, you know that as well as I do."

Yanis Mitroglou agreed wholeheartedly.

Three days before he had received an order to quit sending information to Martel and his team, so he was not surprised to hear afterwards that the case had been transferred to the special commission. He liked Denis. They were both old school and had built up a good friendship, but with retirement three years away he had no intention of wrecking his future for the sake of his friend's good intentions.

"Yanis, you owe me one and you know it. I've saved your ass on occasion. Nobody will ever know. Never. You have my word."

"Good-bye Denis," he managed to say after a deafening silence. "Don't get yourself into trouble, you hear? For your own good."

Yanis Mitroglou hung up.

The sun beat down on the office window. The smoked glass in the smart windows darkened automatically due to the brighter light outside and dimmed the room, which was plunged into a dismal shade.

He could not get rid of that nagging feeling of helplessness. Then again, neither could he quite tell whether it bothered him more that the case was closed off to him, or that he had had to find out from Yanis Mitroglou.

He needed to speak to Coburn. Right now. He could spend no more time wallowing in misery. Sylvie's voice filled the room.

"You've got to see this," she demanded impatiently.

Sylvie handed him a sheet printed on one side. An email hard copy. Denis glanced at the heading. The sender was Luis Contini, chief of the Interpol Central Bureau in Buenos Aires, Argentina.

> *Dear Ms. Prévot:*
> *Re. your request of a few days past, this is to confirm we have an open case that has some elements in common with those contained in the information you have shared about the murder of Vinko Miletić. Please contact me a.s.a.p.*

"We have a conference call with them at 7 p.m.," Sylvie announced with a smile before Denis Martel could open his mouth.

During lunch, Denis made no mention of his talk with Mitroglou: the time was not yet ripe for him to tell her they were off the case. In fact, neither did he try to contact Corbun. If there were new orders, then it was up to him, as the one in charge of the case, to be informed directly by his superior of any changes. Furthermore, in case Coburn did inform him officially of what he already knew, then he would have to cancel the conference call or risk being disciplined for disobeying direct orders from his chief. The hours flew by until 7 p.m. They had found out that Coburn would be out of the office all day. The telephone rang to announce Contini's call with Swiss punctuality, in the conference room next to Denis office. After the formal greetings and introductions, Contini proceeded to give the details for his missive.

At 7:05 p.m., Denis Martel's BlackBerry began to flash. He looked at the screen and switched Corburn's incoming call to voicemail.

Contini spoke hesitantly. His noticeable Argentine accent made his English sound musical, and his voice was palpably enthusiastic. The information Sylvie had sent had re-opened a case he had given up on.

"The events date back to March last year," Contini explained. "A yacht blew up in unexplained circumstances a few miles from the port of Pinamar. The explosion took place about 22:30 hours, killing Guillermo Lavinia —an engineer— his wife Anne, and their eight-year-old daughter, Angélica. The boat, registered as *Le Boucanier*, was literally blown to pieces. It was totally destroyed; the largest bit of the hull that the coastguard picked up was no more than three feet long. According to the forensics, the explosion was caused by a very powerful home-made bomb with a timer, definitely placed next to the fuel tank, which made the blast all the more deadly. The remains of the carbonized bodies were scattered over a radius of 1,500 feet from the epicenter. Traces of nitric acid were also found."

Denis and Sylvie's silence prompted him to carry on.

"We have investigated this case more than thoroughly. We have a police sketch of the alleged perpetrator."

"How did you get that?" Denis asked. "Was there a witness?"

"A suspect was seen several times wandering around the port days before the crime; he even struck up conversation with some of the sailors. He was foreign, probably American. We know he was a young man of around thirty, medium height, of light build and dark haired. One of the Pinamar security cameras filmed an individual that very afternoon, ambling along the pontoon where Lavinia's boat was tied up. Although the picture was blurred, it fits the description given by the port workers. Following descriptions given by the witnesses, we drew a sketch that was broadcast by the media and posted in every air- and seaport, station and border crossing. We checked all records of foreign nationals entering the country that matched the suspect's details for a month after that. But nothing turned up."

"He'll be back home by now, watching *Jeopardy* on TV," Denis jested.

"We believe he entered and left the country on a forged passport, he probably used two different identities. It may be that to avoid detection he spent two or three weeks holed up in some dive before crossing the border with Chile or Brazil."

"Is there any clue as to the motive for the crime?"

"Lavinia was a controversial character, with his detractors and supporters. The crime caused a great upset throughout the country, as Lavinia held an important post during the Videla dictatorship. Although a career officer, he has always been considered an eminent intellectual. While never accused, he was linked to activities in the Navy Mechanical Institute, where all kinds of torture were inflicted on political prisoners. Various organizations have protested that he was implicated in the logistics of the clandestine detention centers and 'death flights'."

"What do you mean, 'death flights'?" Sylvie queried.

"During the dictatorship, many detainees were drugged and dumped into the sea from military aircraft. It is believed that more than four thousand people were exterminated that way, and that the aforesaid practice had the military government's backing."

"And even so there were people who supported him?" Denis Martel's assistant reiterated.

"Indeed, because afterwards Lavinia became one of the main

drivers behind normalizing institutions in order to return the country to democracy. And when later on he retired altogether from politics, he did so to focus on the import business. For that reason a large segment of public opinion reacted indignantly to the attack because it killed his wife and, above all, their eight-year-old daughter."

"The perpetrator had no qualms about killing innocent people."

Denis concluded.

"We have our doubts about that," Contini replied. "Lavinia always sailed alone or with Néstor, one of the port sailors. His family rarely went with him. In fact, according to what we surmised from statements we took from his family and friends, at first he planned to sail alone. He changed his mind at the last minute."

"And unwittingly sentenced his family to death."

Denis concluded.

"That is what we believe."

"The case certainly has parallels with the Miletić slaying. They were both suspected of taking part in atrocities and crimes against innocent people."

"There is another important detail, Denis," the Argentine officer added. "The main reason for our interest in Miletić, and what particularly drew our attention when we read Sylvie's notice."

"Please continue."

"The morning after," Contini added. "In the vacant mooring post normally occupied by *Le Boucanier*, right on top of the bollard where ships' cables are looped, officers found a narcissus with a red string tied to it."

In a gut reaction, Denis and his assistant swapped glances and fought back a sudden feeling of excitement running through their bodies.

"A *Narcissus Poeticus*, " Contini noted.

"Interesting. Most interesting. Was there anything else next to the narcissus?"

"Nothing else. Only the flower tied with string."

Those coincidences cannot be happenstance. There was no reason for them to be. Denis asked in detail about Guillermo Lavinia's life —his main enemies, his activities in recent years— and Sylvie began forthwith to go over the report on the Miletić case in detail, which Contini and his colleagues followed most carefully.

For one hour and a half they keenly shared details and findings. Contini could not conceal his satisfaction, either. At last some light had been shed. After almost one year and a half of fruitless investigation, the case was on the point of being shelved: that was too long for such a high-profile case. The press had their knives out and his rivals at the Ministry could not wait to go for his jugular. They agreed to send Sylvie the police sketch of the suspect and the rest of the documentation, and planned to exchange details regularly on any possible lead. Denis asked Contini and his team for the utmost discretion before they ended the call on a cordial note.

After the conference was over, Sylvie stayed behind in Denis' office. She knew him well enough to realize by the look on his face that something was up. Right away she figured her boss and friend was not in the mood for talking and decided to call it a day. Denis did not so much as hear the door close behind her. He slumped back in his leather chair like a sack of potatoes, and looked out of the window at the darkening tree tops in the Tête d'Or park that surrounded the building.

It was absurd. None of it made sense.

The Organization had on file the best criminal database on the planet, it enjoyed the most advanced criminal intelligence facilities, but for some reason he could not quite grasp, until that afternoon he had had no knowledge of the existence of a similar case as far as the victim's profile went and, what is more, the same signature.

Minutes later he heard the message Coburn had left in his voicemail.

The old man wanted to see him the following morning. First thing.

CHAPTER XVI

Several large boxes were stacked up at the back of the cave. He delved into the cave while trying not to make any noise until he came to the improvised storeroom. The first box looked like a sort of wooden chest, a showy, worn-out rustic curio that was splintered all over. He opened the old box easily and all kinds of items met his eyes: pots, flashlights, cutlery, a small hoe, candles, a tape measure, sponges, detergent, a compass, ropes of varying sizes, and bleach. A random collection of jumble.

Adrian looked behind him. Everything was still in order. Laura seemed to be still asleep, while the Brazilian pair had wandered off to their daily escapades at the bottom of the sea some time before. He had lingered with the patience of a Tibetan monk until the time was ripe: while lying down on his camp bed, he had waited for the Brazilians to leave and the sun's first light before inspecting the terrain.

Next he opened the second box, which was somewhat bigger than the first and had a metal surface. It looked to be made of aluminum, and could well have been an industrial pallet. Adrian was dumbstruck. It had enough tools inside to service an airplane: every kind of wrench, screws and nails, pliers, hammers, chisels, cold chisels, a blowtorch, a gas welder, saws, sharpeners. 'What a box of tricks,' he thought. He rummaged through the three remaining boxes, which were smaller and held fishing tackle, harpoons, fish hooks, diving gear and other devices for surviving at sea.

Right at the back of the cave, the vault that was the roof dropped sharply —it was barely five feet above the floor— and he had to crouch in order to reach the back wall.

Adrian was plunged into darkness. There the gloom completely absorbed what scarce daylight had found its way through the mouth of the cave. He stroked the rough, damp surface of the back wall and shuddered suddenly. The temperature had fallen a few degrees on the inside due to the effect of the rock, which acted as a natural thermostat. He stood stock still by the wall and listened to the dull sound of the sea, its everlasting whisper, a lapping sound that rang around the stone. He felt his leg tingle. A draft of fresh, damp air tickled his feet and ankles like a soft, impish feather. He knelt down slowly and groped around the whole surface until he lost touch with the rock, and shoved his hand into a natural hollow eighteen inches wide that opened up at floor level. Like a blind man groping around him, he stretched his arm out without finding any blockage and stuck his head into the opening.

It looked like a black hole that swallowed up all light. He remembered Stephen Hawking's keynote lecture at Harvard's Sanders Theater during the '99 season. A student audience hung on the invalid's every word as he stripped down science fiction theories about unexplored domains, lost in space, that were dense enough to generate a gravitation pull that could absorb all particulate matter, including light photons.

The draft became stronger and blew his hair back. He walked back a few feet to grab a flashlight from one of the boxes and went back into the hole, while crawling slowly along the ground like a marine in training. The diver's flashlight with its xenon light bulb and polycarbonate lens, cast a shaft of white light that spread out over the thousands of nooks and crannies that covered the surface of the black rock inside the narrow passageway. Adrian closed his eyes for a few seconds to get used to the glare and then crawled a few feet along the tunnel, until the beam lighted up the walls and roof of a spacious natural room as greedily as compressed gas escaping from a cylinder.

He looked in amazement at the cave's towering height. It was a sight to behold.

The rock drew back from itself to form surprising natural shapes, due to the sea having eroded the volcanic rock face. An area of one hundred square feet spread out into an almost perfect circle. The light shone on the crags and majestic vault above to lend the place an almost mystical influence, as if God had hewn for himself a chapel in the bowels of the earth. The very damp feel of the place impregnated his bones straight away. He felt the gentle breeze on his face again and followed it with his hand. It took only a few seconds to find that the air current came from some undefined point in the roof, which was about fourteen feet above the floor.

He looked over every inch of the vault. Nothing, no visible way out. He sighed. Adrian was sure that there was some gap that let the air through, but no light, and linked that space to the outside; maybe a narrow passageway or a breach. He tried to get closer still to the upper part and stood with his left leg on one of the many ledges on the rock face, but a sharp pain ran up and down his back when he placed his splinted leg on the outcrop. He clambered back down on the ground and cursed to fend off the agony. The noise echoed around the inside of the cave like a sounding board. He took a deep breath and shone the flashlight around the chamber.

Something attracted his attention at the back.

A few feet away, next to the only corner hollowed out in the natural cavity, he could make out a couple of sizable shapes amidst the shadows. Adrian glimpsed two rectangular figures and a large plastic bag lying beside them. He moved over and pointed the xenon light that way.

The damp made it harder and harder to breathe the more he delved into the expansive chamber. He pored over his find. Next to the bag were some sort of leather chests: they looked like two trunks whose hide was well worn. He saw that they were the sort of trunks servants of well-to-do families used to stow on trains and ships in old movies, big enough to transport a goodly amount of luggage, but incongruously uncomfortable unless you had the right domestic help. The metallic clasps looked to be open. Adrian lay down the flashlight and knelt in front of them.

Just then an instinctive reaction made him spring back a step.

His glance fell on a strange figure hanging from the wall, one whose profile stood out from the rock like a ghostly shadow. Its contours looked oddly familiar and the play of light and shadow around it seemed to give it a life of its own. When he brought the light closer to the wall, it lighted up a wooden sculpture of Christ on a cross nailed to the wall. He could not help feeling the shivers.

The blackened wood measured eighteen inches from end to end and depicted Christ's suffering on the cross in detail.

He stroked its surface: they had fixed it to the rock with climbing bolts.

The high-quality woodwork could not hide the wear and tear on the surface. It was chiseled out of a single block. Jesus was wide-eyed and his head hung to the right. His crown and serene expression enhanced his divine nature, to convey his victory over death and the salvation of humankind. The body resting on the cross made its anatomy stand out slightly, which from waist to knee was covered up by a *perizoma*. It was a Romanesque image, a far cry from the bloody and agonizing variations that succeeded it over time. He took a deep breath. Every artistic detail of his find had been eclipsed from the first. The cross he had before his eyes was hung upside-down. Christ's head pointed to the ground, and his perfectly vertical feet pointed upwards.

He checked the fasteners again. Whoever had nailed up that wooden sculpture that way had done so deliberately. An inverted cross. Some currents of thought linked the inverted Latin cross to satanic sects, as the symbol of the Antichrist in opposition to God. But it also had another symbolic meaning, that was perhaps less well known:

'The cross of Saint Peter'.

According to the ancient writings of Origen and Tertullian, Peter was crucified head downwards. He chose to face his martyrdom with such an awful ending because he did not feel worthy of dying the same way as his master, Jesus of Nazareth. Thenceforth the inverted cross, the symbol of Saint Peter, the predecessor of popes and heir to the Church, represented Christian humility. He remembered having seen that symbol sometime adorning the papal throne. He asked what on earth that figure was doing there but, as there would be no answer, he knelt back down beside the trunks and left the flashlight on the ground to examine their contents.

The chest was covered with old hunting green cloth, printed with golden lines of *fleurs-de-lis*. Although rusty, the hinges and locks were ajar. He lifted up the lid. A motley array of objects was bundled in its depths. He breathed in a couple of times to tell exactly what was the pleasant smell that unexpectedly wafted out from it. Four days without smoking had made his dulled sense of smell hypersensitive. The intoxicating fragrance of jasmine issued from a blood-red silk handkerchief. A woman's handkerchief. Adrian drew the cloth up to his face and breathed in its effluvia. The smell took him back to civilization for a few seconds, far away from that natural cave, to his artificial urban world, where heightening small details that enhanced the senses were the mark of daily life. Among some items of clothing and documents, he found a good number of books, about twenty copies of different shapes and sizes, new and old editions, in English and Portuguese.

'Our friends' cultural legacy.'

He picked up the Apocalypse of John; a Portuguese edition: *Apocalipse de São João*. The burnished leather binding fell apart as soon as he looked at it so he put it back. A copy of *A Grief Observed*, by C. S. Lewis, bound in a more modern edition, was still in its plastic wrapper; it had yet to be opened. Next to them, strewn any old how, he came across the *Book of the Dead*, *The Divine Comedy* and *Rewards and fairies* by Kipling. Adrian smiled in disdain. 'So the diving kings read Kipling's poetry.'

He put back the books in the same disarray in which he had found them, and picked up a crumpled envelope that stood out a the back of the trunk. Inside there were two passports with tattered covers on which could still be read, in golden lettering, the inscription: *República Federativa do Brasil*. Flávio Azevedo de Souza was born in February 1982, the same month and year as Paul Schotten Machado, but only a few days apart, in São Paulo.

Never in a million years would he have connected the guys in the passport photos to the two hippy hermits that spent their days under water. In their short, slick hair and navy blue suits, they could have passed for derivatives brokers in a multinational investment bank. The entry and exit stamps for several countries decorated both documents from beginning to end in a pattern of different colors and shapes: Thailand, Belize, Egypt, Sudan, Australia... They tended to stay for three months at a time, sometimes more, and the dates and places were exactly matched. Those two guys always traveled together.

He gulped down a mouthful of air to make up for the lack of oxygen due to the damp.

Sat in front of that chest, he had the impression he was

prying into someone else's inner recesses. He had never felt any curiosity for anybody else's lives. They barely mattered to him. He had his work cut out unraveling his own, which was in fact the only one he cared about, but in his quest for answers he felt like a child impatiently unwrapping its Christmas presents. After a few minutes, he decided he had seen enough for now, and got ready to leave behind the stone chamber and end his eventful expedition.

Nonetheless, just before he closed the chest, a notebook bound in cork leather, with neither title nor heading, drew his attention. He untied the red ribbon around it. A good half of the parchment-colored paper pages had handwriting in Indian ink on them, followed by a series of blank leaves. At first sight it looked like a diary, but not any old diary. A date headed every page, below which were two or three notes, a couple of paragraphs at most. That is all it takes. It was written in Portuguese. Adrian spoke reasonable Spanish and could just about understand Portuguese. The diary told of journeys and spoke of God and love. He would need Laura's help to translate the writing exactly. The last page was dated 3 August, 2006.

Right then, a photo trapped in the book fell on his knees with the rustle of a leaf in the fall.

The snapshot showed a woman.

The beauty of her face stood out from the matt paper. Her complexion, hair and eyes were all very dark and elegant. She had a childish, almost virginal expression, and her bright look and white smile beamed life and depth, like a source of pure and natural power. On that day's date, the last written entry consisted of just one line: '[1]*Hoje voltei a dar graças a Deus por tê-la conhecido*'.

---

1. Translator's note: Portuguese for 'Today I gave God thanks again for having known her'

Adrian breathed deep and took a few seconds' break before standing up.

His gaze lit on the inverted Christ again. 'My friend, what are you doing nailed up there like that?'

The sound of footsteps outside the underground chapel broke the silence and stopped his breathing dead. They became louder and faster until they stopped suddenly outside the entrance to the narrow tunnel.

Adrian stood still when he heard a voice echo around the rock face.

CHAPTER XVII

Denis arrived unusually early at the office. He had been unable to sleep well and filled up his coffee cup twice as much as normal. He went through the door into Coburn's office at 8:30 a.m.

"Good morning Al, I didn't see your call yesterday, I was in a meeting. It was too late to call back when I heard your message. My apologies."

"Don't worry, Denis, the main thing is that you're here now."

"OK, shoot."

"Denis, you've done a great job," Coburn asserted, as he took off his glasses prudently. "The report you sent us is excellent. Undoubtedly you are an example of thoroughness and professionalism. Although I believe that, with your track record, that goes without saying."

"Thank you," he answered shortly.

"I guess you are aware, as I have already told Miss Prévot, that the operating commission studied your report yesterday."

Denis nodded.

"As you know, the Miletić case is classified and as such it is directly overseen by the commission, which will assume ultimate responsibility for the investigation."

"I get that, I know the rules."

"It's a delicate case. Perhaps you're wondering why it was

classified as red. Well," Coburn continued, without waiting for an answer. "The basic reason is quite obvious. As the victim was a military man, everything suggests that the crime could be deemed a consequence or ramification of a conflict between two member countries. As you know, under such circumstances, it is outside our remit."

"Yes, of course," Denis acknowledged, as he drank down his coffee.

"Nonetheless," Coburn continued, in his unchanging calm tone. "There could be other explanations about the crime's context. Causes that escape the mere isolated analysis of a criminal act and could involve supranational organizations and movements. Well then, that is the scenario that has led the Miletić crime to be included within our remit. And classified, of course."

"Understood," Denis answered coolly. He had no intention of saying a word more than needed.

"The commission has followed its own lines of investigation and it may be said they have been highly satisfactory, believe me. Along with your report's conclusions, for which the commission asks me to pass on its compliments, we have reasons to believe that we are on the right track."

"Al, that's all very well, but I've been working very hard on this case these past few days, I know and understand the rules, and if it isn't too much to ask, I would like to know what is the 'right track', according to the commission, and what the next steps are to be."

"Hmmm, well, it's a rather delicate matter. I am not at liberty to reveal too many details, as you will understand, although obviously it is not a new issue; indeed, several governments have been working on it for some time. What I can tell you is that we have detected a gradual radicalization of certain Balkan groups in recent years, groups originating within supposedly pacifist organizations, which divert their anti-war activities away from victim support and toward terrorist acts and organized crime."

"Is the Osmanović couple implicated?" Denis remembered that Jasmina was a keen member of Women in Black.

"As I said, I cannot tell you much more. Understand, it's restricted information. I'm sorry, Denis."

"You see, we had a phone call yesterday with the Argentine police and have been informed..."

"Yes, about the attack on Guillermo Lavinia and his family. We are aware of the case."

Denis needed a few seconds to compose himself. He felt like a bucket of cold water had been poured over his head.

"Denis, we have investigated this thoroughly and come to the conclusion that Miletić's killers are trying to mislead us; the narcissus, the whole ritual, it definitely looks like a farce. We have good reason to think so."

Denis was perplexed. The guy in front of him seemed to pull the strings in the universe as naturally as God himself, while he himself was no more than a fucking puppet whose arms his boss moved at will.

"You have done your bit. I should like to truly thank you for your participation and effort."

"Does that mean I'm off the case?" Denis asked in evident disgust, which he could not hide. "Is that it?"

"Allow me to tell you that I do not understand your reaction," Coburn answered condescendingly. "I understood you were not very happy at interrupting your vacation, that it was a nuisance to take on the case so suddenly. Go on, go back to your vacation, you have earned it."

Denis was sure he had never mentioned his annoyance to Coburn. In fact, he had only voiced his almighty anger to Sylvie, nobody else.

A cold sweat ran down his back. He felt an overwhelming urge to get out of there. There was not much left to say.

He took his leave of Coburn with aseptic cordiality.

Minutes later, after he had picked up some papers from his office, he walked along the corridors like a robot and out of 200 Quai de Charles de Gaulle.

CHAPTER XVIII

Denis Martel's apartment was a late nineteenth-century attic in the Croix Rousse neighborhood. He had worked long and hard to revamp its structure completely, by sacrificing his free time at weekends over the past year. He tore down walls and partitions, and rebuilt ceilings and walls with the patience of a saint. There were only two closed rooms; his bedroom and the guest room, which he liked to call 'Cécile's room', for his daughter. The open-plan kitchen, living room and office in the spacious loft had ash parquet flooring, on top of which were scattered designer furniture, antiques and souvenirs.

Sylvie found the door open when the old elevator stopped its annoying clatter, and went in without knocking.

The old paintings and impressionist prints were still leaning against the bottom of the wall, waiting to be hung up some day, while the books were still piled up in the corner, where they had soaked up all the dust churned up by the building work, like sponges. All in order, just like she'd seen it last. She smiled. Denis was on the balcony. The burning dog-day heat had relented since mid-afternoon, and was at least making it bearable to go outdoors.

Sylvie crossed the airy room. As soon as she stood on the cute terrace, the sweet violin music she had heard as soon as she stepped out of the elevator sounded louder. Denis looked vaguely at the neighboring rooftops.

He was slumped on a thick wicker *chaise longue*, surrounded by a row of plant pots of varying sizes that stretched along the red limestone floor and housed hemp plants and dwarf trees. He was knocking back a glass of Jameson on ice, which had now melted. Sylvie guessed it was not his first. Her boss's spells of cathartic musing could be gauged by the bottle. Denis moved the index finger of his right hand in time to the music, gently, up and down, like a metronome.

Sylvie sat down beside him on an old wooden rocking chair.

"Spectacular yet sad, don't you think, Sylvie?"

"What?"

"The music you're hearing. This piece."

The digital sound of the woofers bluntly enhanced the string section, full blast, which was bordering on unbearable for the building's crusty old residents. The start of the second movement in Beethoven's Seventh Symphony wafted throughout the apartment and spilled out like a noble gas, onto the landing and communal areas on the stairs.

"It's like life, so beautiful we should be happy, but we can't because it is sad," Denis went on.

He savored every second of the heavenly score in a state of hypnosis that was almost autistic. He noticed Sylvie's presence, of course, but felt no need to talk to her. No need to be polite. He was not like that with anybody else. His emotions raged for the eight minutes that the allegretto lasted, which had to be enjoyed to the full. There was no other way.

"The sound of the strings begins all by itself," he intoned. "The rest of the instruments join in on the way until the end, *in tutti, in fortissimo*. The *ostinato* is repeated, it hides and then it comes out again, louder than ever. A quarter note, two quavers, two quarter notes. Time and again. So simple and so moving. And so on until the end. Don't you think that's great?

"Denis, what's up?" Sylvie asked when the music died down.

"Do you really want to know?" The booze had taken its toll

on his speech, which was now slurred.

"I've been with you on this one from the start. I believe I'm entitled to know what's going on. You vanished from the office after you met with Coburn. Well then, I want to know what the hell's wrong."

Denis laughed pithily.

"What's up is that we are just two damned puppets on a string. It so happens that we're off the case, that we have to let the 'higher-ups' handle it, as they have information that surpasses our 'limited vision'.

"I don't get it. What about the conference with Contini?"

"They know about it. The coincidences are 'a farce ', 'good reason to think so'."

Sylvie was speechless.

"That's what's up."

"What do you figure?" "Maybe Coburn's right. He has more information than us. We've done what we were asked to. You know how it goes."

"What I think is that there's a truckload of bullshit here and it turns out that —surprise, surprise!— my boss is driving. That's what I think." Sylvie poured herself a glass. She could sympathize with his being upset. For some reason, he had become more involved in this case than others. Maybe it was down to his looming retirement. Perhaps Coburn had gone too far this time. She preferred not to pry: the sooner they moved on, the better.

"What are you going to do?"

"I've spoken to Olivia. I'll go to St. Tropez to join her the day after tomorrow. Then we'll swing by Paris, to pick up Cécile. We'll spend a few days in Brittany."

"That sounds great," Sylvie replied, uttering words she did not mean. "She must be pleased."

"Pleased? Let me think. She seemed more relaxed," Denis said, by way of ducking an answer. "You should take a few days off, too. You're off the hook now. Thanks for coming by. You're always there for me, but I need to be alone now."

Sylvie stood there, thoughtful.

"OK, call me if you need anything," she replied, choking back her dismay at Denis' terseness. She was smothering her sincerity, not rudeness.

"Have a good time with your kids and get some rest, you deserve it."

"Will do."

"Before you go, please take with you the white enveloped that is on the table; it must be filed away with the case notes."

"What is it? It has no return address."

"Well let's see. If I had to bet my bottom dollar, I'd say it's from Mitroglou, whose conscience has pricked him while he was sleeping on it, and has sent us Atkins' passport, although it's too late to make any difference. You'll see if I lost my bet."

"Bye, Denis."

"Take care, Sylvie. By the way, my cell phone's tapped. I wouldn't be surprised if yours was, too."

Sylvie looked at him in disbelief before she went out.

"Trust me."

A light breeze brushed the rooftops. Birds flitted from chimney to chimney, without wanting to lose sight of downtown Lyons. The sound of car horns honking in the streets below worked its way up the flanks of the apartment blocks, more and more often to herald the approaching rush hour.

Denis turned the volume of his stereo back up and gulped down the rest of the bottle. A few minutes later he fell fast asleep.

Sylvie went home and played with her children awhile. Alice, the oldest, was always behind on her homework. As she did every afternoon, Sylvie sat down next to her and patiently helped her work through her high school assignments. She made believe it was her daughter who worked it all out. Alice felt proud and full of confidence when her mother congratulated her.

At 9:30 p.m. the offspring were in bed and the daily round of shouting and playing suddenly turned to a thick silence.

At that dreadful time every day. Sylvie poured herself a glass of wine.

She saw the envelope Denis had given her on the table. She would miss him.

Then she opened it.

Denis had won his bet. The morning after, she would file away William Atkins' documents along with the Miletić case.

CHAPTER XIX

"Adrian, where are you? Say something, please."
Laura's scared voice rang around the cave.

"Laura, is that you? I'm in here," Adrian replied, in relief. "In the other gallery. I've found a passageway."

Although they were but a few feet apart, Adrian's voice sounded as if he had fallen down a very deep pit.

"I'll be right with you, wait for me out there. Stand by the entrance and look out for them coming back."

He realized he would have all the time in the world to probe his find at his leisure. He had been inside that grotto for almost three hours, his leg was killing him and he had no intention of Flávio and Paul showing up unexpectedly in the middle of his ransacking; even so, he decided to give himself another twenty minutes to finish going through the contents of the plastic bag.

The time seemed to drag on forever for Laura, who was still standing watch at the mouth of the main cave and scanning the beach as thoroughly as a lifeguard. She could not help feeling deeply relieved when she saw her boss come limping back a few minutes later.

Adrian sat down on the sand and stretched out his broken leg with a sigh of relief.

"Where were you? What did you find?"

Right when he was about to go into detail over his journey to the center of the earth, he saw the shapes of Paul and Flávio walking toward them between the rocks by one of the cliff edges. An unseasonal summer storm had lashed the coast with wind and rain, so the Brazilians had decided to cut short their daily diving expedition.

"Saved by the bell," he said with a grin.

The rain had turned the sand in the cove to a morass of sticky mud that sucked at their feet and left tracks like clay molds hollowed out of the surface as they went. A thick mist hid the sun for the first time since they had arrived at the cove, and draped a ghostly pall over it that was more usual in other climes. Paul whittled away at a piece of wood with his penknife inside the cave while he listed again and again to *Strange Days*, the second album by The Doors. Flávio sat back on the rock and read a book. That day they had postponed their dip until sunset. Adrian watched the display, seated next to Laura on the shore.

Laura had heard him tell of his discoveries inside the grotto without a blink: the trunks' mysterious contents, the wooden inverted Christ, the woman's photograph and the diary. He could not quite understand what baggage those men had or what disturbances were hidden away in their scrambled brains.

"Forget about anybody finding the wreckage," he added. "They must have taken apart every last bit of it with the arsenal of tools, cold chisels and everything they have in there. They don't lack for equipment."

"What about the bits? They can't just vanish into thin air."

"I don't know. I didn't see anything in there."

They stayed silent for a few minutes. Sunlight began to poke through the mist.

"There was something else."

Laura gave him a questioning look. She rested her chin on her knees and had her arms wrapped around her legs. The sunny days had tanned her skin golden brown which made the whites of her eyes and pink, dried-up lips stand out.

"Next to the trunks I found a black plastic bag holding an inflatable dinghy. It's not very big, but enough, I figure, for one person. There was also a compressor there."

Adrian's eyes glowed brightly, as they did when he had everything under control.

"It's odd how the area hasn't been searched yet. Several days have gone by and we don't even know whether anybody saw us turn off onto the dirt road by the gas station. Damned incompetents. There's nothing for it but to try to escape by ourselves. On our own initiative. Are you with me?"

"Of course I'm with you, Adrian," she answered in a beat.

"Good. The inshore currents are very strong here. I'll cast off into open sea and row southwards, as far as the first spot where the cliff gives way and I can get inland; I'll look for somebody and raise the alarm. We'll give it a try tomorrow, weather permitting."

"Just one of us?" Laura did not at all like the idea of splitting up from Adrian and staying behind, stuck in that rock and sand prison with her weird hosts.

"I don't think there's room for both of us." Laura stayed quiet.

"I know, it's risky, but I assure you there's no alternative," Adrian added.

"With your leg, I don't think you're in any condition to go looking for help. I'll have to go. I'm an excellent swimmer."

"I'm sure you are, but I'm fine," he lied; the pain had been hell those last few hours. "Besides, being a great swimmer counts for nothing at sea."

Laura preferred not to say what she thought about that comment.

They exchanged glances. The situation had gone way beyond the bounds of the unexpected. For a moment Adrian thought it was not real. His eyes could see the waves breaking on the shore, his hands could touch the sand and his ears could hear the background music. And, despite everything, he had trouble believing that it was not all make-believe or that his mind was playing creepy tricks on him. There he was —a world away from his luxury apartment in Paris, from his business dinners, his undisputable power over others— held hostage by lunatics on a secluded beach, with a broken leg and no clean water to get a proper shower in. His quickly cast aside his doubts and worries. He was not made of such stuff. He had antibodies to banish weakness, which he metabolized inside to provide him with a huge rush of energy.

In a reflex action, Laura rested her head on his shoulder and hugged him, gently at first, then hard. Adrian returned her hug while he stared at the sea. He felt the warm touch of her skin and thought he wasn't so thick-skinned after all. She might even be able to breach his defenses. Nobody else could. Nobody wanted to.

Just then he felt nice and warm inside, and clutched the girl to his chest.

CHAPTER XX

'He's dead.'

Sylvie entered Atkins' passport details into the system again.

William C. Atkins, the U.S. Citizen who had sailed from Naxos on board the *My Own* the very night Miletić was murdered, had died little more than a year ago.

No doubt about it.

She went through the envelope Mitroglou had sent again. She found no more than what she already held in her hands: a photocopy of Atkins' passport and a police sketch drawn using witness accounts on Naxos, of the individual who went to the island, which matched the passport photo exactly.

She remembered Denis' parting shot: 'By the way, my cell phone's tapped. I wouldn't be surprised if yours was, too.'

Sylvie Prévot put the envelope in her purse and stood bolt upright as if an electric shock had run down her spine. If her boss was right, they could also track her Internet hits from her computer.

She ran out of the office full-speed, as if a ghost were after her. Although nobody took too much notice of her as she hurtled along the corridors, she felt every person she came across was a budding inquisitor ready to arrest her. Twenty minutes later she parked her car outside 30 Boulevard de Marius Vivier Merle, and after checking once more she was not being tailed, went into the City Library in the Part-Dieu neighborhood.

A deathly silence reined inside the premises, broken occasionally by a giggling bunch of elementary school children on a visit, and whom a young colored monitor hushed up again and again, while displaying priceless patience.

The free Internet access terminals were at the back, of which only one was in use: an elderly lady sporting a ridiculous flowery hat turned around to examine her new companion from head to toe. Sylvie sat down by the computer on the end for the row and began to surf the web.

It was not hard to find search results for Atkins.

He was killed in a dreadful car crash.

William C. Atkins, the only child of a wealthy Maine family, had graduated in economics from Harvard and after a short spell with a multinational corporation, went into the family real estate business. The archetypal rich kid with his whole future before him. His car smashed into a tree in the dead of night. He was killed instantly. The article hinted without going into too much detail that the crash was due to an excess of alcohol combined with speeding. He was driving a two-seater Mercedes convertible, alone at the wheel; it would appear he was on his way back from a party. The car was totaled and the body trapped in the twisted remains. It took six hours to remove the corpse from the wreckage.

Sylvie zoomed in on the photo of the spoilt young man published in the local newspaper. It was a callow, almost famished face, with sunken eyes like two coins on edge behind a blunt, beaked and hooked nose that overwhelmed any other feature and stamped its mark on his facial expression. He had short and slightly curly blond hair.

She gazed at Atkins' photo for a few minutes. It was taken on his graduation day.

Sylvie remembered the day she graduated, a stormy Friday at the Paris V René Descartes University: her happiness, her parents' satisfaction, the family gifts. Graduation day is usually a special occasion, one of pride and joy and, nonetheless, young William looked shy, sad and ashamed; he was almost apologizing for existing.

Two things stood out: first, that kid looked more like something out of a concentration camp than from the privileged background of a rich East Coast family. And second: the face of the alleged "Atkins" that appeared on the Naxos sailor's passport could not be more unlike that kid's, even if he had tried. They had forged the passport by switching photographs.

Sylvie printed the article, closed the session and left the library. She looked up and down the street, but saw nothing unusual or different from the everyday landscape of a quiet summer's day in the city. She got into her car, started up quickly and shot away. She had to tell Denis what she had unearthed. There was not a minute to lose. Her boss would fly to Nice the morning after, on his way to St. Tropez.

A man dressed in overalls silently watched Sylvie leave the library. Right away he picked up his cellphone and made a call. He then entered the building and, after showing his ID, sat down by the computer she had just left.

CHAPTER XXI

Denis had not slept a wink since Sylvie had left, which was after three in the morning. His assistant's recent discoveries prompted a sudden change of plan: he would postpone his trip to St. Tropez.

It was three o' clock in the afternoon and Denis had sat down in seat 26A, on an Air France Boeing 747 that flew the Paris-Boston route. It had been a hectic day and his mind was working as smoothly as thick molasses.

Reveille was at 8:30 that morning and twenty minutes later he was already on the street.

He had decided that first came ensuring a safe communications link with Sylvie. He had been told of a dime store in the depths of the Lyons *vieux* neighborhood where every type of cellphone and prepaid SIM card could be bought, no questions asked. His informants were putting it mildly when they said the old Chinese man was 'discrete'; he handed over the merchandise and took his money without so much as a 'How do you do?'. After dropping one of the 'phones in Sylvie's mailbox, he went back home and finished packing at the speed of sound. By eleven he was entering Terminal 1 at Lyon-Saint Exupéry Airport.

The airplane landed on time in Paris at noon. He decided to spend the two hours left before his flight took off in the Terminal 2 business lounge at Charles de Gaulle Airport. He had unfinished business: calls to make and changes in plan to justify.

Olivia did not pick up her phone. 'Better that way,' he thought. He spent a while mulling over every word before he finally wrote an email that he sent his young girlfriend: 'It'll be just a few days. Things have gotten tangled up a bit, I'll explain. I'll be back with you soon. Love you, darling.' Next, he told Alana of the program change: he would not be able to look after their daughter on the agreed dates. She did not object too strenuously. His ex-wife had already planned on taking her vacations with little Cécile. She knew him all too well. Also, she had taken stock of his continual shocks and sudden disappearances and, thanks to defense mechanisms she had developed, avoided reliving the endless disappointments that had plagued her marriage. Cécile, of course, missed her father. Denis assured her they would soon spend a few days together; even so, his daughter did not hang up until she extracted a firm promise from him that there would be no more delays.

That day the business lounge was packed with executives that placed their laptops on the tables and spoke aggressively on their cellphones, making themselves look important and serious. Those seated in the most comfortable chairs dozed or leafed through the financial papers with feigned interest, as if looking at exam results on a faculty notice board. Various types of sandwich were on display under the glass countertop at the bar; tuna, *foie gras*, boiled egg and mayonnaise, it was hard to tell which was least appetizing. Denis went over to the drinks cabinet and poured himself a Citadelle gin and tonic.

A stocky guy crammed into a suit three sizes too small for him, snored like a chainsaw next to the only free armchair. Denis made as much of a racket as he could when he placed his glass on the table top in order to wake up the hibernating bear, who came back to life with a ridiculous start.

He sipped his drink.

147

After a few hours he began to wonder what the hell he was doing there, about to cross the ocean to follow up a case he had been taken off, far from Olivia and his little girl.

It was not the first time he had been dropped from a case, and neither was he a beginner when it came to Coburn and his cronies' shenanigans. He had not cared about all that for some time —the world was sick and that was no longer his problem— but since the very day he interviewed Jasmina Osmanović, like a man possessed, the image of his brother had come back to haunt him in his dreams every night, just as it had come and gone years ago, to thrive on his misery and remind him there was unsettled business. A messenger from beyond the grave, a witness to his failure to shed light on the truth, to do justice; incapable of even redressing his own flesh and blood.

He was risking disciplinary action or, worse still, getting thrown out. Coburn did not take kindly to his instructions being disobeyed, but Denis was officially on vacation. He did not need to know. God alone knew why the old man had taken him off the case. He was not telling the whole truth, but there was no doubt that, whatever the evidence, the Osmanović couple were in their sights. They had already passed sentence.

His flight was called and Denis headed toward his destination burdened with a load of questions and few clues.

One the one hand, there was William Atkins, the young man killed in the car crash, whose passport had crossed the Greek border into Naxos in the hands of an American sailor.

On the other, the impostor, who was traveling on the dead man's passport and whose photo matched the description given by witnesses on the island; a tall man with light brown hair, brown eyes, a broad nose and thick lips. The waiters in the *Captain Morgan* remarked on his aloof and haughty expression, and his lofty look, head and shoulders above other mortals.

Sylvie had already given him a name, as she usually did. Ever since she had joined Interpol, she had gotten into the habit of nicknaming criminals on the run, and wanted delinquents, as a means of bringing them to life and also as a way to identify them in reports and team talks. In a way, it brought the goal closer and made it more tangible, accessible and real. The odd nagging feeling that the young man in the photo's look gave her was familiar from the very start. It was a recent memory, although the one that inspired it had died almost five hundred years before. It was a profiling assignment from the New York Metropolitan Museum of Art. *Portrait of a Young Man*. An anonymous portrait, as all of his artistic commissions were. A painting by Agnolo di Cosimo, or *Bronzino*, a Florentine Renaissance poet and mannerist painter, who had left the unknown identity of his sitter as enigmatic entertainment for future generations. The mysterious model in the painting has an unyielding and arresting look, full of confidence but lacking in life, bereft of joy. Sylvie had defined his profile as that of a young loner, probable a noble, who behind his exterior hid a deep grief that voided his soul. Some experts had identified him as Cosimo de' Medici, Grand Duke of Tuscany, although there was no firm evidence to support the truth of that affirmation.

Sylvie decided that was what she would call her fugitive. 'Il Duce', that would be his moniker.

And, finally, apart from the late William Atkins, there was a third man: 'The Argentine'. A suspect in the killing of Guillermo Lavinia, of whom they only had the police sketch sent by Contini and his team. The individual was lightly built, dark-skinned, had dark hair and was of medium stature. He was around thirty and his face had smooth and childish features for his age. The police sketch was of almost photographic quality: six witnesses' descriptions had fed the powerful software tool, which handled more than ten thousand different facial characteristics, to draw a suspect's picture with exquisite neatness. According to the report, the statements had been taken in the five days following the date of visual contact, which thoroughly enhanced the document's reliability.

The three individuals had approximately the same age and, if the witness statements were right, the three were certainly Americans.

The only certainty was that Atkins was dead.

Only on occasion did Denis Martel indulge in his boss Coburn's conjectures, and top of that short list was betting on the simplest explanation in order to clarify the facts of the matter. He considered it an article of faith after thirty years' experience. He had always believed in the most straight-forward and obvious solution was the first option for deciphering any case.

'Il Duce' knew Atkins well. Moreover, he figured Atkins belonged to his close, inner circle.

Identity theft usually arises in cases where people have some connection with each other, often a close one. Impostors like to be at ease in their new role, so they can step into the other person's shoes. They are familiar with his life and personality; they study his behavior; they have enough information to get out of any hitch that crops up. Even the coldest and most calculating minds need to take refuge in a basic comfort zone. Our main guidelines are not hidden behind a TV screen but all around us: family, friends, workmates, acquaintances. They all chisel out the contours of our personality. They trigger reactions. We always look nearby, invariably, within the perimeter we are capable of spanning.

Denis closed his eyes.

In seven hours and a half he would land at Boston Logan airport.

CHAPTER XXII

The dawn's faint light bathed the coastline and at a stroke revived the inert colors of the ridges and bushes. Adrian, who had woken up early, filled his cup to overflowing with an overdose of squid ink coffee, that magical brew which Flávio freshly made before setting off to be at one with the sea depths. A semisolid sludge that could bring a whole cemetery back to life.

He went outside the cave and breathed in the damp morning dew, which began to evaporate in the first rays of sunlight.

'Time to get out of here.'

Laura was still lying on her rubber mattress. Her lips were pursed in a smile, as if her dreams reassured her spirit. Adrian sat beside her for a few minutes. He looked at her girlish features, delighted in them and heard her slow and gentle breathing. A halo of naive, almost childish purity hung over her. It was wondrous. He could not remember the last time he had seen someone like that. Everything in his world was rotten, and he was first in line.

He grabbed the flashlight and crawled through the little passageway until he reached the inner chamber.

"Good morning, wish us luck," he exclaimed, as he greeted the carved, inverted Christ with a half-bow.

There was no time to lose, so without delay he headed over to the huge plastic bag containing the blow-up dinghy.

Adrian cursed to high heaven. To call it a dinghy was an exercise in unbridled optimism. That boat-shaped bit of inflatable black plastic was no more than a toy, a plaything for kids on the beach. A medium-sized person could barely fit in it without capsizing.

He shoved his arm into the bag up to his shoulder, and searched around the inside. There was nothing else: no sign of oars or anything like that. He would have to paddle against the current with his hands to propel the dinghy. After spending a few seconds searching the rest of the boxes to check there were no other means of propulsion there, he went back to the main gallery. It did not take him five minutes to blow it up with the compressor, which hardly used up any of the battery. Laura, who had woken up from her peaceful sleep by now, watched her boss from her mattress as he checked the small craft for leaks and punctures, by carefully going over its whole surface.

Adrian realized she was back in the land of the living.

"Good morning."

"Good morning," she answered as she roused herself on the camp bed.

"I hope you slept well. It'll be a busy day."

"How's your leg?"

"Never been better. I could dance the tango on Flávio's head."

He smiled to admit that, even if his leg was worse than ever and he had not slept a wink from the pain, he would indeed love to dance on the Brazilian's head.

Over he walked to the mouth of the cave and looked out to the horizon. The sea currents in the area were as whimsical as a child on its birthday. The Alborán Sea washed the whole coast and connected the Atlantic and Mediterranean: the Mediterranean waters, which were warmer and saltier, moved westward along the seabed, while the Atlantic waters, coming from the Straits of Gibraltar, moved eastward along the surface.

The sea could change in a matter of hours from being as smooth as a millpond to a raging, saltwater, roller coaster.

However, conditions within the stretch of sea nestling by the cliff seemed acceptable. A light east wind blew, which made the surface a little choppy and raised some lesser-sized waves. Once he was in open sea it would be another matter: he could come across anything, like in a Chinese fortune cookie. He had to trust his intuition. Adrian had as much chance of finding a reliable weather forecast for the next few hours as did Ferri, his marketing director, of learning table manners. He smiled. He had not fired him yet because he did a good job and was hard-working, but whenever he appeared in the office of a morning in his gilt tie pin and snub-nosed shoes, it took heaven and earth to stop him. 'Offenses like that ought to be punishable by hard labor, or even death,' he thought.

A few minutes later, when he finally decided that they had a reasonably good day before them for sailing and there was no reason to delay their departure, he went back inside the cave. He decided to take a last look around the rear gallery. He could have sworn that on his last search he had found a kayak oar, one with a short stem and paddles at each end. On his way he saw Laura, who had huddled into a corner to get changed. Among the shadows he could make out her naked, slim and wiry body. While she gathered her hair in a ponytail, her profile showed up curves in all the right places, as if they were air-brushed. He had never taken any notice of her all these years; for him she was just another employee. Before that journey, he had never thought of exchanging so much as two words with her, after the interview. He was aware he kept his distance from people, that he had his barriers, and he guessed that meant he missed out on some things, but that way he also avoided mixing with fools and undesirables that, doubtless, were in the majority. God knew it was a price worth paying.

Once inside the rocky recesses, he shone the flashlight

around it. The powerful beam pierced the darkness like a laser. He explored every nook and cranny again until he finally uncovered a crack that was more than a yard above his head and, alongside several oxygen tanks, was a long bag that was broad at the ends.

He rested the flashlight on the ground and, stepping on the nearest stone with his right leg, he stretched out as much as he could. He could just about reach the part of the bag jutting out from the shelf with his fingertips. He grabbed it between thumb and forefinger and pulled it outwards. The oar did not budge an inch: it was stuck underneath the tanks and diving gear. He needed to stand on his other leg to raise himself a few inches, and use both arms. He cursed endlessly when, on his third attempt, he managed to place his bandaged leg on the stone. The pain was unspeakable and his knees wobbled like a *soufflé*. He took a deep breath for a few seconds and, next, grabbed the end of the oar with both hands. He pulled it with all his might, but the oar only budged a few inches. He still gripped the stem with both arms stretched out, and leaned back a little, to pull with his added body weight. The oar moved outwards a little bit more. Adrian leaned even more and was now almost hanging in mid-air.

A few seconds later the balance of forces and weights finally toppled over; the oar shot out like a scalded cat, and Adrian fell on his back to hit the ground like a sack of rocks, which winded him for a while. In the grotto that was improvised as a storeroom, the rest of the stock was in disarray and the tanks rolled over each other. Those that didn't settle inside the cavity, fell hard to do so outside it. Forty pounds of dead weight in almost ten feet of free fall. One of them landed within inches of Adrian's belly. Seconds later, another hit him smack on his left leg.

His harrowing cry of pain echoed around the whole gallery.

"Adrian? Adrian, is everything OK?"

Laura ran to the back of the cave when she heard no reply, and crawled as fast as she could through the small passageway until she reached the rear gallery. She grabbed the flashlight and lighted up Adrian's body, which was sprawled out on the ground.

"My God, what happened to you?"

His breathing was forced and he nodded toward his limbs. Laura suddenly felt relieved to see he was conscious.

"My leg," he gasped laboriously.

The bandage covering his leg in splints was covered in blood, and a metal tank lay on it. Laura felt her pulse rate hit the roof. He took a deep breath. She had to calm down and keep a cool head. She crouched down beside Adrian and wiped his forehead.

"Take it easy."

She took the utmost care to remove the oxygen tank from his knee and place it on the ground. Adrian breathed a quiet grunt, while his body was twisted and shaken. He shone the flashlight on his leg. It looked woeful.

"I've got to get you out of here. That injury needs treatment. Will you help me?" she asked calmly.

Adrian nodded.

She grabbed him underneath his armpits from behind.

"I will drag your body along. I need you to push with your good leg. I'm not strong enough to drag you in one go, so we'll need to take a five-second breather after each tug. Think you can do that?"

"OK," he answered in a dull voice.

Laura began to count down to her first tug. Adrian's body shifted eighteen inches. So, with infinite patience, little by little, they ate up the distance between them and the cave's outer chamber. The five-second breaks turned into ten, then twenty. Twenty minutes later they had managed to get through the passageway. The daylight bathed them again.

Laura rested Adrian's head on a plastic bag and went over to the first aid kit; she came back quickly with a glass of water and two painkillers which she made him take. Then, slowly, she unwound the bandage and removed the stick immobilizing his tibia. Blood streamed from his injured knee and covered all of his skin. She cleaned the injury with fresh water and soap, and then disinfected it with surgical spirit. Then she sprinkled it with iodine antiseptic, and covered it with a dressing and sticking plaster.

She looked at his face. Adrian lay there, eyes shut. The painkillers looked like they were taking effect. Laura reckoned it was best that he did not pass out.

"Well, I've disinfected the injury. The weight of the tank has broken some tissue, but it's superficial and will soon heal up. I'll put the splint back on your leg. Now you must grit your teeth a bit, because this will hurt."

Adrian opened his eyes and nodded. He cracked a faint smile. Laura looked at him. His look betrayed no emotion; neither pain, nor anxiety, nor fear. He gave nothing away, as usual. Neither did he when he should have shown joy, interest or happiness. He simply opened his big brown eyes, which only seemed to register what happened on the other side by stripping everything of niceties and emotion. Like an automaton. And that smile... At first, when he had looked at her like that, it made her feel worried and small. Now she only felt an addictive feeling of intrigue and curiosity wash over her.

"Try to straighten your leg out as much as you can."

Adrian stretched his leg and tried to fight back the pain that, despite the pills, ran all along his spine. Paul had diagnosed him with a fractured tibia which, as it affected the bone supporting his bodyweight, usually went hand in hand with a fractured fibula. He had no confidence in Paul's ability as a doctor, but his friend Bernard, who was a renowned traumatology lecturer in La Salpêtrière, was a couple of thousand miles out of the

156

way. Laura placed the stick acting as a splint in line with the bone and, gently but tightly enough, she wound the bandage around it again. The splint stuck out above the knee to make sure the whole of his lower leg was immobilized.

"That's that. How do you feel?"

"Give me a jar of that coffee sludge and another painkiller, and I'll be in heaven," he smiled. "Come on, help me get up."

"You need to get some rest now. I'll heat up the coffee for you."

"I've no time for rest, I have to put to sea.Help me, it'll just take a moment."

"Are you crazy? You can't even move, your leg's all busted. Forget it."

Adrian took a couple of deep breaths.

"Laura, come here and listen to me."

She sat down beside him. Her eyes beamed the same refusal as before.

"It's true, I am injured, but in the boat I'll only need my arms, you get me? There'll be no problem, I can hack it."

"I hear you. And the answer's no," Laura stood back up and walked over to the coffee pot.

Adrian snorted in anger. His crippling injuries tortured his insides. He tried to get up but the sharp pains made him lie there.

"Laura, please listen to me. When the Brazilians get back they'll see what a mess I've made in there, and they'll know we've been rooting around in their stuff. I don't think you're up to putting the oxygen tanks back in place: they weigh a ton and the shelf is very high up. And even if you could, we won't manage to leave them just as they were. They'll know we've tried to make a break for it. And can you imagine what they'll do? Tie us up? Chain us to a rock? Don't you get it? We won't get another chance."

Laura made no answer. She lit the stove and ignored what

he said.

"Laura, for God's sake!"

"OK," she said, at last, turning round. "I'll go."

"Don't even think about it," Adrian replied, after being baffled for a few seconds.

"Don't you think I'm capable?" Laura stared straight at him, looking daggers.

"No," he answered curtly.

Laura beamed a wry smile, one that only arises when the rational part of the brain tries to avoid blowing up after a put-down.

"Adrian, look at me. You're lying there, racked in pain with a smashed leg. You cannot fend for yourself. That's the way it is. I'm just fine. I'm a good swimmer and am not scared. Besides, if I stay here alone with those lunatics, I might be in harm's way, mightn't I? Isn't that what it's about? Keeping me out of harm's way?"

Adrian said nothing.

"Why do you think I can't do it? Tell me, Adrian. Is it because I'm a woman?"

'I'd rather not answer that,' thought Adrian.

"The sea doesn't care about good swimmers. You don't get that, either."

"Well look at you, you're in no state to swim at all," she said, in a calmer voice now.

They kept quiet for a few moments. Adrian knew that putting off his attempted escape meant scrapping it forever.

"OK, you win. Go out there, paddle a few feet, but as soon as you feel any danger, you come right back. Otherwise I'll have to go after you, and you wouldn't want to do that to an invalid, would you?"

"I promise."

"Go ahead, go on, before I change my mind," he protested.

Laura was ready to go a few minutes later. She wore the same jeans and sandals as the day of the crash, and had borrowed one of Paul's worn T-shirts. It was not the most suitable attire for her expedition, but they had nothing else to hand and both figured it would have to do in order to search for help. Laura preferred not to use the oar —she felt more comfortable paddling with her hands — and Adrian cursed to himself, remembering what it had taken him to get hold of that goddamned oar. After a last look around to check there was no sign of the Brazilians, they left the cave and walked to the southern end of the cove. Adrian could only move with great difficulty, holding on to Laura's arm, while she dragged the dinghy along the sand by a rope. When they reached the departure point, they looked quietly at the sea, which was only ruffled by the murmur of the waves. That vast expanse of water was their gateway to freedom. The sky was still clear, but the east wind had been growing stronger and was driving waves shoreward.

They ran through the plan again. Laura would have to overcome the undertow and paddle some sixty yards directly offshore until she was level with the end of the cliff. Once she was in open sea, she would head south and in line with the coast until she found a safe place to hit dry land.

"Don't lose your nerve. Take it easy. There's a headwind and it won't be easy to make headway. And when you reach open sea, we don't know what currents you'll come across. If they're with you, use them; if not, be patient and stay the course." He stared her right in the eyes and, with his hands placed on her shoulders, said, "Sure you'll be OK?"

"Yes, I can take care of myself."

"Remember, at the first sign of trouble, please, come right back. I'll be here. Will you do that?"

"I promise."

They slowly fell into each other's arms.

Laura welcomed the shelter and warmth of her boss's body,

and held it tight. She guessed that odd uneasy feeling that ran through her body and made her legs quiver was normal, but she was amazed at the surprising energy that welled up inside her and wiped out any fear.

"Lots of luck, Laura."

"Good luck to you, too. See you back home," she answered with a smile.

"We'll make it."

Laura got into the boat and unflinchingly threw herself heartily into the first waves that crashed on to the beach, waving her arms and legs, which spun like windmills. The wind hindered the little raft's progress, which gained ground on the horizon in fits and starts, as it pulled away from the shore.

Adrian balled up his fists and drove her on by shouting encouragement. Only a few seconds had gone by and already he was quite regretting having let her go.

The waves pitched and tossed the boat, this way and that, up and down, playing with the foreign body that lay on their back. The little dinghy went further and further out of sight with each passing minute, until it was merely a dark speck on the sea when it was level with the cliff's rocky edge. Even so, Laura's body could still be seen from the shore, in between sea spray and slabs of gray water. Her paddling began to slow down and at times she could not see for the waves.

Adrian shouted like crazy, putting all his strength into it to encourage his colleague, even though he knew the roaring wind would drown out his voice and she would never hear him.

Laura took a break for a few seconds. She was worn out.

The concentration of lactic acid in her bloodstream had shot up, her muscles burned inside and her heart beat faster and faster.

The swell in the open sea had risen greatly due to the clash between the two currents. The dinghy was adrift, spinning around and sliding along the waves every which way, like a sleigh coming out of nowhere.

Gusts of wind splashed her face with salt water. She looked up, she was moving away from the rocks and the currents were sweeping her out to sea relentlessly. She held the boat tight. She paddled once more, to try to head the dinghy toward the cliff edge, but she went further and further out to sea, as if lured by an unseen magnet.

The idea of getting stuck on that raft in the middle of a watery desert took on the form of a terrifying nightmare in her mind. Her body began to be seized with dread as she drifted helplessly offshore, and a heart-rending cry for help burst from her throat.

Tears started rolling down her face and mixed with the sea water to blind her.

She grabbed the inflatable dinghy with all her strength.

She closed her eyes and said a prayer, the first one her mother taught her when she spoke her first words.

Her numb muscles would not respond to any prompting. After a few minutes of jitters her body relaxed completely, overcome by an odd lull, as if she were no longer accountable to anybody.

A sudden wave made the little dinghy capsize.

She looked at the sky before she sank and the waves swallowed her up.

CHAPTER XXIII

A summer storm battered Massachusetts Bay all the way from Cape Cod to Nova Scotia, and lashed the entire coastline with gale-force winds that shot the rain around everywhere, like a gigantic sprinkler. Denis picked up the little Chrysler outside the air terminal and drove out of the Avis parking lot to head for Maine. He had now recovered from the bumpy landing and sat back for a few minutes in the ergonomic cloth and leather seat, which smelled nice and new. Then he turned off U.S. Route 1 to take Interstate 95. Both highways ran along the East Coast, from north to south, from Florida to the Canadian border, but the traffic flowed quicker along the new freeway, which was thirty years more modern.

Denis tuned into a 1970s hit radio station and lit a cigarette. The windshield wipers were working full tilt and, even so, he could barely keep at bay the deluge of water falling on the glass. He would reach his destination in three hours' time, and did not want to risk his neck in a storm like that for the sake of a few minutes, especially given his lack of expertise in driving automatics.

The Atkins residence was in Southport, a small town in Lincoln County, one hundred seventy miles from Boston. It covered the whole of the island of that same name. To the south it flanked the cold waters of the Atlantic, and to the north, the Sheepscot River estuary. Furthermore, Southport town was linked to Boothbay Harbor by an old bridge that crossed the river, and acted as umbilical chord between the fishing village and the mainland.

Stella and Alexander Atkins lived for half the year in their beach house on Nickerson Road. Since the death of their only son just a few months previously, they had spent a bare minimum of time in their mansion on Newbury Street, in Boston. Every spring, after the rigors of a New England winter, they moved to their second home, turning a deaf ear to the advice of family and friends that the best medicine for the tragic loss of their first-born, was to keep up with the social whirl that they had always enjoyed. For the Atkins, however, it was too late: the memories tormenting their September years were impossible to leave behind.

The old Victorian house on the banks of the Sheepscot was an oasis of peace and quiet. There was not much for an elderly couple to do there, apart from look out at the estuary from the porch and watch the fishing boats head out to sea, then come back again, in a constant stream from dawn to dusk. Alexander usually went for a walk around the island every morning. Stella, on the other hand, rarely went outdoors. She whiled away the hours reading or knitting on the porch in the company of Beth who, after thirty years' service, was practically one of the family. The old housekeeper's company gave the lady invaluable support in order to withstand her deep grief over William's untimely death.

A huge billboard welcomed travelers to New Hampshire.

Denis put his briefcase on the passenger seat; it held all the case files, statements, photographs, police sketches, etc. He was convinced he had not journeyed five thousand miles for nothing. He had to get answers, and under the circumstances, he alone in the world could find them.

In the first place, he had to win over the Atkins family. He knew their strengths and weaknesses. A half-century of life is enough to know oneself, without deceit or trickery. He knew how to earn people's trust, it was a gift. With his quiet blue eyes and mature, calm expression, he exuded an atmosphere of sincere relaxation. His deep and unhurried words had a narcotic effect that brought about a sort of Stockholm syndrome on even the most awkward of interlocutors. He could read people's thoughts and motives as soon as he opened up the slightest communications channel, and he could wade into anybody's comfort zone, and onto the vantage point needed to obtain his goal.

He reached his destination after three long hours.

The storm had died down at last and a huge sun had taken its place in the sky. He crossed the bridge to burrow into the heart of Southport island. The thick woods cast shadows on the few streets criss-crossing its middle. As he drove along, he passed trees of all shapes and sizes that vied for every yard of ground: red firs and maple trees went by, one after another, between American oaks and shrubs. The ground was waterlogged after the downpour unleashed during the storm, while rows of droplets bedecking the leaves shone like diamonds in the sunlight.

The greenery vanished at a stroke at the end of Nickerson Road, where the Atlantic hoved into view. On top of of a bluff running down to the bay, stood a stately old wooden Victorian house that was painted in shades of cream. The front was covered in windows. The upstairs ones were round and stuck out, and gave shape to the lookout turrets atop the building's four corners, which sloped into the gabled roof, out of which a chimney stuck. Two rows of rosebushes lined the stone driveway leading to the porch, which was buttressed by four neoclassical columns. Again, he checked the photo Sylvie had given him. Doubtless it was the Atkins residence. Denis parked his car across the street and went over to the gate. A gentle breeze kissed his cheeks. Hardly anything could be heard apart from the murmuring of the sea below and the seagulls squawking in the distance.

He took a deep breath and knocked on the door.

After waiting a few seconds, a stout colored lady appeared before his eyes.

"Good afternoon Sir, how may I help you?"

"Good afternoon, my name is Denis Martel," he announced in a noticeably French accent. "I have come to see Mr. or Mrs. Atkins. They don't know me personally. I am acquainted with their son, William. I heard the news about his terrible accident. My work brings me to New England. So I just wanted to offer my condolences. He was quite a guy."

"Please wait a moment." The frown dropped from Beth's face upon hearing William's name and she went inside again. She was back within a few minutes.

"Mr. Atkins is not at home. Mrs. Atkins will see you. Would you be so kind as to follow me?"

"Perfect, thank you," Denis answered, then followed the maid inside.

The ceiling and floor on the first floor were covered in wood paneling. The vast space was split up into several rooms of different styles, and a large dining room decorated with antiques from all over the world: rugs, African statuettes, pottery and tapestry. A huge chimney breast embedded in the central beam was the first floor's cornerstone. Behind it, placed atop an old bureau, were a lot of silver-framed photographs of different sizes. He saw that most were of William. Beth withdrew after Denis went through to the veranda, but not without offering him some coffee, which he gratefully accepted.

The view from that spot, a wooden balcony that looked out to sea and from which the whole of the bay and surrounding forests could be seen, was dazzling. Stella Atkins sat in silence, watching the estuary from one of the wicker chairs around a heavy, rough-cut, wooden table. She had just turned sixty-five according to Denis' information, but could well have passed for ten years more.

"Mrs. Atkins."

"Good afternoon, Mr..."

"Martel. Denis Martel. Delighted to meet you."

"You are not from around here."

"No. I'm French. I live in Lyons. I'm here on business."

"Please sit down. Lyons. I was there thirty years ago, on a trip to Europe. It is a lovely town."

Stella Atkins spoke in a sparing and relaxed tone of voice. She liked receiving visitors. Lately she had not had very many and she enjoyed having a few words with somebody other than her old faithful Beth, and her husband. She was struck by the fact that the mysterious visitor knew her son. She never tired of talking about William; in fact, she felt that doing so brought him back to life for a few minutes.

"It is indeed, but from what I can see, nothing to compare to this wonderful place," said Denis as he sat down on one of the wicker chairs.

"Everywhere has its own beauty."

"Just so. Thank you for receiving me in your home, very kind of you."

"You're welcome. Now tell me. Beth says you knew my son."

"Yes, I did. I wanted to offer my condolences personally. That is what brings me here, Mrs. Atkins."

"You have my heartfelt thanks. It was a heavy blow for us. For the rest of my days I shan't wake up without feeling this unrelenting anxiety, and every hour I'll wonder why, but the affection of those who offer their sympathy and encouragement is always a comfort."

Beth brought in Denis' coffee on a tray.

"Mrs. Atkins, I'm a father and I can well imagine what you are going through."

"Think of it as endless torture. Now I try to think less, to face things another way. William is in heaven and also among us, living on in our memories."

"I understand. My brother Alain died when he was seventeen. He lost his hearing after an incident, and a year later we heard he also had brain damage. He died two weeks later. My parents and I always kept him alive. We constantly remembered his adventures and wondered what he would think or do in every situation. He will be helping us from up there."

"I'm sorry about your brother."

"It's been a while.

"Are your parents still alive?"

"No. My father left us a while back and my mother passed away three years ago."

"Time flies, Mr. Martel," Stella Atkins sighed.

"You must not let grief eat away inside you."

An unexpected silence fell over the conversation for a long minute. The seagulls' squawking made itself heard more on the porch. Boats that had lagged behind were coming back to port from a day's fishing and putting away their tackle for the night. Denis remembered Alain again. He figured Alain had missed out on so many things, that he had gone too soon.

"Tell me, Mr. Martel, how did you know William?"

"I work for Interpol. Wait," Denis gave her a card. "I'm a police officer and I coordinate international intelligence. I also attend congresses and conferences at universities the world over, including the JFK School of Government. My organization is surprisingly unknown, despite being present in most of the world's countries. We do a great deal to raise awareness, or at least we try to. I visited JFK on several occasions. That is where I met William and his buddies. I was his tutor in a working group on International Politics and Security for graduates from other faculties, and we got on well. He was quite a guy. We kept in touch by email until shortly before he died. It was a shock to learn of his loss."

Stella could not remember her son mentioning that man. Neither did it matter much to her. William was quite reserved and not very communicative, at least with her and her husband. He became very introspective as a teenager and more so as time went by, especially in recent years.

"He showed great interest in our work," Denis continued. "He was keen on international relations and police work.

"I guess so," she replied, not especially convinced. "My husband was handing over much of the company management to him. Alexander was thrilled at the thought of our son taking over the reins of the family business," Stella broke off suddenly. "Maybe William was not quite so thrilled."

"Perhaps. I guess we each have our own dreams."

Ever since the dreadful accident, Stella had not been able to help feeling racked with guilt. She did not chide herself for all the things she never said to him —as is often the case when losing a loved one— but rather she regretted not having really known her own son. Or not enough to break down the glass wall around him. Neither she nor her husband had taken the time to know how he felt, or even what he did in his spare time.

"The problem is that we don't bother to discover other people's dreams," Stella concluded.

"You'll never forget William, just as I'll never forget Alain and my parents. Don't torture yourself. That won't help matters. He'll always be in your hearts."

Stella made no reply. They chatted for a while about France, Paris and Europe's cultural wealth. She loved the Old Continent. She could spend hours remembering her trips to France and Spain, but it was getting late and she needed to be alone. Although she enjoyed the company of her unexpected visitor, she had suddenly been overcome by an awkward sadness. The breeze began to blow harder; it was time to withdraw indoors and talk to Beth about some trivial matter.

"When do you go back to Europe?"

"In a couple of days. First I have an appointment at Harvard. Academic business, you know. Furthermore, I'd like to take the opportunity to look up some of William's fellow alumni, who took part in the meetings and lectures we gave some years ago. I need some help for some symposiums we plan to set up," Denis explained. "I've gathered together some details I kept from our last meeting: registration forms, photos, but some names, addresses and telephone numbers are missing. Did you know any of your son's classmates?"

"Not all of them, just his inner circle and the children of some Boston families. On occasion he used to bring friends here in the summer. They used to go fishing and we would have barbecues by the river."

"Perhaps you could remind me of the names of two classmates from a seminar. You never know," he said as he took the pictures out of his briefcase.

"Of course, I'd be glad to, if I can be of help in any way." Denis looked once again at the mysterious expression on the face in the photograph he handed Stella Atkins: that of '*Il Duce*'.

"Here you are."

Denis swallowed and for a second felt most relieved that Alexander Atkins was not there. He wanted to avoid too many questions and was aware they could crop up at any time. That lady could not be bothered querying Denis' curious concerns with her son's classmates, let alone wonder whether there were not more reasonable channels for gathering such information. Stella pored over the photograph for a few seconds. Never in his wildest dreams could anybody imagine that the man in the photograph had stolen her son's identity.

"I'm sorry, Mr. Martel. I have never seen that face before. As I have already said, I didn't know all of his classmates, just those closest to the family, although that doesn't mean much, either. My son was very reserved."

A shudder of deception gripped his spine like a sudden cramp. '*Il Duce*' was still an enigma floating in the void. He began to think that the trip had been a waste of time.

"Don't worry. I'll ask around in Harvard."

Immediately after that, he took out the police sketch that Contini and his team had sent over from Argentina.

"Just one more thing. Please keep this other picture, maybe it'll be nearer the mark. It is time for me to go, it'll soon be dark and you will have things to do. I have taken up enough of your time."

"Thank you, Mr. Martel, it was kind of you to come over and offer your condolences. Like I said, it is appreciated much more than people think." Stella Atkins took the sketch and looked at it carefully. Repeatedly. This time she did not reply right away, then suddenly flashed a look of surprise.

"He looks very much like the Caldwells' son," she answered, finally. "Peter Caldwell."

"Are you sure?" Denis tried to contain his excitement.

Stella turned around to face Denis. Her eyes were shrouded in a veil of sadness.

"Yes, it's him He was William's classmate in school. They were roommates on campus. We are good friends of his parents," she was quiet for a few seconds, while she looked at the young man's picture again.

"Is something the matter, Mrs. Atkins?" Stella did not answer.

"Are you alright?"

"Yes, yes, don't worry. I just think that... It was also a terrible shame. Peter committed suicide three months before William's accident."

Denis was speechless.

"I've been very close to his mother since then. They were distraught, and have suffered greatly. It came about so

170

unexpectedly, so suddenly. Nobody knows why he did it. A tragedy for everybody."

"It's awful, I don't know what to say. I didn't know."

"His parents live on Beacon Hill, in Boston. That was a severe blow to the whole community. It was all anybody spoke of for weeks. He was an extraordinary boy."

Thoughts flitted around like mad inside his head, at the speed of sound, without giving him time to concentrate on a particular idea for so much as a second. He did not know where to begin in order to put it all in place.

Mrs. Atkins rose from the table. The memory of the Caldwell tragedy, and the recurring bundle of distress and remorse that assailed her every time she thought of her son William, had worn her out.

"I must let you go now. Thank you again for your visit," she said in a faint voice, practically a whisper, before shaking his hand and going inside. "Beth will see you to the door."

Denis politely said good-bye and followed the maid to the door.

He drove slowly through the little island's streets to the bridge. It had already gone dark and he had a few hours' driving ahead to get back to Boston. He took a deep breath. He needed some oxygen to process all the information and make some sense out of what was happening.

Mrs. Atkins had identified in a beat the picture of the suspect in the bombing that killed Guillermo Lavinia and his family: it was Peter Caldwell; Harvard alumnus and her son, William's classmate. Peter had committed suicide two months after the bombing. Why? What did that 'preppy' kid from Boston have to do with the Argentine ex-Navy officer? What strange web was woven between them all? Why did he decide to take his own life? It was a fact that William and Peter knew each other, were friends and had even lived together —his own mother had acknowledged that. But neither of them could answer his

171

queries now; they had taken their secrets with them to heaven. Or hell.

'*Il Duce*' and his mockingly indifferent half-smile preyed on his mind, uninvited.

He took Interstate 95 back to Boston. He wanted to call Sylvie, but it was the small hours in Lyons and he did not feel like disturbing his colleague.

The radio kept playing 1970s hits, non-stop. David Bowie was singing the final strains of 'Heroes' as the New England evening died down.

The freeway traffic was surprisingly brisk. Summer was really making itself felt.

CHAPTER XXIV

The TV preacher's exasperating tirade mingled with Denis' dreams until it forced him to wake up.

'God is your guide.' 'Jesus Christ is the answer.' 'Don't let him down, or his avenging fist will smite the sinner.'

He looked at his watch. It was two minutes to six in the morning.

He switched off the TV, which was hanging from the grubby wall in a metal frame, and sprawled back down on the mattress in a final bid to get back to sleep. Minutes later he gave up trying. He was now wide awake. Denis left room 16 in the Holyoke Motel and served himself an appalling *cappuccino* dispensed by a coffee machine in the hall. The brackish brew was thinner than dishwater. The blue light shed by the worn neon tubes showed him the way back along the filthy carpeted corridor.

It was seven hours since he had decided to turn off I-95. The flight from Paris and visiting the Atkins home in Southport had exhausted him. His lack of sleep had begun to play tricks on his driving, so he opted to take the Wakefield exit that led to Salem Street, and look for somewhere decent to spend the night. And then he found that dump. Well, at least he managed to get a few hours' rest.

He opened the room window. Darkness still reigned above and there was a deafening silence outside. After a quick shower he went downstairs while he remembered the Korean receptionist's indications about Internet access when he arrived. 'No wifi, no wifi, downstairs, Internet down there.'

Denis went down to the reception desk. There was no sign of the receptionist. In fact, there was no sign of anybody. He saw a small staircase on his right and walked down it until he came to a narrow passageway that led to a dark, tiny room. He groped along the wall until he found a switch and a pale light filled the room. A four-year-old calendar hung on the two-tone wall opposite, decorated with the U.S. flag and a picture of Uncle Sam. In front of him, two bulky computers stood on a black, particle board desk. He figured those old machines must have been around at least a decade. He sat down on one of the metal chairs in front of a massive Packard Bell, and quickly discovered that the connection speed was of the same vintage as the old-fashioned equipment. He smiled in resignation. At that time of day, he had nothing better to do. He lit up a cigarette with his eyes firmly on the 'No smoking' sign hanging on the wall opposite. The search results appeared on the screen a couple of minutes later.

Articles on Peter Caldwell's suicide appeared all over the net. Coverage was widespread. Every local, even state newspaper website, ran an account of the fatal news. Denis read all of them, one after another. The headlines were not exactly imaginative. 'Beacon Hill tragedy', 'Caldwells' youngest dies in strange circumstances', 'Caldwell clan in mourning.' Most sources agreed that Peter had been found dead in his ensuite bathroom, and that his own mother had first seen the body in the bath tub. The youngster had not come down for breakfast that Sunday morning.

The Caldwells used to have a family breakfast on the last Sunday of each month, which the whole clan would go to. It did not go ahead this time, but was canceled with the whole family present when Stella Caldwell found her son had bled to death. He had slashed his wrists by way of an ice-breaker.

The mainstream newspapers published the details clinically and respectfully. They gave the boy's profile, and testimonials from family and friends that spoke well of Peter: from his being a model student and active member of the community, to his extensive charity work.

A brilliant future cut short, they all said.

The less traditional websites and some tabloid comments sections, on the other hand, mentioned his liking for alcohol, partying and womanizing, or ascribed his suicide to bipolar disorders. The most daring muckrakers even linked the Caldwell's youngest to satanic practices.

After two hours, Denis had pored over more than fifty articles and as many other accounts of the incident. Six of them mentioned a note Peter had left before dying, all of them according to anonymous police sources that appeared in none of the 'mainstream' media. Denis did not dismiss that disclosure. On more than one occasion, confidential information from cases he had been working on had turned up on a few websites and Internet forums, including *sub judice* details. Leaks of classified information were as common as they were hard to pin down, all the more so in a case with such unbounded local impact.

In a notebook he jotted down some details of the suicide, which he had gleaned carefully from among the various articles. Many of them had contradictory sources, but that was no time to weigh up the veracity of the morass of data scattered throughout the net. He had work to do and left the poky little room, while looking Uncle Sam in the eye and wishing him a good day.

The Korean receptionist had come back to life. She wished him a cursory good morning while serving a plump colored man, who seemed to have been squeezed by forceps into a Hawaiian shirt that threatened to burst at the seams. Denis went back to his room and turned the little desk there into his operations center. Denis opened the drapes. The broad daylight cruelly showed up the variety of stains on the wall and carpet. He avoided thinking what had caused them —he had to concentrate— and began to read over his observations, particularly those concerning the alleged note the youngster had left before killing himself.

His experience had shown him that suicide notes always had a reason to them, from a simple farewell, to a justification to dispel guilty feelings around and about: they checked remorse, gave reasons, confessed something that could not be revealed in life. They sent a message, not just the contents as such, but because they dispensed with any idea that the deed had been spontaneous. Young Caldwell's suicide was neither an impulsive nor hasty act, but was planned and premeditated, he concluded.

As far as the general public was concerned, the kid had led a blameless life. Not for Denis, though. It was less than twenty-four hours since Stella Atkins had identified the police sketch as him, the suspect in the Pinamar massacre. The suicide note may have contained a confession. A young man from a good family that commits an atrocity and cannot live with himself. It did not seem far fetched. Then why were its contents not known? They had not been revealed to the media at all. It was odd. Although the Caldwells were an influential family, the American wheels of justice were relentless when it came to cases affecting high society. They were not squeamish over transparency. The Land of the Free took pains to show its children that all were equal in the eyes of democracy and the law. If such a missive existed, he had to know about it. He looked at his watch. First off, though, he needed some proper coffee. He gathered his papers together and put them in his briefcase before leaving the shabby motel.

176

On the other side of the Atlantic, Sylvie Prévot's telephone rang again and again, unanswered, ruining the silence in the deserted offices. Lunchtime in August emptied the Interpol offices for an hour and a half. Sylvie heard the ringing from the elevator and sprinted between the desks to pick up the call. She took it for granted that it would not be her boss, because they had agreed he would call her on the cellphone that he gave her before leaving.

She recognized instantly the female voice on the other end of the line.

A sudden sense of anguish gripped her when she hung up.

'I have to get hold of Denis'.

CHAPTER XXV

Dark coffee and blueberry muffins.

The breakfast in *Simon's Coffee House* had done much to perk him up. The bright morning shone through the joint's broad windows in all its splendor, covered the sky over the city of Cambridge and brought to life Massachusetts Avenue, one of the main arteries in the Harvard University campus. Groups of students of different nationalities went up and down the avenue, dressed in baseball caps and colored summer outfits. Inside the coffee house a bunch of girls sampled jam bagels and orange juice, while giggling over funny tales from the night before.

Summer school in the country's oldest and most venerable university attracted students from all over the world, and kept the campus ticking over during the baking month of August. The place oozed academic atmosphere from end to end. Denis looked wistfully at the carefree laughter and fresh faces. He missed that unsullied and wide-eyed happiness. As time went by, however, other problems intruded and there was nothing to be done.

He checked his location on the Harvard Yard map: he was on the south side. His destination was nearby. Less than a half-mile away, opposite the Memorial Church, was the landmark building that housed the Widener Library.

Harvard had the world's largest university library, and the

second-largest in the United States, behind only the Library of Congress. It had a collection of more than sixteen million books and other valuable documents, spread out over ninety libraries around the campus. The most emblematic was doubtless the Harry Elkins Widener Memorial, an imposing *Beaux Arts* style brick building with one hundred thousand square feet of floor space and fifty-seven miles of shelving. It held more than three million volumes from collections drawn from all over the world, including some copies of the Gutenberg Bible in perfect condition and, as legend had it, some copies of the *Necronomicon*, the Book of the Dead *grimoire*, were hidden away in its endless rows of shelves.

The building was dated 1915 and financed by a donation from the wealthy family of one Harry Elkins Widener. Harry, a young Harvard graduate who drowned when the Titanic famously sank and his family wanted his name to live on in posterity.

Denis examined the library pass Sylvie had handed him when he left; it was properly stamped and validated. Most buildings comprising the library were not open to the public. Only university students and professors were allowed and, in exceptional cases, specially authorized outside researchers. It had not been hard for his assistant at Interpol to obtain such special authorization. Twenty minutes later, after his pass and the contents of his briefcase had been scrupulously examined, he got ready to go through the checkpoint.

He went up the entrance stairway and was immediately struck by the total silence prevailing inside. There were not too many students there at that time of day; a couple of dozen international pupils at most. Some wandered through the maze of passageways and galleries like moles in their tunnels; others read by desks or wrote lengthy messages on cellphones.

A majestic dome crowned the library's high walls. That room could have doubled up as a church cloister. Denis took a seat at one of the middle desks. In the blink of an eye, after quickly consulting one of the librarians, he had the 1999 Economics Faculty Yearbook in front of him. The volume's maroon binding showed the university motto on its front cover in gilt lettering: VE-RI-TAS. 'Truth' That adage was drawn from the Dominicans and was meant to brand the place's reason for being. The seat of learning's magic words appeared everywhere and on every object: books, facades, stairways, notebooks, crests, etc. The university had taken possession of a pure, unfathomable concept with no owner. Centuries ago, the other three words making up the brand's initial motto had been removed. 'Veritas: *Christo et Ecclesia*». Amputating the motto revoked the religious foundational principles and freed its offspring from the sold spiritual straitjacket. Nowadays only the initial word was left: «Veritas». Denis stared at the inscription. How many wars had been fought in its name, and how much righteous blood shed mercilessly by those that claimed to own it.

He looked around. Students were spread out across the room. He had a reasonable amount of privacy. A girl with oriental features plugged into an iPod watched him through red designer spectacles: a fifty-year-old gazing at the cover of a yearbook. He was not a regular. The girl went back to her notes, and Denis to his thoughts.

Of course, he expected to find William C. Atkins and young Caldwell in that book, but it was not them he was looking for. He already knew where to find them. A fatal car crash and a suicide had cut them down in their prime, and he would surely meet them in hell. Nonetheless, he was convinced they would lead him to '*Il Duce*'. He took an enlarged copy of Atkins' forged passport photo and looked at the subject's defiant expression.

He did not take too long to find Atkins —the real one— among the senior year students. Only his name and address featured in the pen pictures. No extra-curricular clubs, no sports activity, no comment. An empty life. Truly surprising.

Yearbooks are meant to be keepsakes for life, no more and no less. Consigned for the duration in a dusty bookstore or in some forgotten corner of alumni's homes. They were veritable epitaphs of university life that recorded forever who and what you had been in the student community. Students went out of their way to look their best in the photos, or to include every detail of their activities and stress achievements and feats, so that one day, in a wistful moment, somebody could turn to the record of your class and remember your existence. But there was nothing there. William C. Atkins had left his little space for posterity quite empty. Merely his photo, his sharp features, his dull look and faint smile.

Denis searched for his second goal. He found it right away.

Caldwell's pen picture was the exact opposite: member of the lacrosse team, president of the Debating Union, on the board of the Speech and Parliamentary Debate Society, editor of the Harvard Crimson Sunday. A real star. The pride of such refined breeding. A high-born social animal who had the world at his feet.

'He even decided when to sacrifice himself,' Denis thought. He looked at the rest of the senior students' photos. Denis scrutinized every face, every feature, to search for a likeness with the picture of the leading suspect. He concentrated on the basic traits in the portraits, and left aside changeable features, such as hair. Two of the students looked somewhat similar, or at least he liked to think so, maybe out of wishful thinking. He wrote down their names. Four hours later he had examined all the senior year students' profiles. He found nothing of note beyond upper class families' ridiculous obsession with immortalizing their offspring by giving them their father or grandfather's forename, then adding a II or III.

The Asian girl in the red spectacles was still absorbed in a stack of books while she took notes ravenously. Denis snorted in disgust. 'Il Duce' was not his presumed colleagues' classmate. He consulted his watch impatiently. If memory served, his appointment with Levissier was in two hours' time. Maybe it was all a mistake, a shot in the dark, a willful attempt to join dots that were not there. He leafed through the yearbook again. The pen pictures for students in lower classes were briefer and the photos smaller and of lesser quality. He would have to go through all of them. Martel could not leave any loose ends.

'Maybe tomorrow,' he thought. His body was crying out for its dose of nicotine.

The closing pages in the book summarized extracurricular activities: sports and students' societies. The Harvard *Crimsons* did not exactly stand out for reporting sports prowess, unless it was in niche sports like rowing or squash. The section on clubs and associations, on the other hand, was endless. Students spent much of their lives on campus taking part in all sorts of activities to fatten their resumes and, more importantly, to extend their social circles. They covered every interest; Latin Club, Liberal Club, Astronomy, Business, etc.

Denis homed in on the Debate Union page. He knew that face.

Peter Caldwell appeared in the main photograph, along with a group of members surrounding —according to the caption— a certain James Richardson, Democratic senator for the state of Massachusetts. The picture captured the moment when they were meeting and greeting each other after a lecture. He stared at a lanky boy sporting a navy blue suit and smiling next to the senator. His light brown hair spilled over his collar in a deliberately disheveled mop. His gaze, framed by long eyelashes verging on the feminine, pierced the paper, while his eyes shone with lassitude and idleness.

And it looked uncomfortably familiar.

Denis glanced again at the enlarged passport photograph.

He sat stock still, like a stuffed animal, without moving a muscle. Endorphins shot around his body.

At last he cracked a smile.

It was him.

'*Il Duce*'

He hurried down the Widener Library stairs until he was outside. Then he took a first pull on his cigarette and called Sylvie. He felt excited and dazed by turns.

Sylvie's voice came through on the other end of the line after the third ring, and was music to his ears.

"Denis, I tried to reach you a few times, but your phone was switched off. I was beginning to get worried. Are you OK?"

"Yes, I'm fine. I was in the library. "I've a lot to tell you."

"Me too."

Sylvie listened carefully to her boss's detailed account: the visit to the Atkins home in Maine and getting a positive ID on Peter Caldwell, William's classmate, as the individual in the police sketch of the suspect in the Argentina bombing.

"Peter committed suicide two months later."

"Suicide? How? Do we know why?" Sylvie could not conceal her amazement.

"He cut his wrists in the bathtub. It seems he left a note. That's all we know."

"This is all like an eerie nightmare," Sylvie moaned. "There's weird stuff going on here, too, Denis."

"There's more, Sylvie", he interrupted. "I've also identified '*Il Duce*'."

"Atkins' impostor? Does it match the passport photo from Greece?"

"Indeed. It's a long story. They appear in a photograph together. They were friends. The answer is always in the background. Always."

"Who is it? A fellow alum?"

"Yes. He graduated the same year as Caldwell and Atkins,

but in Political Science. That's why he wasn't in the Economics Yearbook. He took part in several extracurricular activities, the Debate Union among others. Along with the other two. His name is Adrian Seaten. I need you to find out everything you can about him."

Sylvie jotted down all the details in a notebook. She wrote quickly, and tried not to let her excitement show to anybody around her, although at that time of day she was the only human being milling around the empty Interpol offices.

"I must leave you now, Sylvie, see you when I get back."

"Wait, Denis, don't hang up. Coburn hasn't been to the office in days."

"Well he's a busy man, you know."

"Yesterday I go a call from Jasmina Osmanović."

"Shoot."

"Her husband's been arrested. He's incommunicado."

Denis felt a pang in his stomach.

Coburn had taken him off the case and snatched his prime suspect without delay. Now he would be relishing a neat trophy to hand over to the commission. The old man had never seen justice as anything but a race against time to find a scapegoat, guilty or not, the more so in a case with such repercussions; but that haste at locking up a suspect on flimsy circumstantial evidence was beyond unseemly.

He took a deep pull on his cigarette.

The searing sunlight bore through the trees. Bunches of students rode away on bicycles, looking for somewhere shady to eat in the gardens.

"What happened?"

"They arrested him in Hamburg airport. They were waiting for him."

"They must be interrogating him. I don't think they'll get much out of him."

"Jasmina was very nervous."

"Of course. But Sylvie, avoid any contact with her from now on. Remember that officially, we're off the case."

"OK, I'll do that. When are you back?"

"I'll catch the return flight to Paris tonight, but first I have an appointment."

"Take care, Denis."

Denis hung up. He still had not had time to take in his recent discoveries. By the time he got back, Sylvie would have moved heaven and earth to uncover everything about Adrian Seaten, and Peter Caldwell's odd suicide. Maybe then he could shed some light on the case.

He was exhausted, the jet lag and getting up before dawn were taking their toll.

Again he got the creeping feeling he was a puppet adrift in the vastness of the ocean.

He decided to eat something to get his strength back. He looked around. There was time. His next appointment was not far away.

To his right, right beside the Widener Library building, stood Boylston Hall, a cute three-story brick building. It housed the Department of the Classics, one of thirty-three departments comprising the Arts and Humanities Division, the pride and joy of the Faculty of Arts and Sciences at Harvard University.

CHAPTER XXVI

It was more than thirty years since he had clapped eyes on Phillipe. He was sure his call would have surprised him and guessed that, at least, both would be curious to see each other face-to-face again, and see how time had ravaged each other. They had not exchanged so much as a word in all that time. They understood back then that there was nothing left to say or explain, that at times deeds make words meaningless and useless, and the passage of time ends up smothering all else.

Denis walked into Boylston Hall and gave his name at the reception desk.

The early afternoon light came pouring in through the hall windows. The building had been revamped and its centuries-old stone walls had modern and functional decor on the inside.

The mawkish girl in the pink dress confirmed with a smile that Philippe Levissier would be ready for him in five minutes in his office, and went back to flirting with the young security guard on duty by the entrance.

"Please take a seat, if you wish," she said, pointing to some chairs around a glass table on which several antiques magazines rested.

"Very kind, I'd rather stand, thank you."

Cliques of students went through the reception area, swapping whispered impressions of a recent lecture. A professor dressed in an old checked coat crossed the room and stopped to joke with the students before vanishing down the corridor. That looked like the ideal habitat for Phillipe, a place whose every corner breathed history. The atmosphere of research and learning impregnated every last air molecule. He pictured him as a professor admired by his students, who was friendly and of limitless patience, and felt happy for his old friend: doubtless he had found his role in life. Although he could not avoid feeling again that old pang of remorse in his stomach.

Phillipe walking out of his life was like an amputation. It left a gaping hole after all those youthful years spent together.

"Mr. Martel, will you come this way please?"

Denis suddenly came back to reality and followed the girl along the corridor to Levissier's office.

Phillipe stood waiting for him by the door. Denis watched him for several seconds while the receptionist said good-bye to him in her sing-song voice. His hair had turned gray over the years and he had wrinkles around his mouth and eyes, but he did not look his age. He had stayed slim and kept his upright posture, his curious look and the fringe that flopped over his forehead. The passage of time had wreaked more damage on Denis.

"Hi Phillippe, it's great to see you."

"Great to see you, too, Denis. What a nice surprise! When I got your call the other day, you were the last person I expected to hear from," Phillippe said, in a friendly tone of voice. "But come in, please, sit down."

Levissier's office was large and minimalist, quite the opposite of what was to be expected from a Classics professor, a lover of the secrets of ancient civilizations, who had taken part in dozens of archaeological expeditions all over the planet. Merely a few curious statuettes standing on a shelf upset the extraordinary harmony of geometrical shapes and glass provided by the table, bookshelves and metal desk lamp.

Phillippe sat down in a leather armchair and waited for

Denis to reveal the reason for his unexpected visit.

"Nice office. I see you've done well."

"I really enjoy teaching and, as you can imagine, there is nowhere better for it than this place."

"How long have you been in..."

"In the United States? Getting on for twenty-five years now, since I left Paris," Phillippe interrupted. "And almost twenty in the department, as a professor. I graduated from Stanford and did my doctorate here. How did you find me?"

"Where I work it's not hard to find people."

Phillippe tried to take the enigmatic reply in his stride by changing the subject.

"How's everything? What about Alana? Do you have any family?"

"We got married, had a daughter, Cécile, she's twelve now. We've been divorced for six years."

"You don't say," Phillippe replied with a hint of irony that Denis ignored.

"What about you? "How've you been all this time?"

"I'm married and have three lovely girls. We're a happy family. I can't complain."

"Well I'm pleased for you, really."

"It's been a while. What do you want?" Philippe urged him.

"It's a long story," Denis answered after taking his time. "I'm a police inspector, I work for Interpol and need an expert opinion on something found at a crime scene."

Phillipe could not believe his ears. His boyhood friend turns up out of the blue, after almost half a lifetime and asks for his help in solving a crime. This could not be happening, especially considering what had happened between them. He looked him in the eye. The years had worn down his face and bleached his hair. He held his gaze and kept a straight face. He could appreciate his grief, the kind of toxic grief that only takes root in the heart due to past events that cannot be undone.

"Sorry, Denis, I don't get it. As a matter of fact, I don't get anything."

"I know all this may seem odd. And I'm sorry to show up like this. I'm working on a case."

"A case? And you come to me? After all this time?"

"Yes. The perpetrator left a certain element next to his victim. Our theory is that he means to send a message and that it might be based on classical mythology. We think you can help us."

"Me? Why me?

"Our team drew up a list of leading world experts on ancient civilizations, classics and mythology. You were second on that list. As you might expect, nobody was more surprised than me."

Denis noticed a flicker of academic vanity on Levissier's face.

"Hmmmm, I don't know much about this sort of procedure," Phillippe replied after a pause. "But I don't believe it's the most appropriate way to request technical co-operation."

"You're right, it isn't. To cut a long story short, I'm not here on official business. Neither am I any longer assigned to the case, and that's one of the reasons I've looked you up. What's more, I'd appreciate it if you kept our meeting under your hat, like it had never happened."

Phillippe took in a good dose of oxygen to metabolize that clearly. His life went by in a stifling oasis of calm and he was not vaccinated against shocks like that. Despite all the time that had gone by, he could still see the young Denis in that guy seated opposite him, his old boyhood friend, and retrieve, from his blurred memories, many an alcohol-laced winter evening spent bar-hopping in Paris.

"OK Denis, tell me what I can do for you."

"Like I said, I'm working on a case," he explained, in all seriousness. "We have found a flower in two different crime scenes, a narcissus. It could mean anything, we're ruling nothing out. Maybe it's just some nutjob who might just as well have left a plaster cat or Mayan calendar as a calling card, but we believe it has a concrete meaning, and maybe you could help me out."

"Who were the victims?"

"I'd rather not tell you that for now."

After Denis saw Levissier frown somewhat, he clarified, "Believe me, it's not that I don't trust you, I just want to avoid any bias in your assessment."

Phillippe stared at him for a few seconds while gauging how sincere his reply was.

"The narcissus dates back millennia. It has endless meanings, and many civilizations have adopted the flower as a symbol."

"Yes, we have gathered some information: the myth of Narcissus, Ovid."

"The symbolism goes way beyond that, Denis," he said, cutting him short. "In ancient Chinese civilization, and even for the Hebrews, the narcissus was the symbol of luck and health. In Persian literature it represents the beauty of the eyes, the look, and as it happens, in Wales the narcissus —known by the common name 'daffodil'— has become the national flower. And yes, in classical mythology and western culture, it embodies the representation of vanity. In fact, as you know, Narcissus is the icon of vanity and selfishness. Countless artists have painted him, from the Renaissance to the present day.

"Vanity understood as arrogance or pride?

"Yes. In Christian teaching, vanity is considered a type of pride, one of the seven deadly sins that take man to the brink, a terrible vice whereby God is substituted for oneself. Although as long as man has been aware, it has been considered a moral transgression deserving of punishment and correction."

"The punishment meted out to Narcissus, his death."

"Correct. According to the myth, Narcissus was extraordinarily beautiful, cold and vain. He loved nobody but himself, believed he was the only one that deserved love and despised those that were not beautiful enough to merit his company, as he did with Echo, the nymph. Nemesis, the goddess of divine retribution, sentenced him to fall in love with his own reflection in the water, where he drowned and gave birth to the flower. His affront was vanity, and death, his punishment."

"Yes, I know the old fable."

"It isn't just fable. Mythology is much more than just a handful of fabled tales dreamed up by creative civilizations of old to stage fashionable plays with. Myths are a tool, a setting for harmony, explaining the inexplicable, but above all a source code for behavior patterns. Myths exemplify and explain, they give answers."

"Based on stories of dragons and seven-headed gods."

"That's only the tip of the iceberg. They sustain values, and values are necessary. Man questioned the mythological universe. He divested myths of rationality in his quest for the ascendancy of humankind and nature over divinity, but was forced to recreate the context of values. Without the mystical component, it all falls apart. Today it's exactly the same."

"Nowadays we have laws and standards drawn up by people."

"They are lacking, weak."

"But there's nothing else."

"Nothing further from the truth. Today, right in the twenty-first century, hundreds of millions of people go to a temple every week where they are warned time and again that a life of sin will land them in hell, and they tell them their gods make the dead live again, and multiply fishes and loaves. If they stick to the rules, they get life everlasting." Phillipe's explanations scaled several degrees of passion and enthusiasm, and he continued. "Plato's teachings in *The Republic* set forth that the first task of a city's founder is to forge its myths, which is what groups together and unites those who live in society. The first and most important one. That does not come about through thoughtful participation. It is only possible by using mythical tales, which weave emotional experiences together and build a community that rejoices and is saddened by the same things; a community of free and equal men that feed on the same value system, wherein a citizen's choices as an individual are framed."

"In other words, abiding by the law isn't enough," Denis concluded.

"Yes and no. The ancient Greek *polis* tried to write in stone respect for the law, in order to attain social stability and avoid violent revolutions. Only if citizens made them their own, if they were agreed to and adopted, did the city not have to engage in setting up barriers, prohibitions and law enforcement."

"That's my point. Basically, they were trying to set up a legal framework, like the one we have today."

"But they didn't manage it. The only way to take possession of them was to build a supernatural backdrop. Coercion established in law is merely a useful device to prevent people from committing deeds that undermine social unity, but it will never be as efficient a mechanism as the emotional attachment articulated in myth. Plato sustained that if an individual is raised by means of coercion, they will enjoy their pleasures in secret, and escape from the law as children do from their parents. Most definitely, civil morality prevails over written laws. Divine tales are deserving of the reverential fear afforded to the gods. Laws are not."

"In other words, everything is based on fear."

"Basically, yes. Fear of divine punishment, of what we cannot understand," Phillippe confirmed. "Narcissus died from his sick vanity and his tale shows the rest of humanity where their sin will lead them, regardless of whether it is real or unreal."

"We have assessed the theory that the crime is a punishment

for pride, but that does not fit in with this case."

"That being so, I don't think I can help you, I am not familiar with the details. Pride or otherwise, the myth of Narcissus is yet another example that evil and wrongdoing have their punishment, a punishment that is above the law and mankind. That is all it takes."

The two men remained silent for a few moments.

'A punishment that is above the laws of men,' Denis repeated to himself.

They looked at each other's' faces again. The conversation had melted the initial ice. Even Philippe felt somewhat glad to meet up with his friend again after so many years. Denis looked at his watch. He had no time to lose. His flight back to Paris would be departing in a few hours from Boston Logan International Airport.

"It's time for me to go, Philippe. It was very kind of you to see me. Thanks for your help, really, it's been very useful."

"You're welcome. When do you go back to France?"

"This very night. It was really great to see you again, believe me."

"Great to see you too," he said, as he stood up to show his guest out. "By the way, you told me you had a list of experts."

"Indeed.

"Why did you choose me? The fact you're not here in an official capacity is not an insurmountable reason not to look for another expert. You know how to get things done."

"I guess I needed to see you."

Phillippe sighed and looked down.

"You both really hurt me. I was very young and in love. Alana and I had plans. You were my friend."

"I guess you can't choose in such matters, Philippe. And to tell the truth, I think she never quite forgot you. I tried calling you, but..."

"I know.

"I'm sorry."

"So long, Denis, good luck."

"Take care, Phillipe."

CHAPTER XXVII

Laura vanished into the deep sea.

The inflatable dinghy floated away like a drifting buoy that twisted and turned on the waves, free and unburdened by its passenger, as it headed out to sea and spun around like a demented top.

Adrian watched the scene from the shore. His heart had raced a thousandfold when he saw Laura's body sink beneath the waves. He was petrified, stock still, consumed by his own impotence, that of a passive spectator watching a loved one's demise. And at that very moment he felt that was a new sensation for him. There was nothing comparable in his memory bank. Without thinking twice, he plunged into the water, as if spring-loaded.

The shock of pain that hit his injured leg ran up his spine like whiplash. He gritted his teeth and paddled hard through the waves. With every stroke Adrian gulped down salt water, which went down his throat to choke and make him wretch. He moved his arms forcefully, and joined his fingers together to displace as much water as possible with each stroke. The waves smacked his face and stopped him from locating clearly the exact spot where he had last seen Laura. He moved on blindly over the sea, driven by a strength he lacked and which for all he knew came from hell itself.

Minutes later he had only managed to get a few dozen yards

offshore. His muscles had seized up from exhaustion. He halted and spied the horizon. The boat had faded away to nothing and there was no trace of Laura. He tried to go on, but his body had ceased to respond, it seemed to be disconnected from his brain. He could no longer so much as feel any pain in his leg. He turned his body over and floated on his back.

The blue morning sky struck his eyes.

His heartbeats began to slow down. Silence reigned for a moment. He could go no farther. A pair of impotent tears rolled down his cheeks and fell gently into the sea. He conjured up images of Laura in his mind's eye. One after the other. He cursed himself a thousand and five times.

It was all so unreal.

Laura perishing under the sea by that damned beach.

And he had allowed her to set off alone. He felt an untrammeled urge to end his life. Flávio and Paul deserved to die. He would do away with them, then it would be his turn.

The undertow dragged him shoreward, slowly but surely, as if the water sought to expel him from its domain. Adrian went with the flow, while keeping still in his crucified position. Water flooded inside his ears and blocked all outside sound. Seconds later he heard a dull buzzing noise and an unrecognizable throbbing, which grew louder when he poked his head above the water. He trod water and stretched his neck like a periscope toward the raucous noise, which then turned into a hoarse human voice.

Desperate cries that were yelling his name.

Nearby, just twenty yards away, a black figure was swimming shoreward. It did not take too long to recognize that person.

'Paul'.

Clad in his neoprene suit, the Brazilian was yelling his name. He was begging for help, while towing a body with his left arm, which he had around its neck while he paddled with his fins toward the shore. The look on his face was the living image of despair, but his strokes were as deft and forceful as those of a mechanical digger. Adrian dug deep inside for some energy and swam until he finally reached the shore.

Paul shifted Laura's body and dumped it on the sand. She was unconscious. She lay slumped with an absent look, lost in the distance. Her complexion had turned ashen while bluish shadows began to spread around the corners of her mouth.

Adrian knelt down beside her.

The Brazilian took off his oxygen tanks and diving goggles, then tore off Laura's T-shirt. He leaned her head back, raised her chin, placed his hand on her forehead and squeezed her nose between his finger and thumb. Next he opened her mouth with his right hand, placed his mouth on hers and began to breathe into her hard, every two seconds. Time and again. He alternated his mouth-to-mouth resuscitation with a heart massage, in which he pressed down on her chest to make her blood flow.

He gradually pressed his hands harder and harder. Laura's body was still lifeless, and gazing skyward, like a rag doll. Adrian looked at her face. She was no more than a girl, whose innocent halo stood out even more against the pallor that comes from dicing with death. He uttered not a word, but merely sought in his inner depths a strength that was not there, and to inject it into the Brazilian's arms, while feeling in his own chest Paul's every stroke on hers.

"Ó Deus, ajuda... tem misericórdia [2].

After a few seconds, a portent unfolded before his eyes: water gurgled out of Laura's mouth, between coughs and wretches, to drain her windpipe and lungs.

"Laura!!!! Wake up!!!" Paul slapped her cheeks.

"Come on, breathe."

Little by little, she started to breathe normally again. She

---

2. Translator's note. "O Good, help... have mercy" (in Portuguese).

was still coughing up gobbets of salt water, but less and less of it. She was still deeply unconscious. Slowly the color came back to her cheeks and movement to her face muscles. Adrian's eyes welled up with tears that relieved his pent-up tension. He felt that feeling again like new. For a moment, a unique and boundless joy ran through his body, one that only arises when you recover what you love and had given up as lost. Paul slumped on to the sand, exhausted by tension and his efforts. Adrian attempted to communicate with Laura while seeking some reaction to his voice. Then after a few minutes she opened her eyes and stared into his, in silence, and cast a perplexed and guilty look. She moved her lips clumsily, trying to mouth the words that would not issue from her throat. He draped his fingers over her mouth, held her hand tenderly and cracked a smile that revealed his immense joy at seeing her alive.

Flávio came back from his day's diving two hours later. Laura was in a deep sleep on one of the mattresses, while her body recovered under dry blankets from being starved of oxygen. Neither her vital functions nor her motor skills had been impaired, but she was very worn out. Adrian carried on sitting beside her the whole time and watching over her, like a recruit on guard duty. Paul heard his companion's footfalls, went outside the cave to welcome him and, after a long argument in Portuguese, both went back inside.

"I guess you must be satisfied. Your friend had a close call there," Flávio said.

Adrian did not answer.

"I told you. It is useless for you to try to escape. We have treated you like guests," he continued. "Haven't we? Would you prefer us to chain you up like animals? Do you want to risk your lives? Is that it?"

"This is absurd, it's crazy. We cannot stay here, all locked up while giving no signs of life. Are you really so deranged you don't get that?"

"I thought we'd already been over that. Soon we'll be out of here. All of us. Now tell me, what would you rather do? Spend the rest of your time here tied down or locked up?"

An odd sound from outside suddenly drowned their voices.

Within a few seconds an initial distant throbbing turned into the loud noise of en engine. Its vibrations drew closer by the second and hit the cliff face, driven by gusts of wind blowing onshore from the sea. An intermittent dry snapping noise began to echo around inside the cave, like steel blades slicing through the air.

The three men were petrified.

"A helicopter!"

Adrian stood up, like a jack-in-the-box. They had come to search for them, or their remains.

The sound of the helicopter blades approaching the mouth of the cave had suddenly brought him back to reality. Laura's accident had dulled his senses and lowered his defenses to a bare minimum, but that racket immediately reminded him that he was locked up in a sandy prison, held by two maniacs, and that right then, outside that cave, lay the only means of escape.

He took a step toward the entrance to the cave. The two Brazilians stood rooted the spot, bewildered by the unexpected visit. Adrian stared at them. His look was no longer human. Those two stood between him and freedom, and God knew that freedom was worth dying for... and killing. He had an injured leg and those fellows were fighting fit, but he had ceased to feel pain, like a predator that never backs down, no matter what.

He took another step forward. And another.

Flávio reached out and slowly moved toward him.

"You stay right there."

Adrian took no notice of the warning. Neither did his brain even process the meaning of the words, as if it had not been programmed to. He picked up a harpoon and moved slowly onward. He and Flávio were only a few feet apart.

"Don't do it," Flávio unsheathed a knife by his ankle and held it head-high.

The eight-inch-long serrated titanium edge flashed in the sunlight that had fought its way into the cave.

"I mean it, Adrian. I don't care whether I die, either. If you think it's worth it, go right ahead. I'm waiting for you, buddy."

The loud noise of the helicopter rotors now buzzed above the beach, right overhead.

Flávio wielded the knife firmly. The ergonomic handle fitted his right hand like a glove, as if it were an extension to his arm. There was no tension in his look. He waited stock-still for his opponent to make the first move, and give away his tactics. He looked relaxed and his heart was beating slowly and calmly, as if at rest.

It was the first time since they had come to the beach that he had seen those two as a threat.

Adrian looked into his eyes. He guessed he was not lying: that guy was not scared to die. Maybe he was looking for it. Perhaps it would be his salvation.

The sound of the helicopter drifted away.

Adrian looked toward Laura, who was still lying down on the camp bed, asleep and helpless, while her pulse grew stronger and she came back to life.

Adrian bowed his head and shortly after, threw down the harpoon.

CHAPTER XXVIII

Denis slept for sixteen hours straight after his flying visit to Boston. The jet lag had hit him with a vengeance, and a hot shower was like manna from heaven that brought him back to his senses. He made two cups of coffee to wash down the freshly-made pastries that Sylvie had bought at *Canne à Sucre*, and sat down beside his colleague on the balcony in his apartment. The heatwave had relented and a fresh, gentle breeze blew through the city.

"There's nothing better than breakfast at noon."

Sylvie smiled to see Denis' look of delight, as he made quick work of the sweet little rolls that melted in his mouth.

"How did your trip go?"

"Badly. Too much time wasted between flights and traipsing around flophouses for my liking."

"There's no place like home," said Sylvie, while she poured more coffee into Denis' cup.

"True, but it was worth it. It appears we have tracked down our mysterious American friend, but how about you, Sylvie? What about the kids?"

"Doing good. Bernard is better now, his fever's gone down. I've divided my time between working on the case and vapor rubs, I've had a ball."

"Only a conscientious woman like you can get things done," Denis said with a grin.

"Come off it."

"Trust me. It's the truth. You're admirable, dear. I tip my hat to you, I'm all yours. I don't know where I'd be without you."

"That'll do!" Sylvie protested.

"OK, I'll drop it. Bring me up to date. What have you found out about our friend Adrian?"

"Adrian I. Seaten, aged thirty-two, of U.S. nationality, born in Boston. Graduated in Political Science from Harvard. A brilliant student, straight A's, according to his report card."

"What does he do for a living?"

"He owns an advertising agency that he runs himself: Boreal Life. Its head office is in Paris and they undertake marketing campaigns, branding, etc. Or at least that's what the mission statement says. They have a payroll of about eighty and work with very select clients. The big shots."

"Adrian lives in Paris?"

"Yes. He has dual nationality. He lives alone, next to his office, in a luxury apartment in Saint-Germain-des-Prés."

"He lives alone? Any known relationship?"

A bachelor, but engaged. His fiancée is Helena Brun-Donzel."

"I see. Any relation to the banker?"

"His daughter. She's Didier Brun-Donzel's oldest daughter. A decorator. Or interior designer, as they say nowadays."

"Well the boy won't go hungry. What about his family? What do we know?"

"Not much, for now. His mother's dead and his father has Alzheimer's, he lives in a home in Lincoln, Massachusetts. Before the illness struck, he was a Harvard University professor for thirty years. Quite an authority there. Adrian has no siblings."

"It's weird, the more I hear the less I understand what the hell a guy like that is doing mixed up in this fucking mess."

Denis lit a cigarette and slowly breathed out the smoke. Sylvie objected; he had only just gotten up and was already getting his first fix.

"I'll die, but happily."

"I don't find that funny."

"Let's get back to business; Boreal Life," Denis continued. "Is Seaten the sole stockholder?"

"No, Adrian only holds thirty percent. The other seventy percent belongs to an American venture capital firm. Axis Ventures."

"Who's behind it?"

"I'm working on that. It's hard to get to the bottom of it. It's one of a layer of shell companies that's harder to figure out than ancient Egyptian hieroglyphics."

"There's no hurry. We've already found our objective."

"And what do we do now, Denis?"

"I'll pay him a visit."

"You're off the case! You cannot go officially!"

"Sure. But he doesn't know that."

"You can't tell him you're investigating him; he'll find a lawyer, and wrap up. We'll need a warrant. Besides, he can always argue that somebody used his photo. The Greek fax isn't hard evidence. If he has planned everything down to the last detail, he'll have an alibi."

"Don't worry, I didn't get these wrinkles for nothing. Call him this afternoon. Tell him I'd really appreciate seeing him, that I'll tell him why in person."

"OK, have it your way," Sylvie grumbled. She had no intention of arguing much more.

"Have you heard any more about the Osmanović couple?" Denis asked.

"No, I've had no news since Jasmina told me about her husband's arrest."

Denis sat and mulled it over for some minutes.

"I have to go, Denis, the doctor's waiting. I'll get back to you on the appointment with Seaten. Will you be OK?"

"Yes, don't worry. If you manage to set the meeting, make it for next week. Tomorrow I'm off to Saint-Tropez. It's been two weeks now since I saw Olivia."

"Haven't you talked to her?"

"She can't be bothered picking up my calls. I guess spending the summer alone has been the last straw after neglecting her all these years."

"It'll all work out, you'll see. Take care, Denis." Sylvie left the apartment.

Denis Martel had a think, then called Yves LeBoeuf on his cellphone. He did not want to involve his friend in his undercover investigation, but neither did he have many options left. The Interpol route was restricted and possibly under watch. Leboeuf's tone of voice changed when he heard Denis on a number with no caller ID.

"Denis, is that you?"

"The very same, Yves. How're you doing, buddy? Can you spare me ten minutes?"

"Sure I can. I'm with Claire and the kids in Dunkerque. I've gotten away for a few days. But I didn't have that number of yours."

"Yes, it's a personal line."

"Everything OK?"

"Kind of... The world isn't perfect, never has been."

Yves smiled to hear Denis' stock phrase again.

"I hear you."

"Sorry not to level with you before. It has to do with a restricted case, know what I mean?"

Then he filled in his old lieutenant on the Miletić case in every detail: his investigations, the Argentine connection, Coburn's attitude, his trip to Boston. Denis described every aspect passionately and emphatically, like a prosecutor summing up for a jury.

Yves, meanwhile, paid attention like a little boy listening to an incredible adventure story. A mixture of conflicting emotions coursed through him with every word his old mentor spoke. He needed to calm his friend down a little, he was courting trouble; this was no laughing matter. Disobeying orders and acting without the organization's permission was deemed a serious offense, no matter how fair the grounds. He knew that better than anybody. If he was caught, he would do time or, at best, throw his career away and lose his pension. And that was just from a legal standpoint. Leboeuf agreed with Denis that Coburn was acting strangely. Something was fishy about it. But it would not be the first time an agent had vanished without trace for sticking his nose in the wrong place. Some interests are above the law, they lurk in highfalutin concepts about security, the world order, or the survival of the system.

Nonetheless, deep down, he was glad to hear him talk that way. It was more than twenty years since he had heard his friend turn on that energy and commitment. When he started out in Paris, young Inspector Denis Martel's team would walk through walls for him. He was hated and feared in the Paris ghetto underworld. Then, after his brother's case was shelved, it all faded away. He became a jobsworth.

"What can I do for you, Denis?" Yves LeBoeuf asked at last. Despite his illustrious job as chief commissioner of the Paris Police, he avoided making any call on whether his old boss was out of order, or not.

"Do you still get on well with Zach?"

"Zach Martínez? 'The Animal'?"

"The same. He still with the FBI?"

"Yes. We talk occasionally. About drugs, mainly."

"I need to know the contents of a suicide note written by that kid, Peter Caldwell, and which has not been made public. But whatever happens, it is vital that Zach keeps his trap shut."

"I'll try to get you that information. Apart from that, no worries. I wouldn't bet my bottom dollar on trusting him with a suspect's safety under interrogation, but if you tell him a secret, he'll take it to the grave with him."

"Thanks, Yves."

"You're welcome. And you, just watch your step."

CHAPTER XXIX

"I've got it, I've got it," Laura said, tugging on a fishing line between nervous giggles and cries of help.

"Get out of here! I don't believe it," Adrian exclaimed skeptically, as he went over to the rocky outcrop where Laura sat.

"Help me, I can't..."

The octopus had been lured by the line bobbing up and down, but had gotten stuck on the jig's upper hooks and was flailing all over the place with all of its might.

"Wait."

He stood behind her and grabbed her by the waist. Then he seized her hands and tugged on the line. The creature slowly ran out of strength until it stopped dead.

"It's amazing, this gadget works!" Laura was bursting with enthusiasm.

"I've spent two hours yanking the string up and down, and not a bite."

"Up and down? Are you kidding me? Didn't you hear what Paul said? You have to wriggle it. The bait has to look alive, not like a yo-yo," Laura explained facetiously.

"Fucking Brazilian! Can't understand a thing he says," he complained, while he picked the octopus out of the water. "That's enough fishing for today. This sun's killing me. Siesta time."

After dropping their catch in a bucket, they went to their beds inside the cave, and out of the smoldering sun that pounded the beach.

Six days had gone by since they reached a deal with their unwanted hosts: they would not try to escape again. They would leave the place on the appointed date. There was not long to go. A week, ten days at most. They would help out with everyday chores, although there was not much to do, really: tidy up the cave a little, wash clothes, and help out with the fishing and cooking.

Flávio had provided them with reading material. Some of the classics and adventure stories to keep them amused and while away the hours after lunch, when venturing outside the cave was sheer agony. The Brazilians kept up their daily diving routine and, although the helicopter did not head back their way, they had placed all the harpoons, knives and sharp tools out of reach, in order to avoid all temptation to flee or take undue risks. Otherwise, the new housekeeping rules had been enforced without too much fuss.

For the last few days, Paul had devoted his mornings —and his patience— to initiating his tenderfoot guests in the noble art of fishing. After his first master class, he understood that he would need to go back to the basics —fishing pole, line, reel— before facing bigger challenges. When they moved up a level, they broached strange concepts such as tying a hook, or jigging, and they had involved discussions about how important it was to choose the right lure, which, so Paul figured, depended on the tackle, the water and fishing style. Adrian could not understand how any fish in its right mind would bite such a device. The oddly shaped and colored minnows and bucktail jigs their teacher proudly showed them looked more like insect repellent than juicy bait. He only calmed down when he explained that the best thing for fishing in those waters was to use a simple octopus tentacle as natural bait.

After the dismal practical classes in assembling tackle, Paul decided to set up two plain fishing rigs and leave it at that. After breakfast, of a morning, they would take up position on the rocks and throw themselves into their new job. They could see horse mackerel and scorpionfish in the crystal-clear water, and the odd sea bass that, to the rookies' despair, would wander around the bait but leave it alone. Then, as the sun went down, after their fruitless fishing, they would read in bed until the lapping waves lulled them to sleep. Adrian plumped for an edition of *The Iliad*, while Laura picked *The Talented Mr. Ripley* by Patricia Highsmith. On the second day they decided to read out loud to each other, in turn, until they nodded off.

Fixing supper had turned into a sterling example of team work. The division of labor ran like clockwork. The chores were shared out according to natural ability and Laura, despite Flávio's reluctance, took charge of the stove, for lack of a better word for the makeshift fireplace surrounded by rocks. Adrian and Paul were in charge of lighting the fire. Catching and supplying the food was also taken up by the expert divers, who swept all kinds of fish and seafood before them in their underwater expeditions. There was a strict daily roster for cleaning work.

The minutes that went by after dinner, when the sun dipped down behind the horizon, offered an exhilarating feast for the senses. The temperature plummeted and the gentle sea breeze turned into a natural tonic that refreshed the body and comforted the skin after the long dog-day hours. A unique pale brightness took hold of the cliff and its surroundings, a broken blend born of the fiery orange shed by the sun's dying rays and the sea's grayish-blue. The ebb at low tide shielded the rocks from the battering waves, and everything calmed down while the skyline went out to sea. Adrian silently relished those moments; they cleared his head, as if the rest of his thoughts had better things to do.

Since the night after the escape attempt, Flávio and Paul had been as silent as the grave, and had not breathed a word more than needed for the sake of politeness. As the days went by, however, and fueled by sweet wine, they unwound little by little, broke the curfew and opened up communication. While they ate dinner, they chatted about the ins and outs of their day and held spontaneous discussions on various issues, ranging from art to astronomy, in which an unwritten rule was never to speak of anybody's past, and neither were questions raised that went beyond the bounds of their little world in the cove.

After the heat of the conversation, sleep overcame them within minutes. They slumped drowsily to their cots out of sheer tiredness, lulled by the rustle of the sea and knocked out by the impact of the sun on their skin. Only Flávio, faithful to his nightly ritual, went out of the cave, bottle of vodka in hand, and sought a place on the strand until he slowly blended in with the dark.

It was as hot as hell that night. Breathing was hard. The levant wind had the coast in its grip, a sign of stronger winds to come, and had made the atmosphere overwhelmingly damp and sticky. Warm currents coming from North Africa pitilessly whipped the Mediterranean with their tongues of fire.

Laura opened her eyes. Her body was drenched in sweat. The inside of the cave had become a natural greenhouse and the dampness had covered the roof with droplets. Paul slept like a log, but Adrian's bed was empty. Her muscles were still numb and she took a few seconds to stretch out her limbs before going outside.

She found him lying down, opposite the cave. The moonlight lighted her way toward him.

Adrian noticed her presence. He was awake, he was misty-eyed and had a sad smile on his face.

"Can't you sleep?"

"Seems not."

"Does your leg hurt?"

"No, it's not that. I'm much better, really. And you? What are you doing up?"

"I couldn't get to sleep, I've got too much on my mind. I saw your empty bed, and wondered where you were." They were both quiet for a short while. The sea was quite calm."

"Want me to keep you company?" Adrian nodded.

Laura lay down by his side and put her head on his shoulder. He could feel her breath on his hair.

"At times I have horrible dreams. That's all."

Laura pressed her head against his neck.

"I too have horrible dreams at times," Laura replied after a long pause.

Minutes later, both were fast asleep on the sand.

CHAPTER XXX

Tourists and fishermen were constantly coming and going through the maze of back streets in the *Vieille Ville* neighborhood of Saint-Tropez, with its bars and ocher facades making way for a strong smell of sun cream and brine. In the summertime the population of the former fishing village rose tenfold and it was taken over by well-heeled families and professional Bohemians. Even so, the mood music in the streets remained gentle and quiet, as if the crowds were forbidden from expressing anything above a whisper, or paying respectful homage to the pitiful silence of the local winters, which were almost always hit by the mistral and the northern cold it brought with it.

Denis walked along the Rue Gambetta toward the old port. The Mediterranean sun bore down on the Côte d'Azur and had made it deeply sluggish. The effect of the caffeine pills, which had kept him awake for the seventy miles he had driven from Nice airport, was now wearing off. After he turned into the second street, he stopped to make sure he had gone the right way.

'Rue Portalet'.

To his right, an old man sold oysters and cones of shrimp from a street cart. His face was deeply creased and he puffed away at his rolling tobacco, as if connected to a respirator. A few feet back stood the revamped facade of Marcel and Marion

Grosvenor's summer home.

Journey's end.

Marion had been Olivia's best friend for the past few years, one in whom she confided closely. Her husband, Marcel Grosvenor, was the only child of a major publisher in Paris and lived off the family income. Denis never concealed his contempt for that archetypal spoilt brat, incapable of fending for himself, even though it had earned him more than one telling off from Olivia, who complained about his lack of interest in accepting her friends.

'Not that I needed them.'

The door buzzer sounded like an old bell. He felt his stomach tighten briefly at the thought Olivia was nearby.

Denis! How... How are you? We weren't expecting you." Marcel's tanned face showed undisguised surprise at seeing Denis on his doorstep.

"Hello, Marcel. You see, my friend, I managed to slip away after all. I've had a few tough days, you might say."

"But please, come in," Marcel indicated, after a few perplexed seconds.

"Is Olivia in?"

"Errr... No, no, she's gone down to the beach with Marion, they'll be back shortly. But come in, man, come in. You must be tired from your journey. Would you like a drink or have you got any dangerous fugitives to track down?" he asked, while uttering the last two words in a playfully solemn tone.

"Oh, no, thanks a lot, but I'd rather go and see her. Are they in *Les Graniers*?" Denis replied, ignoring the wisecrack.

"Errr, yes, I guess so, I don't think they'll take long to get back."

"She doesn't even pick up her cell when I call, but I guess you already knew that," he added with a wry smile. "I'd rather see her as soon as possible."

"OK, Denis, I won't insist, as you wish."

"See you soon, then."

Denis took his leave of Marcel and set off to meet his girlfriend.

Les Graniers was Olivia's favorite beach, and always had been. It was small and narrow, right below the *Citadelle*, the old fortress, behind the sea cemetery and although it was close to the old town, it still had a natural, wild look that imbued it with a special charm. Denis walked through the *La Ponche* neighborhood while he devoted his thoughts to working out whether Marcel was a medium-level cretin or simply off the scale. Finally, after skirting the fortress and cemetery, he came to the edge of the beach.

The sea was calm and there was barely a puff of wind. Sunbathers were packed between the parasols and the shore. There was not an inch of sand to be seen between towel and towel, and an endless procession of bodies traipsed in and out of the sea, in search of relief from the torrent of sunshine that hammered the beach.

Denis stopped under a leafy pine tree and lit a cigarette.

He remembered the last time he was there, sleeping on a hammock under a wide parasol while Olivia sunbathed beside him. Whispering sweet nothings in each other's ears. Shared laughter. Those were the days when everything seemed to make sense again. He looked at his watch. It would soon be time for lunch. There was a lot he had to tell his young girlfriend. He would spend a couple of days with her, maybe three, before going back to Lyons.

He approached the beach and went along a boardwalk that crossed the sand and parted the beach in two.

He looked one way and another.

Bodies were spread out all over the place, soaking up the sunlight through skin basted in oil. Motionless, like hibernating reptiles.

In the distance, a young brunette came out of the water. She wiped her hair with her hands, to squeeze the water down her back. She was light-footed, as if walking on air.

It was Olivia. He would have recognized her anywhere.

Her skin was tanned all over, as if she had had the sun all to herself.

A young man there was waiting for her on the shore and wrapped a towel around her. He hugged her affectionately and kissed her on the lips.

Denis could not tell if he felt pain or merely calm resignation over what could not have turned out otherwise.

Olivia hurried over to her towel and picked up the cell phone that had begun to ring insistently.

She took the untimely call for a minute, hung up and rushed to the middle of the beach.

She looked through the crowd, but Denis had gone.

CHAPTER XXXI

Knocks could be heard at the end of the passageway. One, and another. And another. Louder and louder.

He walked along the dark corridor that was lit only by a small candle-shaped lamp hanging from the wall at the back. The lamp shed a dull amber light that scarcely stretched out for a few feet around it. The rest of the gallery was engulfed in a murky darkness through which only the edges of doorways could be seen, which he passed, yard by yard, to the right and left. The wooden floor creaked with every step and gave off a dirty, hollow snap that echoed everywhere, as if the floor was about to fall apart right then under his feet.

He reached the end of the corridor. The orange light turned red, like a traffic light blocking his way.

He could make out a child, with its back turned that was hammering on the door at the end. The child realized he was there, lowered his hands and slowly turned his head round. Two dark shadows filled his eye sockets.

"Help me, Sir. I have to get in. My father's inside."

Without a word he approached him and turned the handle until the door was open a few inches.

He could not help leaping back suddenly, and had to rub his eyes before he could look again. A metal lamp hung from the ceiling and cast a bright, almost blinding light. A wide metal table took up the middle of the room. A trolley stood next to it, on top of which shone a row of scalpels of various sizes and all sorts of surgical instruments. On top of the table was the naked body of a middle-aged man. Standing next to him, the guy in the white coat probed inside the body. Blood poured out over the edge of the table, down through a grid into a drain and was then piped into a plastic drum.

The prone body had its abdomen slit from neck to groin.

Its companion removed, one by one, all of the viscera, while deftly sectioning the tissue and adjoining blood vessels. The monitor showing his vital signs beeped slowly and evenly.

He was still alive.

The child with shadows for eyes tearfully gave a heart-rending cry. He was calling for his father.

The man lying on the table turned his head toward him. He said nothing, but merely let his eyes shed a few timid tears.

Adrian awoke with a start.

He was sweating profusely. His heart was racing, and he had to take several deep breaths for his pulse to get back to normal.

He looked around him. Everybody was asleep, even Flávio, who had stayed in bed all day due to an untimely fever. The heat had turned the cave into a stone oven. Without a moment's hesitation, he left the cave to sit down on the sand, by the shore. He filled his lungs with the sea air and tried to rid his mind of the strange demons that visited him in his dreams. In a while he had calmed down again, and could close his eyes under the Mediterranean night sky.

It did not take long to open them again.

"Did you have another bad dream?" Laura said behind him.

"No," he lied. "I couldn't sleep inside in this damned heat."

"Me neither," she said, as she lay down beside him. "It's so much better out here; at least you can breathe."

Laura cuddled her slim and lithe body up to her boss. Her lips were cracked by the sun, and her skin was dark brown, almost reddish, like cherry wood. Her eyes, inquisitive and as wide as saucers, revealed that she had little intention of sleeping.

"We'll soon be out of her," Laura felt an odd sensation when she spoke those words. She settled her eyes on Adrian. How she would settle back into her Paris routine, she did not know. Or perhaps she did, and thus avoided the thought that soon came to mind.

"Indeed. Only three or four days now, if our friends are to be trusted."

She could see a serious look on Adrian's face, more than was usual under the circumstances.

"At least we've become experts at fishing," Laura jested. In a bid to make him smile. "Well, at least I have."

Adrian did not answer. He stared at the heavens. The darkness of the night at new moon made many more stars come out. It was a real spectacle.

"You don't sound very keen."

"Of course," he answered, unconvinced. "We'll soon be home."

He turned over and lay face down, with his torso on the sand.

"Laura, may I ask you a question?"

"Yes, I guess so."

"How did you come to live in Paris? You're Spanish and from Málaga, aren't you?"

"It's a long story," she answered after thinking it over.

"Do you have any family?"

"No, I mean, yes."

"I have all the time in the world," he said, as he finally gave her the smile she longed for.

"Are you really interested? It isn't exactly a fairy story."
Adrian nodded.

"Let's start at the beginning. I was raised in Málaga. I never knew my father. My mother always told me he died when she was pregnant."

"I'm sorry…"

"Don't be, I never believed her. She never so much as told me his name. I guess she didn't want to 'fess up that I'm the offspring of one of those one-night stands she had when she went out and got drunk."

Adrian said nothing, and just kept staring at her. His dark eyes absorbed every bit of light, like black holes. He thought she was gorgeous.

"She's a nice woman, despite everything," she continued. "Then Éduard came into her life, they got married and he became my stepfather, and no, he was not a nice man. We moved to France, to Saint-Jean-de-Luz. He had to for his job. I guess that was the end of everything."

"Saint-Jean-de-Luz? A great place. I've been sailing thereabouts," Adrian recalled that people there wore decent shoes.

"The greatest place on earth can be hell if the company is unsuitable."

"I know that very well. I'm sorry, a stepfather can never replace a father."

"I wish that it had been no more that that. That animal beat my mother, but she never reported him. I figure she thought she deserved those beatings. She blindly believed in that son of a bitch. When Érica, my stepsister was born, he calmed down, although it didn't last, really."

For a few seconds she took a breather while trying to cast out her anger.

She had no desire to go into detail about the grim night in the camp hut. Those dirty fingers probing her little girl's body. The tearful afternoons. That shame she never came to understand. She had only shared it once in her life. Her mother, angry and agitated, did not want to believe her, although deep

219

down, she did. Éduard was a nice man, he was her husband, and she had to stop wearing clothes like that. She forbade her to bring up the matter again.

"When I finished high school I left home to live with a friend in Paris. I got a scholarship at the ISCOM. In all these years I've only spoken to my mother a couple of times; to see if she was still alive, I guess. The monster is still keeping her captive. Now and again I speak to Érica, to check she's doing alright. That's all that matters to me, that my stepsister grows up happy."

'The monster is still keeping her captive.'

Adrian could not help noticing Laura's expression when she mentioned that fellow. She was thoughtful for a while. Her hands began to shake. He could read between the lines, and interpret shadows. Rarely was he wrong. Laura began to have that feeling again. She took a deep breath. and decided to choke it back. Over the years she had learned to do that.

"And that's that. When I graduated in Advertising, I did odd freelance jobs, until my Boreal Life interview, but you know all about that."

Adrian remembered that interview perfectly.

"I remember that you struck me as being a happy young women, who beamed with enthusiasm. I thought we needed people on board with your optimism."

"Thank you. I must admit that at first you struck me as being a conceited jerk."

Adrian looked skywards and had to laugh.

They hid behind silence for a few minutes. The breeze came as a relief amid the roasting heat.

"Don't you find it amazing?" Adrian ended up asking.

"What?"

"The sky. It's so clear that from here you can see half the known universe."

"True. I never thought there could be so many stars. It's beautiful."

"It is." Beautiful and useful. If you know them, and how to interpret them, you can find your way anywhere on earth. People have been doing it for thousands of years."

"What about you? Have you tried them?

"From first to last. I navigate by them when sailing.

It's very simple, anybody can do it."

Adrian sat behind her back and took her hand, which was pointing at the stars."

"Look, see that bright star? It's the pole star, the closest one to the North Pole. It can be used to find latitude and tell how far north you are. Polaris is the pole star in the northern hemisphere; it's up there, in the Little Bear's tail.

"What's that one, which is shining so brightly?" she asked, pointing to another part of the infinite.

"Vega, in the constellation of Lyra. It's one of the brightest stars in the night sky, and also one of the closest. Look up. You see those two next to it?"

"One on top and the other on the right?"

"Yes. They're Deneb and Altair. Together they make up the Summer Triangle.

"Yes," she smiled. You can see the three corners perfectly."

"Vega is also an emblematic star, it is the sun's apex, where the solar system is heading. It will also be the pole star some day."

"The pole star? But wasn't that Polaris?"

"It is now, but in time that will change and Vega will be closest to the earth's axis of rotation. Indeed it already was, thousands of years ago."

"And when will that happen, if I may ask?"

"In about twelve thousand years. I don't think you'll be around then," he smiled.

"Well no, I guess not."

Adrian rested his chin on Laura's shoulder.

"So you see, everybody has their moment of glory, even

221

stars."

"There's something missing," Laura said by way of interruption.

"What?"

"You said the stars guide you when you sail."

"Indeed.

"And what if there's a storm, or a gale that blocks out the sky?"

"In that case I wouldn't put to sea; I'd stay holed up in some port or other, or somewhere like here, waiting for somebody like you to show up."

Laura stared at him for a few seconds. Her stomach was tingling.

She did not budge an inch when he kissed her on the lips. On the contrary, she let herself go.

The surprise faded within seconds and made way for the most sheer and sought-after desire. First their hands ran over their bodies, in a silent, almost sacred exploration ritual. Then they made real with their fingers what only their imagination foretold, quietly and carefully, as delicately as an art restorer.

Their patience quickly ran out and they tore their clothes off until there was nothing left between warm sand and damp skin. They made love with the fury of thousands of tons of energy pent up for years. Their bodies ended up mingled with the sand, fitting in to each other like parts cast in the same mold. Laura fell asleep in his arms.

Adrian hugged her tight, and felt a hitherto unknown addiction had suddenly grown inside him.

CHAPTER XXXII

The vodka bottle was down to the last dregs.

The morning breeze sneaked in through the balcony and aired the whole apartment, while timidly shaking the papers stacked on top of the glass table in the living room. The city was still in darkness despite the full moon, while the light from Denis' loft acted as a lighthouse amid the gloom of the *Croix Rousse* neighborhood.

Denis felt like a fish in water when drunk. He savored the numbness of his senses as part of a purifying rite, like a redeeming balsam that allowed him to feel happy, or dejected to the depths of his soul, come what may. He preferred to do so alone. He took one drink after another until he lost all notion of time; only then did he put aside the bottle and wallow in a world of pain and torture in which he was lord and master, the sole proprietor. Slumped on the couch, eyes closed. He clutched an old family photo in his hands; a grubby snapshot by a neighborhood studio, in which they posed in clothes borrowed for the occasion, against a horrible background showing an artificial sky.

Denis Martel was the second of two brothers. His parents, both deceased, had been schoolteachers. A typical middle-class Parisian family, from the *Marais* district, with neither pretensions nor fuss about them. He grew up in a reasonably happy atmosphere, with a quiet everyday life and was obliged to get on with his schoolwork. Alain and Caroline Martel did not aspire to much more than ensuring their sons were good people and had enough learning to get by. Denis' brother was four years older than him and called Alain, like their father. Alain Martel Jr. was an extrovert boy, exceedingly responsible, a good soccer player, and very popular with his schoolmates.

For as long as he could remember, Denis had taken tremendous pride in his brother, a pride that verged on worship. He felt comfortable under his wing and protected by him on every occasion, such as when they walked to school together or he saw him play games with older kids in the neighborhood. The training had developed his body precociously, made it stand out and underlined the age gap between him and Denis. He was his guardian angel.

A neighborhood public school has its own laws, and big brother took care of Denis in his parents' stead. Alain would look out for him during recess, to check everything was fine. After school Denis would hang around to play ball with him and his classmates, then they would go home together. Day after day.

Denis could never have imagined that it would all end for good.

They got home earlier than usual on the afternoon Alain turned sixteen. Their mother had a special snack ready for them in order to celebrate with neighbors from the block. They went along the streets fooling around, like every afternoon, running along the sidewalks while laughing the whole time, annoying the pedestrians and storekeepers, especially Thierry the butcher, who cursed like a trooper when they stormed through the crates outside his store.

That day, before they came round the corner leading to their building, they saw three kids harassing Salima, who lived downstairs. Salima was the youngest of Rachid's three daughters. He was an Algerian storekeeper and, as befitted her

224

religion, she always wore a hijab. Occasionally she would walk home with Alain and Denis, but that day she went by herself.

The kids hassling her were older. They did not look like schoolmates, they had never seen them, and neither did they look like they were from the neighborhood. They had torn off the little girl's hijab and tossed it to one another, to make fun of her. They trod on it and wore it on their heads. One of them kicked Salima to the floor when she tried to pick it up.

Denis' memories of what happened next were blurred and only a series of fixed images had stuck with him. His brother bleeding on the ground. Sticks and iron bars whirling around. Shouts for help. When their parents came down, Alain was lying in a pool of dark blood.

The kids that had beaten up his brother had run off without a trace. The police never caught them.

Denis stated that the kids wore military jackets and baseball caps. They were of pale complexion and spoke in a strange accent, which sounded eastern European. The tallest of them had a scar on his forehead. The smallest was hook-nosed and thin as a rake.

Alain came home after a few days in hospital. It had all happened years before and, despite that, he could never forget the moment in which his parents came home with him.

The heart-rending silence.

His big brother's head was covered in bandages. The severe beating had affected his hearing.

He became deaf on his sixteenth birthday.

Alain was transferred to a special education school. A few months later he died; the blows had damaged his brain and a hemorrhage ended his short life. Time went by, and Denis joined the police. For the first few years he was on the force, every night, when everybody else had gone home, he would stay behind after work. He would pore over the files, search every inch of the *Marais* neighborhood, interrogate suspects and informants. He never found a thing; the case was finally shelved.

Those individuals had vanished off the face of the earth.

He fell asleep on the sofa. The vodka had knocked him out completely.

His last cigarette was burning down in the ashtray, while the breeze that came in through the balcony spread the smoke through the room before it billowed its way out and up to the sky over Lyons.

CHAPTER XXXIII

"Denis, are you OK? It's gone noon. I've been calling you all morning."

Sylvie's gentle voice sounded like an awful racket to his ears.

"I'm fine," he lied. His head felt like it was about to explode and his back was killing him. He'd spent too long lobotomized on an uncomfortable sofa.

"Are you still in Saint-Tropez?"

"No, I spent the weekend at home. There was a slight change of plan. Something came up and I had to get back early. But tell me, Sylvie, what have you dug up?" Denis hurried to say, because he was in no mood for group therapy over his dealings with Olivia, especially in his catatonic state.

Sylvie kept quiet for a few seconds. She said nothing, needed no explanations to imagine what had happened and preferred to stick to a strict professional report.

"Friday I called Adrian Seaten's office. Jill Dempster, his secretary, answered. I couldn't speak to Adrian; he was away on business. It looks like he was on a film shoot in southern Spain, on a beach in Almería. He was due back in Paris yesterday."

"Well call him back today," Denis concluded. He was not up for lengthy discussions.

"I've done that. He's not back yet. They're somewhat nervous in his office."

"He'll have changed plans or missed a flight. I don't think

it's a big deal."

"They've been trying to reach him since Friday night. The last person to speak to him was Jill, on Friday afternoon; he was already on his way back, and spoke to her from his car. After that, all attempts to contact him have been useless. His cell is switched off or out of range."

"What about his return flight? Did he have a reservation?"

"No. He was traveling in his own car."

"By car? From Paris? How odd."

"It is, but it seems it's not the first time. Jill said he had some personal meetings to attend; he had been in Spain all week."

"What kind of meetings?"

"She had no knowledge of who he was to see, or what they were about. It was personal business and Jill doesn't handle his agenda outside the agency. She has no access to that information. All she knows is that he had a shoot on Friday."

"He owns the agency, he can do whatever he pleases. Maybe he's changed his mind and is sunning himself in some fancy hotel. He'll be back, sooner or later."

"Helena, his fiancée, hasn't been able to contact him since then, either," Sylvie went on. "She was in the office this very morning, with her parents and a family attorney. It seems the girl was very scared; she was having a severe anxiety attack."

"Another case. He had cold feet about the wedding and baled out in time. Men are rarely smitten with sense, but when they are, it's for sure," jested Denis, who was not taking the delay too seriously. He had seen thousands of similar situations. A few heartfelt excuses, a nice romantic dinner and everything sorted.

"He wasn't traveling alone" Sylvie went on, while ignoring her boss's comments. "Laura Bernat was with him. She works in the agency as a copywriter in the creative department. She flew from Paris to Madrid. Adrian picked her up and they drove down to Almería in his car. Laura was due back in Paris

228

at 12:35 p.m. on Saturday, on Air France flight AF 1305. She had a reservation at the Fénix Hotel in Madrid for Friday night. She didn't show up. Neither did she catch her flight."

"Has she been located?" Denis asked. He was beginning to realize the situation was not at all usual.

"No. Her cell has also been switched off since Friday afternoon."

"Hmmm. Now that is odd."

"Helena's family have reported Adrian as missing, and the Spanish police are already looking into it. Our '*Il Duce*' has vanished into thin air."

Denis was thoughtful. It would not be easy to track down that Seaten character, or whatever the hell he was called. He was bound to show up in a matter of days. There were always imponderables. Everything had an explanation. It was a fucking coincidence, too, that he had vanished right when they had identified him, but frankly he believed in coincidences about as much as he believed in Santa Claus and his flying sleigh.

"What shall we do now? Sylvie queried.

"Wait. There's little more we can do. Let's give it a couple of days and, if there's no news of his whereabouts, get in touch with the Spanish police. We need first-hand information"

"Got it."

"Thanks a lot, Sylvie, we'll talk soon."

"If you want to talk, you know where I am."

"Thanks, Sylvie. I appreciate it. Good-bye," Denis cut in to say.

Denis struggled to get up from the sofa and headed over to the kitchen. His temples and face hurt, as if a jackhammer was pounding away at his brain cells. His backbone burned inside him, like it had a life of its own. He needed to get his strength back so he set about making a power breakfast. So he poured the last bit of vodka out of the bottle, and added tomato juice, salt, pepper, and a healthy measure of Tabasco sauce. He never believed all the baloney put about by morons that a Bloody Mary was the best cure for a hangover, but he needed a drink to cope with the new day. It was years since his hands had trembled after a boozy night, but merely remembering those days drove him to take preventive measures. He filled up his glass with ice, took a swig of the mixture and felt that things were falling back into place.

His private cell bleeped three times to tell him he had a text message.

There was no mystery to it: it could only be Sylvie or Yves LeBoeuf. Nobody else had that number.

Denis read the message. It was from a private line.

Peter Caldwell: FIAT IUSTITIA ET PEREAT MUNDUS.

Yves had been a quick worker. He smiled to think of the grim expression on 'The Animal's' face when he received that strange request.

He repeated the Latin phrase several times.

He looked at his watch. It was 2 p.m. Eight in the morning in Massachusetts.

He would wait another couple of hours.

CHAPTER XXXIV

Philippe Levissier was doodling with a pencil on the agenda while he listened, with the sound of the sea in the distance, to Professor Artest droning on about the convenience of altering the fall courses program. The old academic maintained that including a case study on epistemology and values in the workshop on 'Classical philosophy and ancient civilizations' was nothing short of outright heresy. A betrayal of history. "God knows, my dear fellows, that it was not until the Renaissance, moreover, until the nineteenth century, that epistemology began to be considered as a separate branch within philosophy."

"Professor Levissier, you have a call," the departmental secretary chimed in from the doorway in her shrill voice, to interrupt Artest's heated speech.

"Not now, Lisa, I'm busy."

"He says it's very urgent, and cannot wait."

"Excuse me, gentlemen. Please continue without me," Philippe rose from his leather-backed chair and went through the door to the timeworn meeting room.

As he left he winked discretely at Lisa, who gave him a shy smile in return. As usual she had followed his instructions to the letter: any call during the boring monthly meeting had to be deemed urgent or of the utmost importance.

Phillipe followed Lisa along the corridor to his office.

"Who's it from?"

"Mr. Denis Martel."

"Denis. OK, put the call through and, if you'd be so kind, close the door on your way out."

"Of course, Professor."

When Lisa was gone, Phillippe made himself comfortable, stretched out in his chair and picked up the phone.

"Denis, is that you?"

"Hello, Phillipe. How are you? I hope I'm not bothering you."

"No, don't worry," he answered, not letting it show that he was glad to be interrupted. "Life is full of surprises. We don't see each other for thirty years, and then we speak every week."

"If you believed in fate, I'd tell you that was an ace up its sleeve," Denis jested.

"Great to hear you again. I hope you had a nice flight home."

"Everything's fine, thanks, my trip home was most interesting," Denis replied, as he took a sip from his second Bloody Mary of the day. I don't know if you've the time to chat awhile now."

"Of course I do. How's your mysterious case going?"

"That's exactly what I want to talk to you about. I'm sorry to trouble you again, but I need to consult you on another matter."

"No trouble at all. If I may be frank, I'd be glad to: it spices up my humdrum life. I'd be lying if I said I wasn't intrigued by what you told me the other day.

How can I help?"

"You see, I need your opinion about a motto. It's a Latin phrase: *Fiat iustitia et pereat mundus.*

"Did that also appear next to a body?"

"No. Well, yes. Kind of."

"It's an old Latin saying. *Fiat iustitia et pereat mundus*: Let justice be done, though the world may perish. A devastating expression, don't you think?"

"May justice be done above all, whatever the consequences, above even the world's very survival," Denis paraphrased.

"Indeed. It's not a Classic Roman saying, but was actually coined much later; in the sixteenth century, to be more exact. It was the motto of Ferdinand I of Hapsburg, Holy Roman Emperor, son of Philip the Handsome and Joanna I of Castile. I believe it comes from some Lutheran writings of the time."

'Justice at any price'. He could not get the idea out of his head.

"A classical concept," the professor continued. "That Kant broached later and was then sweetened by many authors who postulated that justice should have certain limits."

Denis said nothing for a few seconds.

"Denis?" Philippe wanted to check the line had not gone dead.

"Yes, yes, I'm still here, sorry. Let's get back to the chat we had the other day. As you were saying, mythology explains why the flower appeared on the spot where Narcissus drowned, as eternal proof of his wrongdoing."

"Right, Nemesis gave him his punishment."

"Nemesis?"

"Yes, the goddess Nemesis. Her origin is somewhat unclear, although some say Zeus himself was her father. She is depicted as a winged woman, bearing an apple blossom and a crown, and depending on the image, she may wield a sword or scales. The goddess of divine retribution, of balance."

"Of vengeance."

"You could say so. All who dare to commit misdeeds or disobey shall be punished. Her mission was to maintain order, balance, and the *Aurea Mediocritas*, which is to say, 'the golden medium' for the Greeks. If this were to be broken, it would put the world's very existence at risk. She became the instrument of divine wrath to maintain it.

"Justice above all, *Fiat iustitia pereat mundus*," Denis concluded.

"Exactly, it all comes back to the same idea. Like I told you last week, having a flower grow where you drown or getting turned into a pillar of salt, is superfluous, a tale. The meaning of myth is above all that. The essence, the foundation of everything, is that crime doesn't pay, evil comes at a price, and punishment doesn't stem from human law, but is of divine provenance, from which nobody can escape."

Denis sat down on the balcony and lit a cigarette. The words bounced around his head time and again:

'From which nobody can escape.'

Nobody. Not even a blood-thirsty Serbian old soldier acquitted by an international court, or a respectable Argentine businessman, a former collaborator with the dictatorship who was later reinserted into society. Nobody, not even those individuals. Punishment had been exacted for their crimes, the punishment no court had been able to mete out, so they would not get away with their misdeeds on this earth. Order had been restored. The executioner had left his calling card.

Hundreds of questions buzzed in Denis's head. Who was behind it all? It seemed obvious that the young Americans were implicated somehow. Too many coincidences: Caldwell's note, the forged passport in Atkins' name with Adrian Seaten's photo in it, on Naxos on the day Miletić was murdered. All that could not be happenstance. Why them? What did those young Americans have to do with Miletić or Lavinia? They belonged to another generation, and it is unlikely their paths had crossed in the past. They were college kids, from wealthy families; they had it made. And to make matters worse, none were around to clear things up. Atkins, dead in a car crash; Adrian Seaten, missing; and Caldwell had committed suicide in a bathtub. Peter Caldwell. What made him take his own life? Was anybody else involved? It was unlikely they did it unaided.

And what about the victims? Were Miletić and Lavinia the only ones? Or maybe in some part of the world there were more unclaimed bodies or unsolved crimes?

"Denis, I must go back to my meeting," Philippe suddenly cut off his thoughts. "If you need anything, don't hesitate to call me."

"Thanks, Philippe. I'll do that."

"I don't know what you're mixed up in, but be careful, won't you?"

"Well, you know, the world has never been perfect."

He hung up and downed the last of theBloody Mary.

He had nothing left to do for the time being.

The first rays of the afternoon sun stole across the balcony, to bathe every corner of the apartment in light. The sky was a spotless azure blue, without so much as a cloud to spoil its purity.

A poisonous feeling of loneliness intruded inside him.

He picked up the phone and called Alana's number. There was a promise he had to keep with the lady in his life.

Little Cécile jumped for joy when she knew her father was going to see her, they would spend a few days together, and this time it was for real.

CHAPTER XXXV

The day had dawned under a torrential downpour, as if heaven were crying bitter tears over the impending farewells. Water raining hard on the coast formed a hazy curtain that turned the sky dark gray and was the perfect backdrop for a dog day afternoon.

A spectacular thunderclap echoed around inside the cave and made the ground shake beneath Flávio and Paulo's feet, while they packed up diving gear and belongings in boxes, fitting each item in with a longshoreman's skill. They worked quietly, from memory, like putting together a jigsaw puzzle they had done before.

The job was done a few hours later. Night had yet to fall but everything was meticulously packaged and lined up by the entrance, ship shape and ready to set off that very night, as planned.

Despite the storm, Adrian and Laura had spent the last few hours walking on the sand. They went from one end of the beach to another, under the rain, exploring every nook and cranny, albeit only to take stock of everything that had really happened, and to prove that the hidden beach was not heaven and they weren't lost souls wandering in it. They had even been bold enough to dive in the sea and feel the Mediterranean waters on their skin. They did not speak very much, and neither did they need to, it took just one look to tell what they had been through there, with the connivance of those that knew nobody else could ever understand. To an extent they felt an odd melancholy they could not quite explain. After their walk, they had a nap under an alcove that the cliff had contrived to make at the other end of the beach. They made love sheltered by the stone ceiling and fell fast asleep, entwined like a ball of wool, until woken up by the sunset.

The storm had blown over now and the sun could be seen searing the horizon. Adrian carefully stroked Laura's hair, while her head lay on his shoulder.

"Where would you like to spend the rest of your life?"

Laura looked at him in surprise. She was not used to point-blank questions.

"If you could choose, I mean."

"I don't know," she replied, after thinking it over for a short while. "I've never thought about it. Somewhere quiet, out of the way, far from the city, where I could enjoy the countryside, and little things. Something like that."

"Idyllic, back to nature. You'll make me cry!"

"Don't mess with me!" she protested, giving him a little punch on the shoulder.

"I wouldn't dream of it; too primitive for my liking. Best leave that hogwash to Flávio and Paul. Living far away from life's pleasures is bad for your health; look at them, they're not right upstairs. They're incurable," he said, tapping his temple with his forefinger.

"*Touché* ," Laura agreed with a smile. "And what are those pleasures, in Mr. Seaten's book?"

"Well now, there's so many they're countless. Sampling a good Scotch, maybe a Balblair, listening to music by the fireside, savoring a charbroiled steak with fresh *foie gras* , watching night fall over the city lights."

"You can have both," Laura objected with a smile. "You can get all that in a coastal town or on Mediterranean island, no smoke or stress, no fuss."

"Now you're talking."

He kissed her on the lips and held her tightly between his arms. It seemed as if everything had vanished from around them and nothing more was needed.

"I must admit you make me feel weird things," Adrian said.

"Weird?" I hope that, as well as weird, they're good."

"Of course," he smiled. Wonderful things. What makes them weird is that they're new. That's all."

"And may I know what things I make you feel?"

"I can't put them into words. I want to protect you, take care of you, enjoy you, love you. They include something like that."

"And that's all new for you?"

"It is."

"What about Helena?"

Adrian took a few long seconds to answer.

"Helena is a bit-player in my life, and always has been. She's a nice girl, no doubt about it. I guess she's one of the theater props in my own personal play."

"But you were going to marry her, that makes her more than a prop."

"I imagine I was groomed for that. It was going with the flow, playing safe. Never did I really wonder whether I was in love with her. I guess I never was. It must be the fucking sunstroke that has opened my eyes." He gazed into the distance, and after a long silence, announced; "In fact, I'm not going back to my life."

Laura looked at him in surprise.

"I didn't know 'not going back to my life' was an option."

"It's always an option," he replied, without looking away from the horizon. "It's an option for everybody, even if they don't know it or haven't the guts to want to know. Moreover, what could be a better time than this? Everybody thinks I'm deader than dead, don't they?"

It was beginning to dawn on Laura that this was not a joke. She did not understand anything at all.

"You mean leaving behind the agency, your house, Helena?"

"I mean leaving it all behind, making Adrian Seaten vanish forever. And don't worry about the agency or the house, they're the least of my concerns. With my money and property, I can get by for several lifetimes. Helena will soon get over it; in less than three years she'll marry some creep with money to burn. I'll take bets on it."

He felt his colleague's naive look full-on; she was staring at him with her perplexed brown eyes.

"There are things you'll never get to understand, Laura," he said quietly, almost in a whisper.

Laura did not know what to say. She did not even know what to think. What she had been through while stuck on the beach since the accident, was light years beyond reality. She was barely capable yet of digesting her hitherto unknown feelings for Adrian, which flowed around her, and much less her future plans with her colleague.

Maybe what she felt was... sadness. Yes, that was it, sadness. But a sadness that was as short-lived as a dewdrop.

"I would like you to come with me."

Laura stared at the horizon with a haunted look. The breeze tousled her hair and brushed her cheeks with a gentle caress. At last it had stopped raining and the beach was now a mud bath. She noticed her body float on air as if she had handed over control of her soul unconditionally, and did not care.

Just then she felt every inch of her skin warming up. A comforting and absorbent warmth, from which she decided there and then that she did not wish to escape.

"I think I need you," Adrian insisted.

In the distance, they heard Flávio shouting that dinner was ready.

"Will you look after me?" Laura whispered.

"Always."

The last dinner they had in the cove went ahead amid lively conversation, like an end-of-summer meeting between four old friends that were about to go their separate ways after living together to the full for a while. They decided to finish off the two bags of sweet wine that were left over, to wash down the strips of dried octopus and sea urchins. Flávio passionately described the local sea bed and told tales about the reluctant guests' fishing abilities. For once he spoke calmly and uninhibitedly, like somebody who had shrugged a huge weight off his shoulders. They laughed at his stories, which were spiced up with his funny Brazilian accent. Then they rolled and smoked cigarettes, and gazed at the starless sky.

Finally, Flávio turned in and left Paul by the fireside along with his two companions.

"Where are you guys thinking of going to now?" Laura asked, while not really expecting to get an answer.

"Far away. Some secluded spot on the planet," Paul answered. "We change our home every three months."

Adrian looked at the fellow in disbelief.

"But what do you live on? Are you running away from something?" Laura added.

"Flávio's father takes care of everything. He has plenty of money." He turned round and stared at Laura. "Who isn't running away from something?"

Laura gave no answer and Paul poked the embers with a stick to revive what flames were left in the dying fire. Paul was not exaggerating: the old man did have plenty of money. Flávio's father bought favors with it. He did whatever he felt like, and was happy to pay the price for keeping his son out of reach of the law and from sullying the family's —and the business's— good name. Paul knew that very well. He took personal charge of dealing with the old man for the exact amounts needed to fund their exile, and the means of moving around. Since Flávio and his father had ceased existing for each other, four years ago now, he had been in charge of everything. But that did not matter. After the accident he decided never to leave Flávio alone. He had been his friend since he was five and was not going to drop him now. Paul would look after him for as long as needed. He would protect him from his own madness and the demons inside his head. Everything would calm down in time.

The drug quickly took effect.

In the space of five minutes they fell unconscious on the sand, after a sudden and intense dizzy spell.

At 11:30 p.m., two semi-rigid Narwhal Fast-110 boats, thirty-six-feet long, arrived on shore, with four crew members on board, dressed in black neoprene suits. They landed using flashlights and in forty-five minutes exactly had stowed away all the boxes of equipment on one of the boats. Adrian Seaten and Laura's bodies were placed on board the other boat, on which one of the men embarked.

At 00:32 a.m. both craft set out to sea. When they were a mile offshore they changed course and went in opposite directions, in line with the coast, and put distance between each other at great speed.

CHAPTER XXXVI

When September came, Interpol headquarters went back to work as usual. The corridors were thronged by inspectors and administrative staff, who ran around the premises at full speed, up and down, like bees in a hive. They had realized that speed of movement was appreciated as a skill more than efficiency itself.

Denis Martel greeted the receptionist and complimented her on her deep tan. He took the elevator and within seconds was seated once more in the leather chair in his office and looking at his computer, like a pilot in front of his control panel. Only a day and a half had gone by since he had said good-bye to Cécile, who had gone back to Paris with her mother, but he already missed her. She was twelve and had become quite the little woman, but was also full of surprises; she unsettled him with her wisecracks and moved him with her sweetness. For the first time in his life he felt truly sad to be parted from her, and was overcome by the unknown feeling that he was wasting his life, although his unease did not detract from the happiness he had felt in spending time with her.

There were no big items waiting for him in his inbox: an operation to investigate online sales of phony medicines in several countries, a follow-up meeting of the piracy group, the quarterly experts' committee on police training, the sound practices working party, and a few emailed reports on updating databases, of which there were more every day. Thanks to new computer applications, updates had been gathering speed notably in recent years: a wanted list of one hundred fifty thousand, fifty thousand fingerprints and DNA profiles, and more than three million stolen vehicles.

He did not dally long. Denis had a meeting to go to and, after telling his assistant he wanted to take no calls, he logged off and headed to 31 Rue Franklin Roosevelt.

Sylvie was sipping a *macchiato* at one of the tables outside the Le Rive Gauche. She had spent a few days in the country with her children. Her hair was worn up and had on a navy-blue two-piece suit. Her green eyes stood out against her light tan. Denis smiled to see her. He admired her chameleon-like ability to change from being an all-round mother to efficient executive. He thought it was a particularly fine morning and immediately set aside the uncomfortable feeling that he was looking at her through different eyes.

They chatted for some time about their vacations. It was a shame that their two weeks off had sped past so quickly. Doubtless it had done them good. Sylvie found her boss to be more relaxed and his old sense of humor was back. She had been missing him. Denis avoided all mention of his sudden rift with Olivia, so they discussed Cécile, and Sylvie's enjoyable trips with her children on the river. After their first coffee they went over developments in the Miletić case. Denis was dying to meet the young American face-to-face.

"He's still a missing person."

"That cannot be, damnit, it's been more than three weeks now."

"I've spoken to the Spanish police several times. There's a search party working flat out. The Brun-Donzel family have pulled strings at every level, even the ambassador to Spain is involved. All the stops have been pulled out. It has turned into a matter of national importance."

"And haven't they found anything?"

"Yes, but it's not good news. They came across the remains of Seaten's car on several beaches, over a radius of twenty-five miles from where he began his return journey; little pieces of the engine and some bits of plastic."

Denis could not believe his ears.

"They have combed over the whole area," Sylvie added. "All the neighboring beaches, dirt roads, cliffs. Not a trace of them."

"That's impossible."

"And that is what the Spanish police think. They figure they left the main highway to avoid a tailback, that they crashed and fell into the sea. That would explain the remains of the vehicle on the coast, but that being so, they would have found more of the wreckage, or at least bigger pieces, and one of the bodies would probably have washed up on the shore somewhere."

"And now what? "What are they going to do?"

"The search party will be deployed for a few more days, as they have promised Helena's family and the French government; then they will drop it. The case will not be completely closed, but the active search will stop. In Spain they are rather pessimistic; by this stage they believe the odds the couple are still alive are virtually nil."

"Great. And what if they don't show up?" Denis felt the case was slipping away between his fingers like a wet fish.

"They will be declared officially disappeared. Spanish law stipulates a period of ten years before death can be declared, but in cases involving an accident, like this, they could be legally pronounced dead within three to six months."

The veteran officer cursed to high heaven.

This could not be happening. Just when they had cornered 'Il Duce', he went and vanished off the face of the earth. It had to be a freaking joke.

"What do we do, Denis?"

"Keep waiting. I guess there's nothing else for it."

They exchanged glances; there was not much else to say. It was Sylvie who broke the silence.

"We have received more information on Axis Ventures."

"Axis Ventures?"

"The majority stakeholder in Boreal Life, Seaten's agency. As I told you, it is part of a very complicated layer of shell companies and figureheads. The main office has its business address in the Isle of Man. Here's a list of names of the leading individual shareholders and board members," she said, as she slipped the paper across the table.

"Let me guess. Our friends?"

"Right, but not just them. As well as Adrian Seaten and Peter Caldwell, Roger Seaten, Adrian's father, is also registered, as is Craig Rosewood, a Harvard professor, and a dozen other professors and retired senators."

"Rather than an advertising agency's board of directors, it looks like a congressional commission," added Denis, who could not help a disturbing feeling take hold of him.

"Axis Ventures is incorporated as a foundation," Sylvie went on. "As well from stakes in several subsidiaries, its revenue comes from donations."

"Donations?"

"Yes, they raise funds from major donors, presidents of multinational, even a former U.S. president's foundation."

"We're just small fry, aren't we, Sylvie?" he surmised with a bitter-sweet smile.

Denis lighted a cigarette. 'Major donors. Donations.' He felt groggy. They were out of their league.

Neither could he get Seaten's mysterious disappearance off his mind.

Sylvie looked at him affectionately. Time waits for no man and it showed on her boss's face. He did not have as much energy as he did a few years before, and there was a careworn look in his eye.

"Tell me, Sylvie, remind me. When, exactly, did you first try to contact him?"

"On the same day he went missing, a Friday. I spoke to his secretary Jill, it would have been 2:15 p.m."

"How did you introduce yourself?"

"As an Interpol consultant. That's what we agreed, wasn't it?"

"True, that's what we agreed."

He had the sudden realization that he had made a big mistake.

CHAPTER XXXVII

He tied his Hermès tie in an even triangular knot. A perfect full Windsor that fitted his blue Italian shirt collar like a glove. Neither too loose nor too tight, in keeping with the rules. Next he put on the blue suit jacket and looked at himself in the mirror, which showed a respectable man in his prime. 'Hello again, Monsieur Blanc.'

It was only the third time he had played his new identity, and it felt like his very own. His acting had been perfect. Worthy of an Oscar. Good enough to have won over Madame Gillet. The sixty-something widow had even gotten her hopes up. That new neighbor of hers who came home about six-thirty, just as she returned with her bits and pieces from her painting class, and helped her carry them to the elevator, seemed like a nice man. No doubt about it. There were no respectable men left on the 'market' with a modicum of class and good manners that could keep a lady of her standing company.

Denis Martel showed up at the usual time at 30 Rue Jacob, in the heart of the Saint-Germain-des-Prés neighborhood. Adrian Seaten's home was in a luxury apartment block and security at the entrance was in keeping with that. The porter worked until 3 p.m. in his lodge, after which a four-digit code and a front door with a lock guarded the elegant reception area. He waited on the sidewalk opposite until, finally, as on the last three occasions, Madame Gillet approached the entrance to the apartment block. Without delay he crossed the street and gave her a polite and gentlemanly greeting, to which she replied by beaming a syrupy smile.

"May I?" Denis asked, as he picked up one of the bags, out of which poked a little easel and several pieces of canvas.

"Of course, Monsieur Blanc."

"Please call me André, I insist."

"Thank you, André," she answered, and kept smiling.

Madame Gillet tapped in the code and opened the iron door, then she got out of the elevator on the second floor and said a friendly good-bye. She decided not to let another chance go by without inviting him in for coffee. One day she would have to come out of her shell, be bolder. She was not going to spend the rest of her days alone.

Denis got out on the top floor. Everything had gone according to plan. Monsieur Blanc had found his way into the building properly and was now but a few feet away from the door to Adrian Seaten's apartment.

'Il Duce' was still missing; maybe he was languishing in hell. The Spanish police had called off the search party a week before, while Helena's family and the agency staff had arranged to hold a mass for his soul, which would take place the day after. They had not given up all hope of finding him, but life goes on and they could not prolong the agony much more. Didier Brun-Donzel, the top banker, was unbending. The situation was tearing his daughter's delicate health to shreds. Legal proceedings took their time, but it was also time to start taking decisions, to cut losses and try to move on.

As Denis approached the door, he took a small case of tools out of his jacket pocket. He held his breath. You could hear the silence that spread out all over the floor. A tension tool and a lock pick would do. He had found out the last time he was there that the door to Seaten's luxury apartment only had a pin tumbler lock fitted. Not so much as an additional bolt.

He guessed that Seaten knew as well as he did that you could pick any type of lock, given skill and patience. That is all it takes. You can learn anything with the right connections in the Paris underworld. He breathed in, then out again, slowly. Denis crouched down, poked the tension tool into the slot and turned it gently around while gripping the cylinder. Then he inserted the lock pick into the top of the slot until he could feel the tumblers. He pressed his ear to the lock and pushed up the pick. The first click did not take long. Then the second, and third.

The elevator buzzed then began to go down quickly.

The sound of something like dogs barking on the ground floor made its way upstairs. Denis was frozen to the spot. The elevator began to come up. One floor. Two... Three... It was heading for his floor. He tried to pull out the lock pick, but it was stuck between the tumblers.

There was no time left.

The elevator door finally opened and out came a little girl with a dog on a lead. Denis watched all this from the stairwell. He had jumped up there at the speed of light. The tension tool and lock pick were still in place, and stuck out about four inches, like weird metal branches growing out of the lock. The little girl went to the apartment next door and rang the doorbell. The ringing upset the dog, which leaped from side to side as if possessed. At last somebody opened up and let them in.

Denis waited for a few minutes.

Nobody had noticed his tools stuck in the lock, but he had to get a move on. He could not delay, otherwise all bets would be off.

Back he went to the door. Within a few minutes he had heard the fifth click.

He gripped the tension tool and slowly turned the cylinder until the door opened altogether.

CHAPTER XXXVIII

'Damned hippies.'

The old fisherman with the wrinkled, blackened face walked as spritely as a teenager and as knowingly as an old-timer who was familiar with every grain of sand for miles around. After a good many run-ins he was more than used to young backpackers sleeping on the beach, but his vast experience did nothing to sooth his anger. In the summertime, the Gata Cape National Park filled up with greenhorn tourists that hiked along its trails in the lonely wilderness to get away from it all. Nonetheless, he never could fathom the mysterious reason why, in all the forty miles of coastline, they always settled on the half-mile of beach at Almadraba de Monteleva for their peace and quiet, and moreover, brought their fishing tackle with them.

"Hey, you there!" he growled. The couple were still fast asleep. Who knew how much booze they had put away. "You two, get up! Get out of here. Away from my nets!" he shouted, insistently now.

Adrian finally opened his eyes. He had a headache worthy of a thousand hangovers, and needed a few seconds to emerge from his murky dreams and come back to life.

The scene that met his eyes could not have been more surreal: for some reason that escaped his understanding, a grumpy old man was yelling words at him that he could not compute, in who knew what hellhole.

Instinctively he rolled off the net and placed Laura's body on the sand. The old man went back the way he had come and cursed all the while.

Adrian sat on the sand and began to gather his wasted brain cells together, and not without difficulty. He cast his mind back to the last thing he could remember and, little by little, he could picture the cove, and the dinner with Flávio and Paul.

Then everything went blank. There was nothing else in his memory bank.

He hadn't the faintest idea how they had washed up on that beach, but that mattered little now. His nerve endings were still gripped by the aftereffects of the drug, but his body was floating on air. At last they were free. What's more, they were officially missing, dead in the eyes of the world. You could not be freer than that.

He looked around him.

They were on a narrow beach of fine sand just thirty yards wide that stretched out into the distance at both ends. A single-track road skirted the whole coastline and bordering it was a row of huts with little boats and nets in between. His gaze lit on a weird-looking church set aside from the cluster of huts, which stood proud and alone next to the sand. It looked burnt out, like the remnants of a nuclear disaster.

Laura was still asleep. He looked at her tenderly. His partner. Adrian stroked her hair and whispered in her ear until at last she opened her eyes. He noticed a black backpack next to her. After rooting around inside it, he found a bag of fruit and a plastic wallet with three hundred euros in it. A gentlemanly touch. The memory of the two Brazilians' faces came back to him fleetingly. God alone knew where in the world they had gone with all their peculiar madness and inexplicable torments.

"Where are we?"

"We're free, somewhere, but free."

Soon after they had rustled up some energy and walked

toward the huts that were a hundred yards off.

The little village consisted of a handful of simply built houses. 'Wild West houses must have been just like this,' he thought. A few locals, all above fifty, wandered along the street or sat quietly in the doorways to their homes in wooden or wicker chairs, to take refuge in the scant shade under the eaves. It only took them a few minutes to walk along the three dusty streets that made up the village, under the curious glances of the denizens, more than enough time for Adrian to realize that they would find all it took to put his plans into practice. The Hostal del Mar guest house only had four rooms. The old receptionist, a fat lady with huge breasts, was patching some pants behind a wooden desk in the faint breeze of a worn-out fan. She did not so much as ask for ID: the usual ragged guests merely had to pay up front. The room alone deserved to be included in the House of Horrors, but the hot shower and a mattress that was soft to the touch, made that dump seem like a presidential suite, worthy of the Peninsula in New York.

There was no time to lose, so Adrian went out straight away. He could still see Laura's naked, freshly showered body slipping like a Greek goddess between the sheets. The young woman had yet to shrug off the hypnotic effect of the powerful narcotic that was still wreaking havoc in her bloodstream.

Adrian headed for a phone booth on the other side of the street. He cracked a smile, for he could not remember the last time he had used one of those contraptions. He called a number in Paris. The call was picked up immediately. After a fifteen-minute chat, he went to a little grocery store that, as he guessed, was practically a small supermarket where you could buy just about anything imaginable. There was a multicolored mosaic in the doorway, made from boxes of fruit stacked up. Two refrigerated display cases contained fresh fish and cuts of meat. In back, on metal shelving, were all kinds of toiletries and cleaning products, and a rack with beachwear. He gathered together scissors, shampoo, razors and shaving foam, blond hair dye, two pairs of denim shorts, flip-flops and two white tee-shirts. He bought cheese sandwiches, cream rolls and a two-quart bottle of ice-cold Coca-Cola Zero.

Laura was coming round by the time he got back to the hotel room. He hugged her tight and kissed her on the neck.

"Good morning, sweet stuff. How's that cute little hangover of yours?"

"Errr, my eyelids are heavy. I'm hungry."

"I've brought something to eat. You won't believe it, cream rolls!"

Laura smiled wide-eyed and savored one of the rolls as if it were the last scrap of sugar left in the whole world.

"It's just me and you now, Laura, nobody else. Are you sure about this?"

"I am."

"Well you should know I've taken the liberty to christen you. We'll have all of our documents by tomorrow."

Laura gave him a surprised look then smiled in approval. Deep down she was thrilled at the idea of changing skin.

"Well then, nice to meet you, Mrs. Cooley."

"Mrs. Cooley?"

"Alexandra Cooley, age twenty-eight, U.S. Citizen, partly raised in Spain. Born Lafayette, Louisiana, to be exact. Hope you like jazz."

"I love it; well I do now," she jested. "And to whom do I have the pleasure of speaking?"

"Martin Cooley, your doting husband. Delighted to meet you," he said, while kissing her on the lips.

"This calls for a celebration."

Laura undid his shirt, taking her time over each button, and hesitated a few seconds when she got down to his belt buckle, which even so was no obstacle. When he was completely naked, she dragged him under the sheets. She kissed him all over his neck, his chest and then stopped inside his thighs. The ends of her loose hair obediently followed the trail left by her kisses on his skin, which traced imaginary lines with surgical precision and as softly as a paintbrush. When she straddled him and began to move her hips as if swayed by the sea waves, Adrian lay back and enjoyed her breasts slapping rhythmically against his chest. He lovingly watched her closed eyes, her slow panting and an expression that looked pained but was not. Tenderly he hugged her slim, olive-skinned body when she collapsed on top of him and he cuddled her until she fell asleep beside him.

After a few minutes he got up and went to the bathroom without a sound.

In the mirror he looked like a castaway. Years ago he had discovered that a quick and suitable change of look could work wonders when it came to saving his ass, and he had become somewhat adept at using hair dye and haircuts. He clipped his hair with the deftness, concentration and ease of a barber. Then he applied the dye and left it awhile. Shaving was such a delight. His beard had become as thick and rough as a bundle of barbed wire. He got out of the shower and looked in the mirror again. Tanned skin and platinum blond hair. As if by magic, the ragged castaway had turned into a genuine Australian surfer.

Ten hours later, a Lexus LS 460 parked outside the Hostal del Mar. The fat lady in reception said a fond farewell to them: her friendliness went ballistic after the hundred-euro tip they gave her. The chauffeur kindly opened the door and beckoned them inside, then he handed Adrian a leather briefcase and they drove off.

"Good morning, Mr. and Mrs Cooley. I hope you have enjoyed your vacation."

"It's been great, thank you," Adrian answered in a dull tone.

He checked the documents inside the briefcase. They were all in order. He took out a couple of passports and gave one to

Laura. Hers had a copy of the photo posted on the company website, along with her new personal details. Laura looked askance at Adrian. It had only been twenty-four hours since they escaped from the beach, and already she had a fake passport with a stolen photo in her hands. She guessed this was no time for questions and there was nothing for it but to trust him. She would do just that. It was too late to turn back. The briefcase also contained files and documents that the newly baptized Mr. Cooley decided to check out later.

After checking in at Almería airport without incident, they boarded a private Hawker 800. They landed at Paris-Le Bourget two-and-a-half hours later, from where they were chauffeur -driven in a spectacular upmarket Mercedes to the George V Hotel.

Mr. and Mrs. Cooley took the presidential suite. Following Martin Cooley's instructions, room service had prepared a private dinner: duck *foie gras* with black pepper and roast lamb. They had decided to hold the fish and anything that came out of the sea for quite some time. They washed it down with an Argentine Malbec that tasted like nectar of the gods to them.

When they finished eating, Adrian said he had to step out. Unfinished business, he explained. He would be back the day after, at night, but not to worry if he was delayed, because everything was under control. They would leave Paris upon his return. He spoke to her softly and with that odd, unblinking expression that, as usual, gave nothing away.

Laura nodded, not altogether reassured.

Before he left, Adrian tossed a file onto the bed.

"Take a look at this," he said. "You're sure to be interested."

CHAPTER XXXIX

Laura lay back on the bed in the presidential suite and picked up the file Adrian had given her before leaving. She tried not to dwell on where he had gone at that time of night, and what mysterious business he was up to. Rubbing out an old life would be as complicated as drawing up a new one from scratch, she guessed. An uncomfortable feeling of worry overcame her for a second. 'Rubbing out and drawing up lives.' How on earth had she gotten into all this?

She felt the soft touch of the silk sheets on her skin. The suite was decorated in a blue and white pattern, from the carpet to the wallpaper. The refined furniture was spread around several rooms in the best possible taste, chic but not overdone. Never in her life had she been anywhere like it.

She closed her eyes, and had to pinch herself to check she was not dreaming. Laura felt worried and overjoyed by turns. Scared and hopeful. She had leaped into the void with no safety net.

She looked back at the envelope she held in her hands, and opened it.

It contained a sort of file, some fifty pages long, and spiral-bound. A bar code was on the cover along with the following inscription in large font characters: 'Doc 611—confidential. (Requested by AS).'

Her curiosity was much aroused so she got stuck into the text. The first page showed two copies of Brazilian passports.

Flávio Azevedo de Souza, born 2-12-82, São Paulo;
Paul Schotten Machado; born 2-21-82, São Paulo.

'Flávio and Paul,' she thought.

She read through the pages of report that followed the passports as avidly as an explorer. They were full of photographs, like some kind of album. A family album with family pictures in it: little children at play, birthday parties, picnics on the beach.

Two boys always appeared together, from the first fading snapshots onwards.

Those boys were Flávio and Paul.

It was them all right. The same features impressed upon their childish faces and unformed bodies.

Just the two of them appeared on some photographs, smiling and pulling faces at the camera; in others they posed with what looked like their relations; fathers, grandfathers and friends.

The album was in strict chronological order. The kids grew up with each passing page: they graduated from high school, then university, they even appeared with a couple of girls, maybe their first girlfriends. It also included pictures of their first diving trips: ships' decks, fabulous colored fish and huge turtles they stroked under water.

After that, the report on the young people's lives stopped dead, as if a watch had stopped once and for all.

They were only to appear again in another photograph, a much more recent picture. They were pictured clean-shaven and with short hair, but were now the spitting image of the fellows she and Adrian had met on the beach.

In the snapshot they wore tee-shirts with the slogan '*Eu pertenço a DEUS*[3]' and stood either side of a man dressed in a white tunic. He was an aging man, certainly more than sixty,

---

3. Translator's note. 'I belong to God' (in Portuguese).

257

and clasped a Bible in his hands. Behind them was a white altar presided over by a huge crucifixion figure.

All the following pictures were of that same man. He was addressing a vast crowd, hands held aloft. He was a priest, a mass preacher that kissed babies and touched sick people's foreheads.

The next section of the file was composed of photocopied press clippings.

THE EVANGELICAL CHURCH IN BRAZIL. CULT OR BUSINESS?
(Le Figaro)
Alain Lombard. São Paulo (Brazil), May 17, 2004.

Nobody is unmoved by the exponential growth in the number of followers of new evangelical churches. According to a study by the World Christian Database of ten different countries, Brazil has more evangelical followers than any country in the world.

The staggering rise in evangelical churches has taken place mainly in slum districts, where they have garnered support among the Brazilian people. The 'new' evangelicals are recruited from those lowest down on the social scale, especially in shanty towns, where the influence of Catholicism, seen as more intellectual and middle class, has lost its grip. Catholicism, in general, has lost interest in the disadvantaged, who feel more welcome among evangelical groups, where they get more support and attention to problems that the Catholic church has ignored. While Brazil may be the most populous Catholic country in the world, the number of evangelical followers grows every year; they now total around 24 million and some estimates predict they will be more than half of the population by 2045.

With a presence in more than forty countries, The Universal Church of the People of God is the biggest proof of this. Founded in 1977, along with the Assembly of God, it is the most influential church on the street and in Congress. Its founder, Edir Macedo, owns Rede Record, which is second only to Rede Globo as Brazil's largest TV network, with a 16% audience share. It controls 30 radio broadcasters, two newspapers and a magazine. Its evangelical network has 2,000 churches all over Brazil, 10,000 pastors, 4 million followers and is also present in more than forty countries. Some sources estimate its revenues at more than one billion dollars. The huge media presence of these institutions has always been clouded in controversy. In the past two decades they have survived several scandals and corruption charges, but their leaders have always been acquitted and the charges have either expired or been dropped.

A multi-million-dollar business.

Evangelical churches enjoy legal and tax breaks denied to other institutions. Their business is exempt from countless taxes that the average citizen has to pay. As well as the mass media, the churches' business lines extend to every type of product aimed at Christian consumers, from music and books to support services. Their followers are obliged to hand over one-third of their income.

These institutions' contentious financing has been the subject of controversy in recent weeks and a hot topic in public debate.

In this light, João Azevedo, founder of the new

God's Dawn church, which has more than one million followers, has stated:

'Our big family lives in faith, shares a common hope, and feeds from God and his Scripture. Glory is not to be found in heaven, but on earth. God cares for and protects whomsoever comes to him. He shares joy and hope among the faithful and their families, cures the sick and watches over our health. Our brothers know it, they feel it and it is a great joy to help and be part of his church.'

Worship or business. Therein lies the controversy. All that is certain is the unstoppable rise of the new church in the land of samba and carnival.

TRAGEDY IN EGYPT

(A Folha de São Paulo - Stop Press)

Felipe dos Santos. Dahab (Egypt), August 3, 2006

The most terrible tragedy has struck the family of João Azevedo, well-known founder of the God's Dawn church.

A diving trip involving his only son Flávio, who was on his honeymoon with his newly-wedded wife, Sara Rocha, as well as his friend Paul Schotten and his fiancée Marcela Leiva, has met with a fatal accident.

According to local authorities, yesterday at 17:35 local time the emergency services received a call in Dahab, a small coastal town in the southeast of the Sinai Peninsula.

The young holidaymakers were scuba diving in the renowned Blue Hole, a coral sinkhole which is linked to the open sea by an arch whose ceiling is 180 feet deep and which has become a Mecca for divers from all over the world.

Witnesses say the fatal accident occurred after Flávio and Paul successfully completed the first dive. Sara and Marcela went down into the chasm together and, for reasons still unknown, they never came back up to the surface.

Efforts are currently under way by rescue teams to search for the bodies.

The Azevedo family have declined to comment.

SEARCH EFFORTS OVER
(A Folha de São Paulo)
Felipe dos Santos. Dahab (Egypt), August 7, 2006

Still overcome by the terrible undersea accident met with by the young Brazilian women Sara Rocha and Marcela Leiva, rescue teams have called off search efforts. The Egyptian authorities, who had mobilized a substantial team of army divers along with an underwater vehicle driven by remote control, have announced that it is impossible to reach the body of Marcela, located at a depth of more than 460 feet in a rocky sinkhole.

As reported yesterday, the body of Sara Rocha, daughter-in-law of the famous evangelical priest João Azevedo, was found mid-afternoon at a depth of 360 feet and taken to the forensic medical center, where an autopsy was performed. The first indications are that the most probable cause of death was nitrogen narcosis, which caused the divers' impairment of judgment and loss of focus that led them to continue diving into the depths until they met their death, in the belief they were approaching the arch and a way out.

Including this fatal accident, more than one hundred divers have now died in the Blue Hole in recent years. The so-called 'divers' grave' still holds in its recesses more than forty bodies that have never been found.

DREADFUL FIRE IN THE TEMPLE OF LIGHT
(Jornal da Tarde)
Luca Moratti. São Paulo (Brazil), September 12, 2006.

Last night at 11:15 p.m., a massive blaze destroyed much of the Temple of Light, the God's Dawn evangelical church's main place of worship, located in São Caetano do Sul, in the São Paulo metropolitan area.

Two women died in the accident while doing cleaning work: A. L. S., aged 31, and C. M., 42.

The fire, whose causes have yet to be established, broke out at the main altar and reduced the famous crucifix to ashes, and then spread quickly to the roof and nave. A team of firefighters arrived on the scene a few minutes after the alarm was raised, but found it impossible to rescue the victims or avoid the building's almost total destruction due to the intensity of the blaze.

Nothing could be done for the victims, who choked to death there and then.

Some witnesses said they had seen two men loitering in the building's immediate vicinity minutes before the accident. The Church's spokesman, on the contrary, has said in a press statement that the fire was caused by a short-circuit and they will lodge no official complaint.

The police have already begun their investigation, which according to official sources, is on track, and may implicate members of the evangelical pastor's family.

This tragic event has brought more grief to what is already quite an annus horribilis for João Azevedo, the illustrious founder of the God's Dawn church, who lost his daughter-in-law in a diving accident last August in Egypt and who, according to sources familiar with the autopsy, was three weeks pregnant at the time.

Laura closed the file and felt sorry for those fellows. They were on the run. They had committed manslaughter, but she figured that settling accounts with the courts would only be part of their punishment. Their hearts would be forever marked by an irreparable loss.

She thought of Flávio's continuous wailing by night on the beach, which would cross the cave and flood her dreams. It is hard to understand a man's reactions when God turns his back on him, and reason itself is shattered to pieces.

Despite everything, deep down, she hoped that one day their souls would be at peace.

Laura called her step-sister on her cellphone, and she was unusually pleased to receive such an unexpected call. It had been a while since she had heard from her. She was still living in Saint-Jean-de-Luz. And she was fine. Laura surmised that Éduard had not touched her. Next she told her about her adventure and spared no details.

From that moment on, Laura had officially vanished off the face of the earth.

Érica swore never to reveal her secret. Ever.

Laura would call her from where she went next. And never, ever, would they lose touch.

CHAPTER XL

It was very dark inside the apartment. You could only make out a few shapes in the faint glimmer that seemed to come from the kitchen, and a few shafts of light that poked through the Venetian blind.

Denis lit his flashlight and crossed the little hallway.

The parlor had a dark brown parquet floor and the few pieces of furniture spread around the room —two white leather sofas and three designer bookcases— lent it a minimalist, almost oriental appearance. A huge plasma screen hung from the back wall, and on top of it a video conference camera jutted out. Rows of books were on the shelves —novels, art catalogs— and a few framed photos of Adrian and Helena. All of them showed the same smiling faces and entwined bodies, but against different backgrounds, whether they were beaches, ski resorts or yachts. The very picture of happiness.

He went down to the end of the passageway.

There was a large bedroom to his right. A huge double bed stood on the floor with a closet at the back, which held an endless, orderly row of suits and shirts of various colors and fabrics, several tie racks and a very long shoe rack.

Denis returned to the passageway and shone the light at the room opposite. It looked like the office. A wide glass desk stood in the middle of the room surrounded by book shelves and filing cabinets, advertising books, agency document files ordered by month and plaques for winning some prize or other.

Denis stopped to look at a large photograph, the size of a painting, hung on the wall. It showed three twenty-year-olds laughing and toasting with beers. He recognized a very young Adrian as one of them. Peter Caldwell was next to him.

A dull thud made him freeze. It came from the bedroom.

Denis crouched and sheltered behind the desk, like an animal stalked by imminent danger. Acting on instinct, he grabbed hold of the firm body of his faithful traveling companion, a 9 mm Heckler & Koch USP Expert. He could feel the pistol's rubber grips, the sweat on his hands, the forgotten sensation of being in the front line when dicing with death.

Denis slipped off the safety catch and slid his finger over the trigger.

He had to keep a cool head. *He* was the intruder here, and he was not on official business. Accidentally shooting an innocent party could put him behind bars for the rest of his days.

He waited a few minutes.

It was completely quiet and time ticked by slowly, at a lower-than-real pace.

One minute, two, three... Nothing.

He took a deep breath.

Anything could have caused the noise; it might even have come from outside or the apartment next door. The walls in the old apartments were wafer-thin, and would let through even the slightest sound.

He crawled a few inches, enough to be able to see through the door and check everything was in order. The most absolute silence reigned once more, and he decided to carry on with his search.

Inside the files and binders were invoices and Boreal Life papers; account statements, tax certificates and other official paperwork. Stacked on top of the desk were photographs of beaches and logo blanks, in what looked like a design for an advertising campaign. Denis rifled through the documents, file by file. He found nothing that was out of place on the work desk of an advertising executive.

He turned to look again at the photograph on the wall. Those college boys were brimming over with innocence and joy. Their carefree faces showed that their concerns were split between making it to graduation and the best place to drink the next beer. Now one of them was dead and the other suspected of murder. The third individual could be Atkins, but he was not sure. He lifted the picture off the wall to examine it close up.

A dark shadow appeared before his eyes.

It was a black cavity hollowed out of the wall, a perfect square, something a safe could fit in to, which he had uncovered by removing the photograph.

A kind of black briefcase was inside it, wrapped in a red velvet cover. He put in on the desk and deftly untied the drawstring, and withdrew a portfolio of white files. On the cover, stenciled in black ink, appeared the symbol of the goddess *Iustitia*: a woman dressed in a tunic, blindfolded, holding a balance in one hand and a sword in the other. Underneath it were two gilt engraved initials, a large-sized 'I' and 'V'.

He waited for a few seconds before opening it up, as if for a moment he did not want to know what was hidden in there. The tension had made sweat run down his back.

Finally he opened the file.

His face was twisted in surprise.

Filed away inside it were single-sheet dossiers. There were at least sixty dossiers, maybe a hundred. Each dossier was headed by a six-digit code number, next to a date. The date on the first sheet was 14 October, 1966: the dates on the following sheets were in ascending chronological order, although there was no concrete pattern in the spaces between one date and another.

Everything entered below the heading was totally unintelligible.

The text was in code, broken down into blocks of characters of equal length, in which one letter followed another, without any apparent rhyme or reason. He sighed. The Interpol team could crack the algorithm and produce the raw text in a week, but he would have to take away several sheets as a sample and, worse still, as he was no longer on the case, he could not file an official request to have that done.

It seemed evident that the dossiers described events that had taken place on different dates. But what were the encoded texts all about? He mulled things over for a few seconds, until a light bulb switched on inside his head. March 5, 2009. The date Lavinia was killed! He went over the dossiers, flipping quickly from one to the next. If he had guessed right, the date of the bombing had to be there.

Just then a handwritten sheet slide between the pages and fell into his lap.

It was a letter.

Bro,
There's not much time left. I don't feel bad about this, and I really want you to know that. Every day spent in this world is agony for me. There is no cure or treatment for the grief I get up with every morning, and I will find no balance here. There is no other way out for me and I know you will all agree. I deserve it. Justice will be done in a few days' time and I shall be free at last. I hope God will grant me the chance to redeem my guilt in the afterlife, and to beg forgiveness and clemency from my innocent victims.
Take good care of yourself, buddy.
Iustitia & Veritas
Peter Caldwell:

He could not hold back his astonishment.

It was a farewell letter that Peter Caldwell wrote his friend Seaten before taking his life.

Iustitia & Veritas. 'I&V'. The letters stenciled on the cover.

'Redeem my guilt,' 'I know you will all agree'...

His suicide made sense, to him at least.

And to his colleagues, whoever they might have been.

The late William Atkins' mother had identified the Argentine police sketch as Caldwell. His face was a perfect match for the leading suspect in the yacht bombing that killed Lavinia and family.

The words spoken by Contini, the Argentine Interpol office, suddenly rattled around inside his head: 'His family rarely went with him,' 'at first he planned to sail alone,' 'He changed his mind at the last minute.'

Denis looked up again at Caldwell's face on the huge photograph.

'You went over the top, my friend, and took out an eight-year-old girl and her mother.'

'You turned into one of them.'

He recalled the suicide note. 'Let justice be done, though the world perish.'

'And you did it, you little son of a bitch.'

The floor creaked again behind him. This time just six feet away.

In an endless split-second he spun round and aimed his weapon, but right then he felt a heavy blow to the head.

A dazzling light blinded his eyes and the curtain slowly fell on his consciousness, all the way to the floor.

Everything went dark.

CHAPTER XLI

Denis called out for his mother. Time and again. He was drenched in sweat and cried because she never came. He was scared and hugged his pillow. He swallowed the tears that were welling up in his throat and choking him. He looked at the empty bed beside him. Anxiety gripped his chest, like a spider weaving a dark thread around his soul. Now and again his mother appeared in the doorway. She was dressed in black and watched him wide-eyed. But she said nothing to him. She merely watched. Then she went away. Denis shrieked in anger. He begged her not to leave him again.

Sweat flooded his eyes. He felt the sheets chafing his dry lips and a throbbing headache, from his forehead to the nape of his neck, which crushed his skull like a hydraulic press. He tried to move, but his limbs did not respond to his brain's orders. At last he managed to prise open his eyelids, which were as heavy as lead.

He could not fathom where he was.

The blood ran thickly through his veins, as if some drug had adulterated it. Finally, he forced his head around and could see his bedside table. His pistol and documents were on top of it. He felt immediate relief to see he was in his apartment. He looked around. The blinds were down. He could not remember lowering them. That was not what he usually did. The only light in the place came from the living room. Neither could he remember how he got there, but he hadn't the energy to cast his mind back. As the minutes went by his limbs woke up, but the awful headache would not let up. The sheets were damp and had a strong smell to them. He had wet the bed. He rested his head on the pillow and slowly chewed over his stunned state.

Gradually, more and more clearly, he began to have flashbacks of the last few hours: the lady in the doorway, Seaten's apartment, the folder. But what had gone on? Why was he now back in his apartment? He could feel a big bruise on his head that hurt like hell.

Somebody had slugged him good and hard. He could remember nothing else.

Denis sat on the edge of the bed and tried to stand up. He was weak at the knees, but managed to get up on his third attempt. He walked through the door, following the weird light that spilled in from the living room. He rubbed his eyes. He must have been seeing things. For a moment he wondered if he were still in dreamland.

'Good God, what's going on here?'

Denis went over to the living room table.

The windows were shut and the blinds down.

The whole room was in darkness, apart from the middle, which was bathed in a flickering, ghostly light, a hazy brightness that spread throughout the parlor. A row of candles sat on the table, of differing height and width, arranged in a circle. It looked like Candlemas, to bless the Virgin, or an altar to Satan himself. The flames shimmered in a draft that wafted in from the doorway and shone concentric circles of light on the ceiling.

Three framed photographs stood next to each other in the middle of the wax and fire altarpiece, arrayed like a religious triptych. The pictures showed three lifeless faces, of men in their late middle age. Three corpses with grotesque, open-mouthed grimaces, wayward eyes and pallid skin.

At the bottom of each was an inscription engraved in silver:

Mihai Barbu, 1952-2010 — Galați (Romania)
Bogdan Cristocea, 1952-2010 — Craiova (Romania)
Marius Cristocea, 1954-2010 — Craiova (Romania)
In Memoriam
I&V.

His heart rate soared a thousandfold and he had to gulp down air to keep his body supplied with oxygen. Tears flooded his eyes like those of a child. He looked at those faces again. One of them still had a scar on his forehead. The same one that haunted him in his dreams. He had had his throat slit. When he looked at one of the other photographs, he remembered the shortest man's hooked nose. His eyes were out on stalks. He had a noose tightened around his neck while his tongue stuck out of his mouth, as if it were trying to escape from his swollen body.

Denis's legs buckled under him and he fell to his knees. Nervously he looked around him, gripped by anxiety, but saw there was nobody else in the apartment. He began to retch, and crawled to the bathroom, like a wounded animal, until he could not go on and lay sprawled on the floor.

Hours later, the phone rang insistently. Time and again. He dragged himself along the floor then picked up the phone.

"Denis, it's me," Sylvie said on the other end of the line. Denis gave no answer.

"What's the matter with you? Are you OK?"

"Yes, I'm, I'm OK," he spluttered in response. "Tell me, Sylvie, what time is it?"

"It's twelve noon. Denis, I'm worried about you. Have you been drinking?"

"When's Seaten's mass?"

271

"Today, at 6 p.m., in the Père-Lachaise chapel."

"I must hang up now, Sylvie. Take it easy. Everything'll be just fine."

CHAPTER XLII

Père-Lachaise cemetery is on a hill on the east side of Paris, in the 20th *arrondissement*, and is built on an old plot of land that was formerly covered in vineyards. It covers 106 acres of landscaped terrain, whose chestnut and willow groves are criss-crossed with graves and vaults, and all kinds of motley epitaphs underneath the unruly ivy. It opened in 1804, when it welcomed its first guest, the body of a five-year-old girl. Today, more than a million bodies lie buried in its ninety-seven divisions, and more than seventy thousand funeral monuments have been installed, making it an unmissable sight on the tourist trail. Visitors walk around its nooks and crannies, and take photographs of each other next to the graves of famous painters, poets or musicians, like in a fun fair, spell-bound by the many immortal souls they imagine they are close to.

Despite its mystic leanings, what was originally known as the Eastern Cemetery still has a brisk everyday routine, although funerals are confined to those who die in Paris or were residents, and it has a long waiting list. Masses are held one after the other while its crematory oven works full-blast until it closes in the early evening, and whose chimney spills out a plume of black smoke that, on windy days, spreads northward along the Avenue Gambetta.

Denis Martel walked down the Avenue Feuillant toward the chapel, watching as he went the endless trail of tourists and passers-by that shuffled in groups toward the way out, as it was now almost closing time.

He knew every inch of that graveyard like the back of his hand. During his years on the Paris police force, the pathways and alleys crossing the place in between graves and niches became the ideal habitat for all sorts of petty crime, from theft to desecration and others listed as public order offenses, such as sexual practices on graves or the frequent casual encounters between gays behind the columbarium, which had become a popular venue for cruising.

Denis stopped to take breath. He was still groggy from the drug's aftereffects and had not so much as begun to digest the macabre find in his apartment. He tried by all means to delete it from his short-term memory. Denis was convinced that Adrian Seaten was still alive, and if so, that he would show up at his own funeral mass. He would not miss it. Not him. Denis had studied similar profiles. They liked to gloat at their own doings, they sublimated the overdose of cold-bloodedness in their genes, which was beyond the reach of other mortals.

He looked ahead. The chapel was just a few feet away.

He had come early, the service would start in twenty minutes. He decided to stand among the trees, so he could see properly and without being seen.

There was nobody left around him; well nobody alive, anyway. The cemetery was completely empty and only the sound of the flock's responses and the rustling breeze broke the silence of that sunny September evening.

The service would take place in the garden outside, next to the chapel entrance. Several rows of benches had been set up with an altar in back, next to which was a microphone on a stand. Brun-Donzel's string-pulling and his close friendship with Gaillard, the parish priest at Our Lady of Perpetual Help, to whose congregation the chapel was attached, had paved the way to an open-air service held after hours. Helena had been distraught for weeks and living on tranquilizers, so the inside of a gloomy, early nineteenth-century chapel was not the best place for a daughter to pray in, in such a fragile state.

Even in death there are class distinctions, Denis thought. He lit a cigarette and coughed repeatedly.

The guests came along in a constant trickle, dressed in their finery. Strict mourning was not called for —because strictly speaking it was not a funeral— so the cemetery's alleyways were full of Armani suits, Versace dresses and hair specially done for the occasion. Most of the select gathering had, with some humane criteria, avoided bright or unseemly cheerful colors, but the stench of perfume and lively chatter of those present made the occasion look more like a summer cocktail party than a mass for a departed soul.

The inflow of personages on their way was still in crescendo. The *crème de la crème* of Paris. Nobody had wanted to miss the event: bankers, politicians, noteworthy architects. Neither had the agency employees failed to show up, nor Adrian's wealthy friends, who discussed yachts and beams and could never have imagined how much contempt their departed friend held them in.

All the benches were full within minutes. Helena's family and friends left not an inch to spare, so the rest of the guests had to mill around the garden and stand beside the improvised altar.

Father Gaillard kissed the altar and welcomed those present. Before he began the service, he spoke a few words to explain the reason for the gathering. "Adrian, your friend, your companion, is with us here, in the eyes of God." In a solemn voice he expatiated on earthly living, immortality, the need to maintain hope, "firmly and blindly, like the faith of Jesus Christ when he gave his life for us all."

Next he made the sign of the cross and proceeded to begin the penitential act.

"I confess to Almighty God, and to you, brethren, that I have sinned exceedingly in thought, word and deed. Through my fault, through my most grievous fault," he exclaimed, beating his breast three times.

Denis stood up and took a few steps toward the crowd gathered around the altar. The shrine was headed by a black marble carving of Christ on the cross. Above his head the sky was endlessly blue. In back a couple of cypress trees watched over the entrance, like soldiers on everlasting guard duty, who bore witness to decades of tears.

"May the Almighty and Merciful Lord grant us remission of our sins and lead us to eternal life."

The priest's deep voice boomed off the wall and the breeze swept it across the surrounding hills, that were still thronged by gardeners and cleaning staff on the late shift. The metallic sound frightened away the cats that usually came out of their lairs at that time of day, to scavenge around the graves.

The crowd hearing the service had its back to Denis. Only Christ on the cross seemed to stare him in the eye.

"Save us, Savior of the world, for by your Cross and Resurrection you open the way to heaven. Lord, have mercy on us."

Denis felt a pang in his stomach. The drug was still playing hell with his bloodstream. For a moment he lost his bearings and, suddenly feeling faint, he doubled over and was sick at the bottom of a tree.

He could remember every detail of his father's and brother's funerals, as if in times of grief the recording quality of his hard disk was enhanced in order to play everything back in high fidelity. His mother's burial was the last to be held, but he only had a faint recollection of it. It only came back to him as a happy day. The woman who gave him life found eternal peace at last. She had drowned in a sea of pain during the last years of her life and it all ended that morning, forever.

"Jesus, fill our hearts with your grace. Lord, have mercy on us."

The day his brother was cremated was, nonetheless, indelibly branded on his memory, as if it were only yesterday. It came back to him every night to gatecrash his dreams. He relived that infinite rage. His parents' grief-stricken faces. His blind hatred for the killers, for God and his very existence.

"You, Jesus, who give us cause to live and die in hope. Lord, have mercy on us."

How many times had he wished that if only he had departed, if only he had been remembered at the funeral, and had vanished forever from this world. If only, then maybe things would have been easier all round.

Jesus kept staring him in the eye.

He suddenly felt overwhelmed by the odd feeling that everybody gathered there was staring at him, too. They had their backs to him, but were all looking at him. Coburn too, and Seaten, and all the senators, businessmen and Axis Ventures donors. That obscure society that controlled life and the sign of the times. How far did their tentacles reach? God himself would have a seat on the board. Or the devil. They could have done away with him in Seaten's apartment. Why didn't they? He alone was prying into their inner secrets. They all knew it. And they were watching his every step. Old Coburn was surely in on it, too. They had been riding him like a horse. Instead of executing him, they had given him the offering he had longed for all these years. Decades of searching in vain and then, in just days, they gave him his brother's killers' heads on a plate in his own apartment.

We're everywhere.

Don't you ever forget it.

"Oh Lord, ever merciful and ready to forgive. Hear the prayers we raise for Your son Adrian, whose faith is known to You alone. Welcome him to Your kingdom that he may find eternal joy with You. For Christ, our Lord, Amen."

The first dossier, the first case, was dated October 1966. It was the first of almost one hundred. More than forty years ago. How much blood had been shed? Why all that damned impunity? In whose name? Miletić and Lavinia were hardly innocent. Neither were the bastards who rubbed out Alain in broad daylight. But who had the authority to judge them? Whoever was behind all this did not act alone, or in passing. They had insinuated themselves into every level of power. They had access to every scrap of information. They controlled the lives of mortals and decided on their very mortality.

There was no escape.

"From the Book of Isaiah: And in this mountain shall the Lord of hosts make unto all people a feast of fat things. And He will destroy in this mountain the face of the covering cast over all people, and the veil that is spread over all nations He will swallow up death in victory; and the Lord God will wipe away tears from off all faces; and the rebuke of his people shall He take away from off all the earth: for the Lord hath spoken."

Denis felt very faint again and almost passed out. He slowly stood up straight again.

The gruesome pictures of the Romanians came back to him. All his life he had enforced the law of men and now, at last, his soul felt liberated and cleansed now that those three fellows had been executed.

There was no guilt. Neither was there remorse. Merely peace.

He looked into the marble eyes of the man on the cross. 'Who are you? What kind of impostor are you?'

The sun was setting slowly in the Parisian sky and shadows began to cover the cemetery hill.

The priest began his sermon on the resurrection and the fleeting life on earth. The congregation listened to his words in silence as they devoted their thoughts to their daily business:

money, relations and appearances.

He did not pay too much attention the first time that fellow turned to look at him.

Denis was merely on the fringes of the group. Anybody could have wondered what that odd character was doing there by the trees, the balding one with a pale face and in a cheap suit.

The second time the man watched him, he had all of Denis' attention.

It was a tall, slim, broad-shouldered young man, dressed in a smart, well-cut navy blue suit that fitted him perfectly. His hair was short, almost spiked, a dazzling platinum blond color, and he hid his glance behind a pair of dark sunglasses. He stood a few feet away from the group surrounding the altar.

After a few seconds the man turned around, stared at then walked toward him, in sure-footed strides.

Denis stood still. He looked around. The man was doubtless heading his way. Shivers ran up and down him.

That man's face looked familiar to him right away. The grin on his face betrayed unnerving self-confidence.

Denis prodded his jacket to feel his old friend's grip. He placed his index finger on the trigger and aimed at his target from inside his suit pocket.

The blond man was now standing next to him. At last they met face to face.

Denis gripped his weapon inside the suit, and showed his expected guest the barrel.

The man took off his sunglasses. His face exuded harmony and he was enveloped in calm composure. His heart rate could not have been higher than that of an iceberg.

"Hello Denis, great to meet you," he said at last, in a calm, collected voice, as he reached out to shake his hand.

Denis did not return his greeting.

He merely stared at him, the same way one looks at a ghost just back from the underworld. He could not move a muscle.

He was overwhelmed by the odd feeling that he had worn himself out by following his trail, and now just wanted him to get out of his sight forever.

"Drop it," he added. "You're very lucky. You have a lovely daughter to take care of."

Denis spoke not a word. He did not blink. As if he did not believe this was really happening.

"The world is far from perfect, although you already know that. Deep down, you and I are the same, if you think about it, and I don't mean that we both love classical music," the platinum-blond young man finished off before vanishing from sight and walking off slowly along the pathway behind him.

A blast of cold air struck the whole hillside and whirled around the first dry leaves that heralded the imminent arrival of fall.

The black marble man on the cross was no longer looking him in the eye. Now he was gazing skywards.

"I believe in the Holy Spirit, the holy Catholic Church, the communion of the saints, the forgiveness of sins, the resurrection of the body, and the life everlasting. Amen."

CHAPTER XLIII

Cambridge, Massachusetts
June 4, 1999

He looked at his watch, nervously.
Graduation deserved a wild party. The boys would surely have kicked off by now and anything other than being with them was a real waste of time, Anything other than meeting up with his buddies.

He leaned out of the window.

The thin, stubborn, unseasonal summer rain fell on the maple trees, while soaking the garden outside, where a huge black Cadillac was parked. He figured he had seen hearses looking less funeral than that land yacht there.

He looked at his reflection on the wet glass. His skin burned by the first of the summer sun. Bags under his eyes after the sleepless nights. Doubtless it had been an awesome weekend on Cape Cod. He glanced around him. A shaft of pale, ashen light spilling through the huge window lit up the corners of the ancient and faint parlor. Time had stood still between those four walls.

The musty decor, based on old wooden furniture with leather upholstery, could have been that of a Victorian tea room some decades ago. He got something of a kick out of meeting up in that old mansion house on Brattle Street, instead of a faculty building on campus.

Just then, the sound of footsteps on creaking floorboards told him his host was turning up at the appointed time.

"Good morning, Adrian. I trust I haven't kept you waiting long."

Adrian stared at the old professor's peculiar fringe.

"Good morning, Mr. Rosewood. You haven't kept me waiting, you're on time, as ever. How are you?"

"Well, Adrian, well," he answered in a measured tone of voice. "The semester is over and God welcomes us with rain, which is bad news for my rheumatism. But please come with me."

Adrian followed the professor down the corridor. The shelves covered in old books and a strong smell of damp lent that passageway a somewhat solemn —almost sacred— air, very much in keeping with Harvard. It was incredible that four years had gone by since he had started school there. Time had flown by. Now it was drawing to a close.

"It's a lovely mansion. I didn't know it, I wasn't aware it belonged to the campus."

"We'll soon have time to satisfy your curiosity, Adrian." At last, they entered a hall.

The wall was covered from end to end with old portraits, whose canvases showed elegantly dressed gentlemen from the early twentieth century, depicted in pomp and circumstance, as if perhaps they were masters of the universe. In back, a big marble fireplace lay idle after a hectic winter, and a bronze statue rested on the mantelpiece. The figure of a woman, blindfolded and balance in hand; the same figure that appeared in courtrooms and law books: the goddess of justice.

Rosewood's croaking voice interrupted his thoughts.

"Please take a seat," he beckoned, as he pointed to one of the armchairs surrounding what looked like a conference table.

"You might well be surprised to hear that I cannot stand graduations," the professor added in his warm tone of voice. "Indeed I cannot, Adrian, just as I cannot stand the beginning of the semester. The patient welcoming of impertinent squirts who, when they become respectable people, walk out of your life. The life cycle is cruel. It always is. The effort to train minds to fashion rational thought, minds that furnish creativity and that, when I begin to enjoy them, fly away. A fact of life. But maybe I come across to you as selfish."

"No sir, I can appreciate it," he answered after a pause. "Although it must also be comforting."

"Comforting. Hmmm, I don't about that. Comforting is the New England fall rain, the soft touch of a woman's skin, the ability to discover youthful years. But enough of that. I haven't asked you here to psychoanalyze this old professor, my dear Adrian."

The young man cracked a wry smile and looked admiringly at his illustrious companion.

Curiosity had taken hold of him from the second Rosewood had summoned him, almost a week before.

The old man in front of him was a veritable institution, a kind of legend among Harvard alumni. He was deemed an eminent authority on Political Science, a world expert on modern political theory, which he used to explain history and the spirit of the times, what he dubbed, 'the evolution of world character'.

Craig Rosewood's legend had been built on rumors and stories doing the rounds of the campus, which centered on his influential role with the White House's last four occupants. They held that within his small, decrepit and scrawny body, were hidden unrepeatable state secrets, which were enough to explain the world political order over the past twenty-five years. He had published dozens of articles, essays and books across five continents and, although his liveliness had waned over the years, his occasional lectures drew massive crowds in which what he hinted at was valued more than his learned talk.

Adrian had bumped into the old man more than the other students. Rosewood had been his father's faculty colleague until the terrible illness struck and, despite the age gap, they became close friends from the start. From afar and in Professor Seaten's absence, he had followed young Adrian's academic progress, without interfering at all, just as his father would have wished.

"I have to say I shall miss you. You have been a bold and distinguished student," he admitted. "You have been granted that special gift that allows us to see reality through a different prism, to doubt what is written by others, to set up your own criteria. Always far from the long gray line. I guess you know what I'm talking about."

Adrian nodded slowly, and somewhat timidly. He mistrusted the compliment; he had always been like that.

"I am old now. My days are more and more fleeting, and my body is wearing out. Time waits for no man. Nature is wise, it controls the opaque mechanisms that keep life in balance. Life and death. Everything reaches its proper end at the right time. Natural balance is the watchdog that guards and ensures the progress of life and the species. It forces us to hand down knowledge to future generations."

The old professor turned his tired eyes toward Adrian. Rosewood's speech, like his lectures, was measured and didactic. His words moved with feather-like smoothness.

"It is the mission of good men, the elect, to maintain the balance," he added. Without it we find ourselves headed for destruction and chaos. Only man in his pure, earthly state can struggle to attain it. Weak men seek balance in supernatural belief, which they call religion. They become mere supplicants of the so-called gods, they seek answers from them, solutions to their conflicts, they cry over their fears, unaware that the survival mechanism of the species resides in themselves."

Rosewood tilted his head and stared at one of the portraits on the wall. Adrian looked at the picture. The man in oils was the man himself, the old professor, a few decades back.

"Life is not perfect, Adrian. Existence brings about conflicts, conflicts lead to decisions, decisions engender actions, and actions have consequences. And those consequences must only converge in the balance of existence itself. The vain hope in the restorative faith of contrived gods, or corrupt laws drawn up by man, grinds down, ounce by ounce, that which we know as human nature; it leaves us in a weak position, in a risky position. Therefore we, the elect, must act, and maintain order."

'The elect.'

Adrian stayed quiet for a few seconds.

He knew the old man and it was by no means usual for him to devote his time to enlightening a recent graduate about the balance of the universe or dead children, even if he was the son of his old friend, his former colleague that was confined to a hospital with his memory all dried out.

"And what can we do to maintain order, professor? Man is already in action. We choose those that govern us, we enact our laws, we set up our courts."

"The justice of men will never be perfect. An axiom that is self-explanatory when we share the imperfection of human beings, don't you think, Adrian?"

"It is imperfect, but necessary."

"So it is, necessary but insufficient, as we know it. Courts are corrupt and biased; at best, they are not infallible. The only true law is the law of nature, but it is slow, extremely slow, and waiting for its judgment entails non-negotiable risks."

"I don't get it... What risks do you mean?"

"Imbalance, impunity; ultimately, the destruction of society."

Rosewood struggled to his feet from his chair and took a book from one of the shelves.

"I want you to read this. Maybe it will help you to find the answers."

Before he handed it over, the old man made as if to hold it back.

"You should know that we wish to share it with you as the ultimate test of trust. Eternal and unconditional trust. You are our chosen one. The secrets hidden in these pages are to be protected with your very blood, and the slightest leak will cost you your life. You must know that before you go any further."

'We wish to share it with you.' 'You are our chosen one.' Who the hell were they? 'Will cost you your life.'

Adrian was taken aback by his words, as on those occasions when you are not aware whether all around you is part of a farce in which you are an unwilling player. For a moment there he thought the old professor's age had fried his brain cells. Maybe it was the effect of the weekend's Afghan hashish, which was rushing back to his head. What the heck, he thought, at least it was amusing.

"Understood, Mr. Rosewood. You can trust me," he replied, as he took the book in both hands.

The copy was leather-bound and the cover had a gilt-tooled Latin inscription on it: 'Aurea Mediocritas: *Iustitia Universalis.*'

It was a relatively recent edition, dated 1998.

A kind of memorandum could be read in the first few pages. It analyzed the state of civilization, all the way up to God himself. It explained what had caused the conflicts of recent decades and the patent risk of destroying the human species as we know it. There followed a call to action by the scientific community: 'The need to take a step forward.' The involvement of thinkers and academics in 'times to come and the future of new generations.' It firmly berated the attitude of governments and courts of justice that were, 'more focused on vested interests and wealth' than on maintaining society and nature in permanent and sustainable balance.

A veritable harangue against the system.

The text that followed consisted of articles, in which appeared the wording of a constitution or the clauses in a contract. It was underwritten by six signatures, one of them underneath the title of 'The Rector.' The constitution dated back to 1965.

"They're the statutes of a society," Adrian deduced.

"Just so, our society. Our work."

The articles set out, one after the other, the system of governance, and members' rights and responsibilities: 'The Brethren.' They broached the willingness of the signatories: 'With total freedom of choice and wholly without coercion,' the obligation to keep their activities most secret, 'with our very lives as endorsement and warranty,' and they proclaimed universal justice and fair balance as the sole aim of its existence. The foundational charter's ultimate end was the only goal, to which all ends and means were contingent.

The list of patrons and sponsors took up several pages. Adrian took a deep breath.

The names of leading politicians, economists and even a few Nobel Prize-winners were interspersed with exalted foundations, some of them government-backed. The presence of businesses on that list was hardly conspicuous by its absence: it featured more than twenty multinational corporations drawn from the Dow Jones Industrial Average. Donors, actors, journalists. They had all done their bit for the cause.

That weird society had more support and donations than the Vatican itself.

'The activities log.' Adrian began to feel weak at the knees.

The dossiers on events were arranged in chronological order. Each one detailed somebody's biography, headed with a photograph taken while living. There followed a technical report giving details of violent crimes and offenses against humanity attributed to them. Finally sentence was passed.

A death sentence signed by all the Brethren.

He leafed through the dossiers. His heart beat faster and faster.

Shocking pictures were displayed of those executed. Some showed freakish grimaces, they appeared to have been strangled or shot in the head. Others that had been blown up showed only bloody limbs and body parts strewn on the ground.

He felt a terrible urge to be sick.

Rosewood had remained unmoved, without changing his expression one bit, while he watched Adrian's reaction. Doubtless it was as expected. It had happened before.

The roll of those executed included known war criminals, Nazi officers whose whereabouts were unknown, mafia bosses whose deaths were never solved. The accounts showed whether the society had carried out the sentence using its own means or had indeed sponsored or provided logistical support to the executioner.

As time went by, page by page, the faces became more and more familiar. The coverage extended to more and more countries and the targets were more noteworthy.

Adrian looked in horror at the photographs of some president or other torn to shreds, or of a well-known Italian politician whose bloody corpse was dumped in a car trunk.

That was enough.

He placed the book on top of the table.

"This is criminal," he said at last, in a choked voice that struggled to issue from his throat. "You're murderers."

"You are mistaken, Adrian. Those men were condemned for crimes against humanity, and for that they have been executed."

"Executed? What court has tried and sentenced them to death?"

"They avoided the courts of men. I told you they are not perfect. We take on that task, in the name of God. Civilization cannot allow crimes to go unpunished or impunity to prevail. We would put the natural order at risk and the credibility of the system itself. Let alone for such criminals."

"But by what authority? You're the same as the supposed monsters that you liquidate."

"Of course not! Decisions are taken jointly or unanimously. We have available every piece of information that may be analyzed from one end of the planet to another. Our network of participants and sponsors stretches to every organization, and all walks of life throughout the whole wide world. From countries' police forces to the United Nations. From Interpol to Mossad. The most brilliant thinkers and humanists sit on our board. There can be no mistakes, Adrian, believe me. It is not possible for there to be any."

"Just like that? Without a trace? Nobody investigates anything? This is madness."

"We do our duty and no, once done, we leave no trace. None of our actions has been legally uncovered. Moreover, they have always been 'dropped'. We have made sure that innocent people blamed for our actions are released. Our machinery is swift and effective. We don't control the system. We are the system. We make up security forces and governments. We do and undo at our discretion."

"*Lex talionis.* 'An eye for an eye.' Very academic concepts in the end, aren't they, Mr. Rosewood?"

"I understand your reaction perfectly, Adrian. It is not easy, I know that very well. We do not advocate *lex talionis*, and neither is everything so simple, although I must admit that it was the most important advance in the history of the realm of law. It was applied in the Hammurabi code and later on in the Law of Moses. For the first time they established proportionality between crime and punishment, a limit to the response, a criterion. It is the basis for our laws."

Adrian listened carefully to the professor's explanations. His disbelief had made way for a devastating disquiet.

"We believe in retributive justice," the old man added.

"History has taught us that the established order, the natural balance, is only feasible when transgressions have consequences, when crimes are punished, and much more importantly than all that, when that punishment, that consequence, is public and manifest, known and seen to be done by all humanity. Only thus are the mechanisms embraced that guarantee control of evil and the supremacy of good. Nothing new there. It has been that way since the dawn of civilization. From classical mythology to Plato, from Plato to Kant, from Kant to the present day. Punishment is an end in itself, the key to balance. We deride the inimical theories that defend restorative justice, which pursue rehabilitation and redress, instill everlasting hatred in the victims and undermine the foundations or order. The relativism that destroys our society. That is the only plague."

"Allow me to ask you a question. Why are you telling me all this? What on earth have you seen in me, if I may ask? How do you know that as soon as I leave I won't go to the nearest police precinct I find?" the young student asked, more and more beside himself.

"First of all, calm down, Adrian. You have nothing to worry about. Take a deep breath, please."

The professor waited a few seconds for his young guest to get a hold of himself.

"I won't answer your last question. That is needless. I think that in the course of our talk you will have clearly seen what would happen in such a case. Don't take it as a threat. Were you to do so, they would surely think you were crazy and, if they didn't, within the hour instructions from above would be handed down to extinguish any spark you may light. And not for the first time. Some have paid with their lives. We have eyes everywhere. We cannot allow any leaks, as I'm sure you will understand."

Adrian shuddered.

"Nonetheless, I can answer your first two questions," he added. "There are two reasons for that. Two essential, weighty reasons."

"I'm listening," Adrian interjected, in a fractious tone of voice.

"As I told you earlier, you're different. You have your own criteria, you are not swayed by preconceived notions or conventional attitudes. You home in on what is essential, rather than tangential. You are brave and daring, and..."

"And you can tell all of that from a few lectures?"

"Not particularly. We have been keeping a special eye on you. We cannot allow ourselves to make mistakes."

Adrian was struck dumb.

"There's another reason you should be aware of. Our rector, our guide, our founding father, is my friend Roger Seaten, your father."

Adrian's blood ran cold.

"That's impossible."

The boy gave his teacher a penetrating glance, in disbelief. But Rosewood remained silent.

"That cannot be, it's not true. You're lying!" he screamed.

"His withered mind is now void of memory, but before that he left you his legacy, you can check for yourself in the deeds. His sole conviction was to leave the world a better place."

A tear rolled down Adrian's cheek. Everything around him vanished, while the image of his father stuck in a wheelchair with his faraway look hit him like a hammer to the head. Dozens of childhood scenes ran through his mind. He felt his father's hands ruffling his hair again when he was a toddler, and stood barely three feet tall. Again he basked in the warmth of his father's words, which always managed to allay the demons that stalked him by night. But his tears were short-lived. A moment later his spring-loaded eyes dried his tears away. His face was composed again, as if time had gone back a few minutes. He took a deep breath and gave the professor an idle, almost animal look.

"You must carry on his work, Adrian."

The young man remained quiet.

"We need new blood. You're the chosen one. You will be able to call on people you trust that, as you will appreciate, we shall need to assess beforehand."

It had stopped raining when he left the mansion and drove silently to the Cave.

Jeff, Will and Peter were waiting for him, seated around the table.

'Bizarre Love Triangle' began to pour out of the lounge's powerful loudspeakers. The party would get under way soon in The Ocean House.

CHAPTER XLIV

Capri (Italy),
December 2010.

Laura lovingly mixed the colors on her palette. First some yellow, then a dash of red. She took a few minutes to get the right mix to match the hue of the wonderful sunset. They had a picture-postcard view of the Tyrrhenian Sea from their balcony. The hanging houses ran downhill like a natural amphitheater, built on terraces with limestone facades, where they boldly intruded between the rock and the Mediterranean bushes. Behind them, a few dozen paces further down, fishing boats were moored by the quay, unmolested by tourists that no longer thronged the ferries from Naples now that winter had come.

Adrian walked up the stone stairway that led to the spectacular swimming pool that was built into a rocky outcrop. He had said a prayer for his friend Atkins. William had had a good heart, but he was weak and cowardly, and was putting the whole organization at risk. He remembered the last time he had seen him alive. He was completely drunk. That afternoon, after the Higgins's party. The same one when he had fixed Atkins' car's brakes and his life ended when he crashed into a tree. He looked out to sea. His memories went back for a moment to their halcyon days on campus. He smiled to recall Jeff's face. A fellow with a strong personality. For some strange reason, the organization had dismissed the idea of taking him on. They barely stayed in touch. He hadn't heard from him again, although something told him his old friend was destined for greater things. When he reached the terrace he hugged his lover from behind. He gently brushed his hands over her belly, which was bigger and rounder every day.

"How are my two girls doing?"

"What makes you so sure this one'll be a girl?"

"Not a girl, a princess," he replied, as he kissed her neck.

"There's a parcel for you, Mr. Cooley. A messenger brought it this afternoon."

"I know. I was expecting it."

"Do you have to go away again?"

"Yes, but it'll be the last time, I promise. I'll be back in two days and then there'll be no more trips."

He crossed the living room in their vast apartment.

The white leather sofas reflected the fantastic light and spread it throughout the place.

He went downstairs to the first floor for a bit of privacy and carefully opened the FedEx box. He checked that everything was in order: tickets, hotel reservation and false passport. The machinery was still running like clockwork. He smiled.

The flight would take Mr. Priemer to San Sebastián airport. A chauffeur would pick him up on arrival and take him across the French border to his final destination, his unfinished business.

'Saint-Jean-de-Luz'.

Kemal Osmanović, his faithful comrade-in-arms, would be waiting for him, having just gotten in from Mostar. A man with convictions. He had always fully trusted him. He was elegant and discreet, cold and calculating. Except when seized by hatred. Then his cruelty knew no bounds. 'Like everybody,' he thought.

He looked in the mirror in the hallway. Then he cracked a half-smile,

"Adrian, come here, quickly. Your princess is kicking."

CHAPTER XLV

Off the Cambodian coast,
December 2010.

Paul went back to the hut. The palm-thatched roof was thick and hardly let in any rain. 'Good job,' he said to himself. He was worn out after a day's diving, so he ate a bit of fruit and lay down on his camp bed.

It was almost supernatural the way the deluge had poured down so much, because the rainy season had been over for two months now.

The water battering the roof was deafening. Unable to sleep, he got up and went outside the hut. It was now in the small hours and the whole coast was smothered in darkness. At last he saw Flávio. He was lying on the sand huddled around his bottle of vodka. He sobbed in silence and, every now and then, spewed up a heart-rending cry.

His eyes filled up with pity, as they did every night he saw him like that.

Flávio could only find peace at sea. The only place on earth where he felt close to Sara and the baby he never came to have. When he was on dry land grief struck with a cruel intensity that only arose when its devastating ax-blow had never fallen before, no holds barred. He had spent his whole life cocooned

296

by a church that had never let him look beyond his gilded cage, not even at the daily tragedy of thousands of families that gave what little they had when it appealed to them, while seeking the same god that had turned them away like dogs. Like his own father, who had bankrolled his forced exile as the only possible way to keep his son's problems with the law from harming his lucrative business.

Paul looked in front of him. The sky and the sea had blended into a scattered dark blot.

He was fit to be tied at losing Marcela. All his life she had been his soul mate. But the wounds would heal. They had to.

He saw Flávio slump to the ground. He would have to make his friend see sense. Pay his bills. Come back to life.

CHAPTER XLVI

*Lyons (France),
October 2010.*

The phone would not stop ringing. Little Bernard toddled along the passageway, crying; he was after his sister, who had taken Pipo, his favorite teddy bear, off him.

At last she picked up the phone.

"Hello, who's there?"

"It's me, Denis."

"What's up?" Sylvie answered curtly, barely concealing her annoyance.

"Sorry, I should have called."

I haven't heard from you in a month! "You should have called? You had me worried there."

"I know, I'm sorry."

"But where've you been?"

"I've been away for a few days. I needed to be alone."

"I thought something had happened to you, Denis. I didn't know what to think. That damned case."

"I am well, and you?

"How am I supposed to be? I've been worried sick."

"How are things at work?"

"No big deal. Coburn has assigned me to a working group.

Training agents in the Third World, you know. He asked me to tell you that Kemal Osmanović has been released, for lack of proof against him. He's now back in Mostar. He thought that you'd want to know.

Denis gave no answer.

"What about you? When will you be back?" she asked, to change the subject.

"I won't be back. I quit. I've taken early retirement, one of those deals for aging rockers. I guess I'm old now."

Sylvie said nothing. She did not know whether to feel glad or upset at her boss's move. She just wanted him to be happy.

"What are you going to do with yourself now?"

"I haven't thought about that. Make up for lost time, I guess. There are too many things I've let slip by without paying proper attention to them. I've been blind. I'm a jerk, you know. I'll try to spend more time with my daughter, and I'd like to spend more time... with you. I must confess I've missed you these past few days."

Sylvie felt a warm glow inside her.

"I'd like to have dinner with you tonight or whenever you like. Although I guess it's the last thing you want, and I... Well, I'd understand," he added.

Sylvie kept quiet for a few seconds.

"We could also go to the park with the kids on Sunday, if you'd rather, or..."

"Tonight at eight," Sylvie interrupted him to say.

"OK."

"And no talking shop."

"I promise."

The first of the fall rain began to pour on Lyons that early October morning.

Dry leaves began to carpet the city streets, and crackled underfoot and fluttered in the fickle north wind. Kids waited on corners for school buses while several mothers sheltered under umbrellas on their way to the market.

As it did every morning, the traffic began to clog up the avenues and the bustle of passers-by drowned out the silence left over from dawn. The city was slowly coming to life and waking up to just another day.

———

AUTHOR'S NOTE

Thank you very much for reading The Nemesis Factor. I hope you enjoyed the journey.

I have always believed that each one of us is born with their own ghost and obsessions. There are children who from an early age wonder about death, their relationship with their parents, or the nature of God. In my candid mind I highlighted a subject: justice. When I was a brat and watched the news or flipped through the front page of the newspaper, I always wondered why evil actions often didn't have what they deserved, or why the bad guys often got away with it. And, above all, who would end this mess. Would it be man through his courts? God in the final judgment? Who has the legitimacy and capacity for it? These and other reflections have bubbled up in my head to spin the stories you just read. I hope you enjoyed them and have made an impression on you to some extent.

I would also like to invite you to explore, if you have the opportunity, the wonderful settings that host the adventures of our characters, from the magical lunar landscape of the coast of the Cabo de Gata-Nijar Natural Park, the bittersweet magic of Mostar and its bridge, or the Mediterranean peace of Naxos.

New adventures of our characters will arrive soon. Meanwhile, I am available for further comments in:

Instagram: www.instagram.com/inakimartinv

Email: imarvel@telefonica.net

Finally, will always thank you if you take two minutes to leave a review of the book in Amazon or wherever you acquired it.

Cheers

CONTENT INDEX

Printed in Great Britain
by Amazon

81517382R00181